'How much does it cost for a kiss, Athena? And don't try telling me again that you're not for sale.'

He was drawing her closer. She could feel the heat of his body now. See the texture of his skin, his lightly stubbled jaw that her fingers ached to touch...

'Let me tell you,' he was saying softly, 'that on closer inspection I'd have paid twice the usual rate—for *this*.' His eyes never leaving hers, he lowered his head and brushed her lips with his.

It was a fleeting caress, but even so Rosalie had never experienced anything like it. A sweet, melting sensation was pouring through her nerve-ends. A moment later his strong arms were cradling her even more securely and he was kissing her properly, his mouth possessing hers, his tongue stroking her soft inner moistness in a sensual dance that stirred the blood in her veins to white heat.

He was masterful. Dangerous. Exquisitely provocative. The worst of it was that she wanted more, and he knew it. She felt one of his strong hands slide up to cup the back of her head so his tongue could continue its rhythmic thrust, the slight roughness of his stubbled jaw providing a sensuous counterpoint to the silken sweetness of his mouth. His other hand slid tighter round her waist, pulling her closer against the hardness of his powerful body, his chest, his thighs. The urge to succumb to this dark magic and open herself to his potent masculinity was irresistible. Her hands crept upwards of their own volition to cling to his shoulders, feeling and savouring the vital force of his body.

This should not be happening...

AUTHOR NOTE

Those of you who have read THE RETURN OF LORD CONISTONE might remember Lucas Conistone's best friend, Captain Alec Stewart—yes, the brave officer with a ready smile and an eye for rich and pretty heiresses!

Readers have asked me, 'What happened to Captain Stewart? Did he find his heiress?' I wondered, too—especially as I knew that England's soldiers often faced a harsh return to reality once Waterloo was fought and won.

Alec is the son of an earl, but life is still throwing problems at him—notably in the alluring shape of Miss Rosalie Rowland, who is no heiress, and who accuses Alec of ruining her beloved sister.

How does Alec face this new challenge? Here is his story.

THE CAPTAIN'S COURTESAN

Lucy Ashford

First published in Great Britain 2012
by Mills & Boon, an imprint of Harlequin (UK) Limited.
Large Print edition 2013
Harlequin (UK) Limited, Eton House, 18-24 Paradise Road,
Richmond, Surrey TW9 1SR

© Lucy Ashford 2012

ISBN: 978 0 263 23249 3

Harlequin (UK) policy is to use papers that are natural,
renewable and recyclable products and made from wood grown in
sustainable forests. The logging and manufacturing process conform
to the legal environmental regulations of the country of origin.

Printed and bound in Great Britain
by CPI Antony Rowe, Chippenham, Wiltshire

Lucy Ashford, an English Studies lecturer, has always loved literature and history, and from childhood one of her favourite occupations has been to immerse herself in historical romances. She studied English with history at Nottingham University, and the Regency is her favourite period.

Lucy has written several historical novels, but this is her third for Mills & Boon®. She lives with her husband in an old stone cottage in the Peak District, near to beautiful Chatsworth House and Haddon Hall, all of which give her a taste of the magic of life in a bygone age. Her garden enjoys spectacular views over the Derbyshire hills, where she loves to roam and let her imagination go to work on her latest story.

You can contact Lucy via her website— www.lucyashford.com

Previous novels from Lucy Ashford:

THE MAJOR AND THE PICKPOCKET
THE RETURN OF LORD CONISTONE

Chapter One

Spitalfields, London—February 1816, 8 p.m.

'The Temple of Beauty?' echoed Captain Alec Stewart, lifting his dark eyebrows as he eased his foil into the nearby sword rack. 'How old are you, Harry—twenty? And still wet around the ears, my young pup. The Temple of Beauty is nothing but a den of harlots, take my word on it.'

For the last half an hour, this dusty old hall at the heart of the east London mansion known as Two Crows Castle had echoed to the click of gleaming blades, to the muttered curses of Lord Harry Nugent, and the curt admonitions of his tutor. Now the fencing lesson was over and Harry collapsed on a bench to mop the sweat from his brow and make his plea once more.

'Oh, Alec, do *please* say you'll come! It's my birthday after all. And the girls are as sweet a bunch as you'll find in London!'

Alec laughed aloud. 'Trust me, they're whores.' Pouring out two brandies, he handed one to his pupil. 'I'm not coming. But—happy birthday all the same.'

Harry Nugent, inordinately rich and a truly hopeless fencer, sighed and sipped just a little of his brandy, which was rough. He let his gaze rove with a certain amount of trepidation around this lofty hall, where the chill February wind rattling at cobwebbed windows sent shadows from the candles leaping across the smokestained rafters. Then he glanced at his fencing master, who, tall and looselimbed, looked as though the exertions of the past half-hour had affected him not one jot.

Harry took a deep breath. 'Alec!'

'Hmmm?'

'It's really not right, you know, Alec, that you should live in a wreck like this and make your living by running a sword school. You're a war hero, man!'

Alec shrugged. 'War hero or not, I've scarcely sixpence to scratch with, Harry. Anyway, I quite like it here.'

Harry watched as his fencing tutor idly pulled another fine rapier from the rack and tested its balance. Alec was one of the best swordsmen in London and used to hold an enviable reputation as a captain in the Light Dragoons. Once, they said, he was light-hearted, never serious, even on the night before battle. London's ladies used to adore him; he'd had his pick of the *ton*'s heiresses, and for a brief while was betrothed to one. But now... Now, he was a stranger to London's social scene and his once-merry brown eyes were etched with cynicism.

'Even so, to live like *this*!' Harry couldn't stop himself blurting it out. 'You should take up the matter with your father, you really should! Everyone says so!'

Alec made a gentle feint with his rapier. 'Do they indeed say that?' he asked softly. 'Do you have fun discussing me with your friends around London's clubs and watering-holes, Harry?'

'No!' protested Harry Nugent, rather flustered. 'Well, we say nothing we wouldn't say to your face, Alec!' He spread out his hands in entreaty. 'You needn't actually—you know, *do* anything with any of the girls tonight. Just join us at the Temple for a bit of fun! And perhaps,' Harry went on innocently, 'a night away from this place would do you good. Your brother said—'

Alec's well-shaped, flexible fingers suddenly went very still around the hilt of his rapier. If Lord Harry Nugent had fought at his side at Waterloo, he'd have known to be wary of that look.

'When, exactly,' said Alec in a deceptively soft drawl, 'did you see my esteemed brother?'

'Why, it was mere chance, at Tellworth's tables in St James's last night!'

Still in London, then. 'And what in particular did he say?'

'He said...' Harry hesitated '...he said you are a little too fond, like all former soldiers, of the brandy bottle—which we all know is a lie!—and that is why, he says, you tend to avoid decent company.'

'Decent company, eh? And will my delightful brother be at Tellworth's again tonight, do you think, my fresh-faced, intriguingly honest Harry?'

'Not as far as I know...' Suddenly Harry's face brightened. 'I say, Alec, are you thinking of making your peace with the fellow? That's surely what your father wishes, ain't it? Now, that really *would* be capital!'

Alec reached across and ruffled the younger man's fair curls. 'Make my peace?' he echoed. 'Harry, let me tell you something. If I come across my brother tonight, I shall take very great pleasure in slicing whichever expensive coat he's wearing into precise, inch-wide strips.' The rapier in his hand gleamed as he thoughtfully practised a *coup de pointe*. 'I don't much care for his taste in clothes, you see.'

'Oh, Lord,' muttered Harry. 'Oh, Lord.'

'No bloodshed, though. For which my brother should be profoundly grateful.' Decisively, Alec put the weapon away and started to propel Harry gently towards the door. 'Enjoy the Temple of Beauty, my young and innocent friend. And if you really consider there'll be any girls there who *aren't* whores, then you're an even greater gudgeon than I thought. Now, here's your...' he blinked at the wide-brimmed creation '...I think it's what you'd call a hat. And your coat.'

'Very well.' Harry nodded. 'Same time next week, Alec? And Alec—do you think I'm making progress?'

Silence. Then, levelly, 'Your technique, Harry, never ceases to amaze me.'

'Oh. Oh, I say.' Harry left, looking rather pleased. Alec shut the door on his departure a little too hard and brushed the ensuing shower of ceiling plaster from his shoulders.

The damn place was falling to pieces. Rather like his life.

Alec was the younger son of an earl, and had served in the army for seven years. He'd returned home with a reputation for gallantry, and his future should have been bright indeed.

But here in London, the very air was tainted. Tainted by his own *brother*.

'Beg pardon, Captain!' A small but tough-looking man with a black patch over one eye had entered the hall. 'I've got three fellows here, wantin' to speak to you.' Hovering behind Garrett were some men who were plainly ex-soldiers, though their uniforms hung in rags from their half-starved bodies. And—they saluted Alec. That got him. In spite of their pitiful condition, they saluted him.

'They're old 'uns from the Fourteenth, Captain,' Garrett explained. 'Want to know if we've got any room to spare.'

Two Crows Castle was full to bursting. Alec sucked in a deep breath. 'Garrett, I really don't see how we can—'

'We could squeeze some extra pallets in the top attic, Captain!'

'Right.' Of course. How could they turn away these brave men, any one of whom might have fought at his side on the bloody battlefields of Spain? 'Right,' he repeated, 'see to it, Garrett, will you?'

'Straight away, Captain!' Garrett saluted and turned smartly to escort the ex-soldiers to their new quarters upstairs. 'Look sharp now, lads!'

'God bless you, Captain!' they were trying to say to Alec. 'You're one of the very best! A Waterloo hero and more!'

Alec waved them away. Then he sat down and raked his hand through his dark hair.

A hero and more? In his father's opinion, far from it.

'My own son.' The Earl of Aldchester had looked stricken—no other word for it—as Alec had stood before him a year ago in the luxurious drawing room of his Mayfair mansion. 'Alec, I cannot believe you have come here to try to destroy my new-found happiness with the woman I love!'

Alec had been in his uniform, the famous blue jacket and white breeches of the Light Dragoons. It was February 1815, and all the army's senior officers had been quietly warned that the Emperor Napoleon was bent on escape from Elba, but Alec had other matters on his mind, for he'd just heard that his father was planning a June wedding.

'Please believe me, sir.' Alec had stood very straight, hating every minute of this interview. 'It's your happiness that I wish to preserve…'

The Earl had got slowly to his feet, suddenly looking every year of his age. Once, Alec knew, he'd dreamed of a military career for himself, and historic paintings of famous British victories a hundred years ago—Blenheim, Ramillies, Malplaquet—were hung around the walls of his beautiful house.

He would await Alec's brief periods of leave from the army with almost painful eagerness. 'Ah, this fellow Wellington!' he used to say. 'At this rate, my son, he'll be snatching the Duke of Marlborough's title as the greatest British general ever!' He used to listen to Alec's accounts of Wellington's campaigns with his eyes full of pride.

But he hadn't been so proud though on that ominous encounter last February.

'You surely realise,' the Earl had said heavily, 'that I used to live for the times you came home to me. For your news of the war. But—to come to me instead with scurrilous *tattle*...'

'Father,' Alec had said quietly. 'Father, I only wanted to ask you if you have *known* her for long enough. If you are sure that she can be trusted, in every way.'

'Trusted?' The Earl looked wretched. '*Trusted?* Oh, Stephen warned me, so often, that you were jealous of my marriage and that you were afraid of losing my favour!'

'Sir, that is not so, believe me!'

'Enough.' The Earl sat down again abruptly. '*Enough.* You must see that what you have just tried to say to me means that I can no longer receive you in this house as my son.'

Fateful words. Irretrievable words. And his father had sounded quite broken as he uttered them. Indeed Alec's voice betrayed his own emotion as he replied, 'Sir, I am sorry for it. And please believe me when I say I will always hold you in the deepest esteem. But I must beg you, one last time, to listen—really *listen*—to what I have to say! Sir, this marriage must not take place!'

His father had stared at him. Almost dazed. 'I just don't *understand*. Perhaps if you were to meet her. Meet her properly, I mean, and talk to her.' He was on his feet again, pacing to and fro. 'Yes, that's it. And then you would realise for yourself how badly you have misjudged her.'

'I will not change my mind, sir. I'm sorry.'

The Earl sagged with despair. Then his eyes grew hard. 'Very well. So be it. One last thing, then. My future wife requires a London base for her mother. She once mentioned that the Bedford Street house I've let you use for the last few years would be suitable. And now I must ask you to vacate it, as soon as possible. Needless to say, your allowance will cease forthwith.'

Alec stood very straight, his face expressionless. 'There's the matter of the home for old soldiers in Spitalfields, sir. I trust, however sorely I've displeased you, that you'll continue with your plans to fund it?'

'Do you know,' said the Earl, his voice breaking a little now, 'I'm beginning to think that it's associating with men of that kind that's made you lose all sense of family duty!' He gazed at his younger son in utter anguish. 'I suggest that you run it yourself, since you obviously care more for your—your lowly battle comrades than you do for me!'

'That is not so, sir—'

'Enough!'

Alec, his jaw clenched, had given a curt bow and left.

His brother had his wish at last. This was a breach between son and father that surely could not be healed.

Soon afterwards had come Alec's recall to duty, for Napoleon had escaped from Elba, and under his leadership the swelling French army had swept northwards to meet the allies in the last and bloodiest battle of the long war: Waterloo.

Then Alec had come home. Only he had *no* home, of course. His father had married in the summer while Alec was away fighting, and Alec's new stepmother's relatives had delightedly appropriated the smart house that he had once occupied.

So Alec had made the decision to move into the home for old soldiers in Spitalfields himself. It had once been a grand mansion, built by a rich Hugue-not silk weaver called Ducroix, but the house, like the district, Spitalfields, had fallen on hard times; the name the locals had given to Ducroix's pre-tentious home—Two Crows Castle—seemed more than ever like an ironic jest.

Before their estrangement, it had been his father's idea to buy it and refurbish it. 'I cannot enjoy my wealth when I see injured and destitute soldiers begging at every street corner,' he'd explained to Alec.

The Earl had bought the lease, but the refurbish-ments had never started. And now it was up to Alec to try to keep the crumbling mansion habitable by using the money from his army pension, together with a small inheritance from his mother and the income he earned from fencing lessons. Quite sim-ply, he felt he owed it to these men. They had given their all for their country and were left with noth-ing, often not even their health.

Alec had not heard from his father since that day of their terrible argument and refused all invitations from the *ton*. He had built a new life for himself and in a way he was content.

Or would have been, had he not got his damned brother to deal with.

* * *

Garrett's return broke abruptly into his abstracted thoughts.

'That's them sorted up there, Captain,' Garrett said with satisfaction. 'Makes six lads in the attic now, bit of a squash, but they was all in Spain, so they'll have plenty to talk about.' He eyed Alec warily. 'And I've some more news for you.'

'Yes?'

'Apparently,' Garrett went on in a rush, 'that brother of yours was seen in the Park this afternoon, large as life in his fancy curricle. And he had a lady with him.' Garrett hesitated again. 'A prime 'un, Captain. Dark hair, blue eyes…'

Alec felt an ominous pulse throbbing in his temple. *Steady, now.* 'Do you know,' he said softly, 'I feel a sudden urge to speak with my brother, Garrett.'

'So I thought, Captain. That's why I asked around about his lordship's intentions for the rest of the day. And he's decided, all of a sudden it seems, to visit some place in St James's tonight. The Temple of— the Temple of…'

Alec went very still. 'Not the Temple of Beauty?'

'Aye, that was it. The Temple of Beauty, in Ryder Street. Now, I know he's got that grand house of his barricaded against you like a fortress, but he's likely to be heading to this Temple place alone…'

And he would not be expecting to meet his younger brother. Alec did not hesitate. 'I'm going out, Garrett. Expect me when you see me.' He was already pulling on his greatcoat.

'Sure you don't want company, Captain?'

'Quite sure.' Alec was flinging open the door when he came to an abrupt halt, for outside in the passageway a large, golden-haired dog was watching him expectantly.

Alec swung round, eyes ominously narrowed. 'Garrett, do you know what this creature's doing here?'

'He's been hangin' about outside for days, Captain. No food, no 'ome. Thought we might manage to fit him in.'

Alec raked his hand through his dark hair. 'Do you realise how much dogs this size eat?'

Garrett remained imperturbable. 'He's nowhere else to go, Captain. His name's Ajax.'

'Ajax. Then, Garrett, you'll oblige me greatly by *finding* Ajax somewhere else to go!'

'Very well. Gently now with that door, Captain!'

Too late. As the door slammed shut after Alec's rapidly departing figure, flakes of ancient plaster pattered down from the ceiling. Garrett, with a sigh, fetched a broom to sweep them up, then ruffled the dog's head. 'Blasted place is fallin' to bits… Don't worry, lad. Our Captain's all heart. Most of the time.'

Ajax gazed up at his new friend and wagged his tail happily.

Chapter Two

The Temple of Beauty, Ryder Street, St James's
Later that evening

The first-floor dressing room was crowded and smelled of cheap perfume. Rosalie Rowland edged her way towards the nearest door and opened it a few inches, hoping for a breath of cooler, fresher air.

Oh, fiddlesticks. She shut it again quickly.

Men. Dozens of them, queuing from the ground floor all the way up the staircase. Men, tall and short, rich and poor, plump and thin, all filling the air with the smells of tobacco and strong drink. Men, queuing to see—amongst others—*her*. On stage tonight, in the upstairs hall of the notorious Temple of Beauty.

Rosalie fought down a renewed wave of panic. If she didn't catch her death of cold in this—costume that was as flimsy as a bride's veil, she'd catch something horrible from the dirt. Not that such a minor detail bothered the proud proprietor, Dr Perceval Barnard, or his wife. Or the other girls, who chattered and giggled as they clustered to paint their faces in front of the looking-glasses hung askew on the walls.

'On stage in ten minutes, Greek goddesses!' squawked Mrs Patty Barnard. 'Make sure you're all looking ravishing, now!'

'Think she means—ready to be ravished,' drily put in dark-haired Sal close by. Within minutes of Rosalie's arrival here earlier today, kind Sal had promptly taken her under her wing. And people to watch out for, Sal told her, most definitely included Patty Barnard, a shrill, domineering forty-year-old, whose dyed red hair dazzled the eye.

Mrs Barnard didn't hear Sal's comment, but her sharp eyes shot to Rosalie. 'You. New girl. Pull your gown lower. Our gents haven't paid to see a bunch of Vestal Virgins!'

Rosalie kept her expression demure. 'Certainly it's the last place on earth they'd expect to find any, ma'am.'

The rest of the girls sniggered. Mrs Barnard looked at her, frowning, uncertain, then swung round to the others. 'Girls, stop squabbling over those Grecian arm-bracelets. There should be sufficient for you all… Charlotte, my dear, what a truly exquisite Aphrodite you make!'

And the normal hubbub of chatter and preparation resumed.

The Temple of Beauty was, Dr Barnard liked to declare, a gentlemen's club. But there were no rules for membership, merely an initial payment for the evening's entry, after which the clients could indulge in the usual pursuits of dining, drinking and gaming. Many other clubs in London offered the same. But here, at the stroke of ten, all the patrons moved as one to join the queue for the upstairs hall, because the Temple of Beauty was known throughout London for its classical *tableaux* featuring scantily-clad girls in costumes who posed in what Dr Barnard called 'attitudes' for around ten minutes while the gentlemen in the audience, already mellow with food and wine, feasted their eyes.

'I have an exclusive clientele, my dear, most of them highly educated in the Greek and Roman myths,' Dr Barnard had earnestly assured Rosalie yesterday morning when she'd called about a post. 'And I pride myself,' he went on, 'on my own knowledge of those ancient times of glory!' He'd waved an expansive hand towards his crowded bookshelves, though his lecherous appraisal of her face and figure had rather spoiled the effect of his lofty words.

Rosalie had dragged her eyes from an oversized volume called *The Myths of Apollodorus* and gazed back at him brightly. Now she looked anew round the crowded dressing room. Greek goddesses? Well, the chief of his girls, Charlotte—'the star of our firmament!' was how Dr Barnard had introduced her to Rosalie earlier—looked more like a Covent Garden street-walker than a heavenly deity. Tonight, as Patty Barnard adjusted Charlotte's dyed locks fondly, Sal hissed to Rosalie, 'D'you think our Mrs B. would find Charlotte quite so exquisite if she caught her romping in bed with 'er husband whenever Mrs B.'s back's turned?'

Rosalie felt laughter bubbling up. But it faded, as she glanced at herself in the mirror and thought, just for a moment, that she saw another face—pale, wistful—gazing back at her.

Her sister. Oh, her sister might have stood here. Might have looked into this very mirror…

She jumped as Mrs Barnard's harsh voice rasped in her ear, 'You, girl. Take that ribbon off!'

Rosalie's fingers flew up to the pale blue ribbon with which she'd tied back her silvery-blonde hair. 'But I thought…'

'Do you think,' went on Mrs Barnard, 'that the

Ancient Greeks tied back their hair in that fashion, my girl?'

Rosalie rather suspected they did and was prepared to argue the point; Sal stood heavily on her toe.

As it happened, Rosalie was now quite happy to let her long hair hang free. It meant she could hide behind it. And heavens above, looking at this garment they'd given her to wear, she'd need to.

When she'd first seen her dress, laid across Mrs Barnard's plump arm, it had looked perfectly respectable. She was Athena, the goddess of wisdom, after all, so a long white-muslin tunic girdled with a turquoise cord seemed appropriately demure. 'The turquoise will match your eyes, my dear!' had simpered Mrs B.

Up until now, Rosalie had never really considered that she had much of a figure to hide. She was twenty-one years old, of medium height, and rather too thin; her legs, she considered, were too long and her bosom decidedly undistinguished compared to the voluptuous figures that were on display around her. Besides, she'd always made a point of dressing to deter any roving male eye. She'd never in her life up till now worn her hair loose and tumbling to her shoulders, had never worn a gown remotely like this one. Demure? That was before she got it on. It was sheer, it was clinging… For heaven's sake! How could she go out on stage like *this*?

She'd done her very best to adjust the ridiculously low neckline by quickly threading a turquoise ribbon through the scalloped lace that edged the yoke and pulling it together into a bow just above the curve of her breasts. But Sal, who was busy powdering her own extremely well-displayed plump bosom, turned to her, powder puff in hand. 'Ma Barnard will never let you get away with *that* cover-up, darlin'. Not in a thousand years.'

Rosalie protested. 'I've no intention of going out there *half-naked*!'

'What did you expect, in Dr Barnard's Temple of Beauty? Gawd, dearie, I wish I had your looks. Your face and figure, that gorgeous hair of yours—'

'My figure? My hair?' echoed Rosalie.

Sal sighed. 'Own up, now. You ain't done nothing like this before, ever, have you?'

'Well, no. Not exactly…'

'Not on the run, are you, from the law, or some cross husband?'

'No! Not at all, Sal! And anyway, I don't suppose that any of them will be paying much attention to me. Will they?'

'New girl at Dr B.'s Temple of Beauty? Course they'll be lookin' at you!' Sal drew closer. 'And after the show—did Mrs B. explain? There's a bit of music in what they call the Inner Temple on the next floor up, and it's there that the gents pay to come to dance with us.'

'*Just* dancing?' Rosalie enquired rather faintly. She had already discovered that this place was like a rabbit warren, with five floors of rooms and various twisting staircases.

Sal winked. 'Just dancin' to start with. Then— who knows?—you might end up with a nice rich lord to milk for a while, if you just shut yer eyes through all the grunting and heaving. But watch out, gal. If they promise love, they're lying through their teeth.'

Rosalie nodded, her heart sinking. She knew that. But so many didn't.

Rosalie, I'm in London. I'm in trouble. Please help me. That was all that was in Linette's pitiful letter last October. Nothing else—no address, no other clue—except that Rosalie knew Linette had always wanted to be an actress.

Now emotion squeezed at Rosalie's throat like a necklet of iron when she thought what had become of that dream, and a touch of fear also; Linette had been only two years younger than Rosalie, and though Linette's blonde locks were more luxuriant and her figure more shapely, the sisters did bear a resemblance. At the interview yesterday, Rosalie had worried that Dr Barnard might spot it.

But his gaze had been one of cursory approval. 'Oh, they come and they go, our girls!' he'd said airily, when she asked him why he had vacancies. 'A world of opportunities awaits them, after all!'

Opportunities. Anger, as well as despair, surged through her. Then the door flew open and Danny, the lad who helped backstage, burst in. 'Three minutes to go, *lay-dees*!' He looked straight at Rosalie and winked.

'Dirty little rascal,' said Sal amiably. 'Always hopes he'll catch us with nothing on. Here—have some rouge.'

'No thanks.' Rosalie turned to face her. 'Sal, how long have you worked here?'

'Feels like a lifetime, but I've been here all of six months! What with Mrs B.'s sharp tongue and her hubby docking our pay at any excuse, no one sticks it more than a year.' Sal was piling on more rouge. 'Why are *you* workin' here, gal? Standin' about on stage in next to nothing isn't what you was brought up to, anyone can see that! You're clever, you speak like a lady. You could have bin a governess or something, surely!'

'I have a child to care for,' Rosalie answered simply. 'Governesses with children don't get hired.'

Sal looked at her quickly. 'How old's your lit-tle one?'

'Two. She's just two years old.'

'Ah, bless! She's lucky, then, havin' you to watch over her,' said Sal wistfully. 'Me, I was put on the streets by my ma when I was ten. To think I'm playin' Hebe, the virgin goddess— Lord knows I can hardly remember bein' a virgin meself. But I've learnt lessons. I know the ways of the so-called gen-try like the back of my hand. And remember, the best way to make life comfortable for yourself and your little 'un is to open your legs to a rich man— but get his money first, you hear me?'

'Ladies!' shrieked the boy Danny, flinging the door wide open. 'Ready to go on stage!'

'Here we go.' Sal grinned.

Here we go indeed, echoed Rosalie silently.

But not before Mrs Patty Barnard, inspecting every goddess as they filed through the door, ripped open the bow securing the neckline of Rosalie's bodice and tugged it down to show the curve of her breasts. 'Told you before, Athena. Think you're in a damned nunnery?'

Rosalie pressed her lips firmly together, but a faint flush of defiance rose in her cheeks.

With the curtains still closed, all the girls hurried to take up position on stage. Charlotte was carefully seating herself on a damask-covered throne and preening her dyed golden locks, while the others clustered around. Now Rosalie could hear Dr Barnard standing in front of the stage and announcing to the gathered audience, 'For your delectation, my honoured friends! A scene of exquisite and ennobling artistry—the Greek goddesses!'

Rosalie had kept as far to the back as she could. *Oh*, she wondered, the breath hitching in her throat, *what had she let herself in for?*

The heavy curtains were gliding back.

There must be nigh-on a hundred men out there.

She felt rather sick. For Linette, her beloved sister. She would see this through, for Linette—and for Linette's child, Katy.

Chapter Three

'Dear Rosalie, why on earth are you asking me about such a place?' had been her friend Helen's startled response when Rosalie mentioned the Temple of Beauty two days ago. They were in Helen's printing shop, and all around them were heaps of freshly printed broadsheets. 'From what I've heard,' Helen went on, 'that Temple is nothing but a glorified brothel!'

'Bwothel,' little Katy had lisped. 'Bwothel.'

Quickly Helen turned to the two children, who were drawing stick men on some scraps of paper. 'Toby, darling, take Katy to the kitchen and get her a glass of milk, will you?'

'And a treacle bun?' Six-year-old Toby, always hungry, asked the question hopefully.

'And a treacle bun each, yes, if Katy wants. Look after Katy, now!'

'C'mon, Kate.' Holding out his hand, Toby had

valiantly led the toddling two-year-old past the for-once silent printing press towards the kitchen. Katy was still lisping, *'Bwothel. Bwothel...'*

Rosalie watched them go with a catch in her throat, then said quietly to Helen, 'Toby's wonderful with Katy. I'm so very grateful to you for letting us stay here with you, Helen. I wish you'd let me pay you for our food, at least!'

'And I wish *you'd* take my advice and stop going round these dreadful places on your own.' Helen had sighed. 'Men who visit the Temple of Beauty have only one thing on their mind! Are you going because you've heard that Linette might have been there?'

'Exactly. You know how Linette always talked of being an actress? Well, now I've found out she may have worked at this Temple of Beauty, three years ago.'

'That place! Oh, poor, poor Linette!'

Helen had been a teacher at the little school in the village where Rosalie and Linette grew up, then she'd married and moved to London, where her husband ran a small publishing press in Aylesbury Street, Clerkenwell. But a few years later he'd abandoned Helen and their little son, Toby, for a singer from Sadler's Wells. Helen had always kept in touch with Rosalie by letter, and after her husband's departure she wrote to her young friend that she'd resolved to make a success of the publishing business on her own. When Rosalie's search for Linette brought her to London last autumn, it was to Helen that she turned.

'I will pay you, Helen, for my accommodation,' Rosalie had insisted when she arrived outside Helen's door.

'Nonsense.' Helen had hugged her warmly. 'I'll do everything I can to help you find your poor sister. As for payment—well, how about writing for *The Scribbler*?'

'*The Scribbler*? Helen, what's that?'

And Helen had gone on to explain.

The Scribbler was a weekly news sheet Helen produced, a round-up of London events and advertisements, which Helen also used from time to time to denounce the greed of the rich and the plight of the poor.

All this Helen had told Rosalie as she'd unpacked her bags last October. 'What I really need,' Helen had said, eyeing her former pupil thoughtfully, 'is someone who'll write a weekly diary of London life. Something light, about the theatre, for example, or an amusing commentary on the latest women's fashions… How about it, Rosalie? You have talent—I realised it when you were my pupil.'

'But I've never thought of writing for *publication*!'

'Why not? I remember you write with such charm, such humour—just try it, please?'

Helen's suggestion certainly paid off, because Rosalie's weekly articles—published under the pen name of Ro Rowland, a fictional young man about town—had become resoundingly popular. In other circumstances, Rosalie would have revelled in her new life. She'd come to love this little Clerkenwell printer's shop with its ancient hand press that rattled away merrily in the front parlour. But Helen could be stubborn, and every so often Rosalie had to make clear what she was after. What her purpose was.

'All I want is to find out the truth about Linette,' Rosalie had repeated steadily in the face of Helen's objections. 'I thought we'd discussed this. My sister might have met *him* at the Temple of Beauty and I cannot leave any stone unturned.'

'Then...' Helen had hesitated '...it might just help you to know that Dr Barnard keeps a secret register of clients. Names, addresses, the dates they visited, that sort of thing. I only heard about it because once I was offered the chance to publish some of it by a man who worked for Dr Barnard and showed me some pages he'd copied. I refused, of course—I'd have made too many enemies. But I learnt that Dr

Barnard keeps this register—he calls it his green book—in his office, hidden inside a hollowed-out copy of a big old book called *The Myths of Apollodorus*. And since you know, roughly, the dates that Linette was there, it just might help you! It's such a tragedy that you don't know the name of her villainous seducer—'

Rosalie cut in, giving Helen's hand a squeeze. 'Thank you for the news about the register. You are such a good friend.'

Helen shook her head, sighing. Though over thirty now, she still looked just like the village school-teacher she once was, with her brown hair pinned up tightly and her eyes behind her spectacles shining with intelligence. 'Just look after yourself, my dear, won't you? Get out of that "Temple place" just as soon as you can. *Men.*'

'Men don't worry me, since I've got a foolproof defence, Helen,' Rosalie said lightly. 'I'm simply not interested in them. Though we mustn't forget that there are some good men in the world!'

'Not that I've met lately!' snapped Helen.

Rosalie put her head on one side mischievously. 'What about your friend Mr Wheeldon?'

'Francis! Oh, well, he's different.' Helen was busily putting the latest copies of *The Scribbler* into piles for distribution. 'And you certainly wouldn't find *him* at Dr Barnard's Temple of Beauty!'

True. Rosalie had chuckled at the thought of the kind, middle-aged churchwarden Francis Wheeldon visiting such a place. She picked up a *Scribbler.* 'Shall I take some copies of this to the news vendor in the Strand for you, Helen? You usually sell quite a few there, don't you?'

Subject changed. But Rosalie hadn't wavered in her resolve to visit the Temple of Beauty. If appearing on stage for a night was the only way to get further in her quest, then so be it. That register could be a breakthrough—because Rosalie had lied to Helen. She *did* know the name of the man who had ruined her sister. But she was keeping it to herself, for she had no doubt that he was not only hateful, but dangerous.

Now Rosalie was looking down from the stage at all these lecherous *roués* in fresh disbelief. How could her darling sister have fallen in love with someone who came to a place like *this*?

'Athena!' Mrs Barnard was hissing at her from the wings. 'You, new girl, stop glaring down at our guests like that! And pull your bodice lower, or I'll come out and do it myself!'

Rosalie muttered a retort under her breath and

dragged down her bodice just the tiniest fraction. Sal winked at her. It was going to be a long ten minutes. Lifting her chin, deliberately staring at a fixed point at the very back of the hall, Rosalie mentally started composing a piece for *The Scribbler*. *'Tonight your fellow about town Ro Rowland took himself to the well-known Temple of Beauty. And there he observed that a large number of the male spectators, being over fifty years old, were alas too short-sighted to fully enjoy the beauteous goddesses on display...'*

Suddenly, the door at the back crashed open. A latecomer strode in and halted abruptly. He looked around, not up at the stage, but at the men in the audience, some of whom had turned in irritation at the slam of the door. Rosalie caught her breath.

He was not an old, fat lecher. He was tall and dark-haired, thirty at most. He was quite unmissable.

'Now, there's a sight for sore eyes,' Sal murmured appreciatively at her side.

Rosalie nodded mutely. Most of the men in here favoured the current fashion for fancy tailcoats in blue or bottle-green superfine, padded at the shoulders and adorned with ridiculously large silver-gilt buttons that would lend themselves to the cartoons of Cruikshank or Gillray. But he—her man—was dressed casually, almost roughly, in a long grey overcoat that hung open to reveal a rumpled linen shirt and a horseman's tight buckskin breeches tucked into worn leather riding boots. Instead of a high starched cravat, he wore a simple white neckerchief knotted loosely at his throat.

He looked angry, determined, and—absolutely gorgeous. His wide-set eyes smouldered with fiery challenge beneath jet-black brows. And his careless attire served only to emphasise the masculine perfection of his body—that broad chest, tapering downwards to lean hips and muscular thighs... *I'm sorry to let you down, Helen, but perfect is the only word for it.* Fascinated, she let her gaze rove back up to his face, noting how his untamed dark hair lent dramatic emphasis to those lean, sculpted features and that amazingly sensual mouth.

His firm jaw was shadowed with at least a day's stubble. He looked as though he didn't give a fig for the company he'd disturbed. An aura of danger emanated from him, together with the cynicism of a man who'd already seen rather more of life than he should.

Yet—you only had to look at him to imagine being in his arms. To imagine doing things a well-bred girl shouldn't even be thinking of. What was he doing here? *You know the answer to that, you fool.* Yet somehow, he—her man—looked as if he hated all this just as much as she did.

Don't be an idiot, Rosalie. She could just imagine Helen proclaiming with a snort of derision, 'Of course, a man prefers to pay for a woman, because the act of purchase means he can discard her the minute he's had enough of her!'

Just for one incredible moment, his gaze met hers so searingly that she felt as if he was undressing her with his eyes. The warm colour suffused her skin. Then he turned his back on the place with a shrug of scorn and walked out. She felt, ridiculously, a sense of loss. A few minutes later the curtains were gliding shut and the girls, chattering avidly, were being shepherded off the stage. Back in the dressing room Rosalie put her hands to her flushed cheeks. Sweet heaven, who *was* that man?

And then Sal came over, and was digging her in the ribs. 'Isn't he just about the most gorgeous creature you've ever seen? Don't try to deny it. I saw you staring!' She chuckled.

Rosalie's heart plummeted. 'Does he...come here regularly, then?'

'Lord alive, never seen him in here before, more's the pity. Shouldn't think *he* has to pay for his pleasures, should you?' Sal put more powder on her nose. 'But I've just heard one of the girls saying he teaches sword fighting to the gentry and is known as the Captain, because he was in the army for years.'

Never seen him in here before. Rosalie was already scraping her long hair back into a tight coil. That was as well. Because she could just imagine Linette—anyone—going off with him at one beckoning glint from those wicked, slanting dark eyes.

Then she reached for the everyday clothes she'd arrived in and started towards the changing room. Sal jumped in front of her. 'Now, just a minute. What are you doing, gal?'

'Going home,' answered Rosalie calmly. *Just as soon as I've paid a quick visit to Dr Barnard's office.*

'What? You're not stayin' on?'

'I was only hired to do the stage show, I made that quite clear… Whatever's the matter, Sal? You look worried!' In fact, more than worried—Sal looked almost frightened.

'Dr Barnard spoke to me about you earlier,' Sal whispered, glancing round to make sure they weren't overheard. 'He said I had to make sure you stayed on for the dancin', see, even if it's just for a bit!'

'But *why*? I told him I'd appear on stage and nothing further, at least for the first night!' In fact,

Rosalie didn't have the slightest intention of coming back here at all if she could help it.

Sal bit her lip. 'Dr B. was hopin' that perhaps you'd change your mind. New girls are always a draw, see, especially ones as pretty as you. And—' her fingers knotted together nervously '—if you don't show upstairs, I get the push, Rosalie.'

'Oh, Sal…'

'But it's all right,' went on Sal bravely, 'you go, it's not your fault—it's a lousy place, this!'

Rosalie was desperate to get at that secret register. If not tonight, then she'd come back tomorrow and endure the stage show yet again; there was nothing else for it. But to go upstairs, on offer to all those men…

'Well, look at little Miss Prim and Proper!' It was Charlotte, sneering at Rosalie's drab cloak. 'So you're disappearin' already, are you? Of course, you won't want to face the fact that nobody out there is going to be in the slightest bit interested in paying out good money for *you*!'

'That's as well, isn't it?' answered Rosalie calmly. 'Since I never wanted them to.'

Charlotte glared. 'I told Perceval—Dr Barnard—you was too high in the instep for this place! He's just doin' his accounts, down in his office, but soon as he arrives up here, I'll tell him you ain't nothing but a stuck-up troublemaker!'

Down in his office. Botheration. Rosalie put down her clothes and shook her hair loose. 'Actually, Charlotte,' she said, 'I've changed my mind. I *am* staying.'

Charlotte's mouth opened and closed. Sal swung back to Rosalie. 'Oh, my Gawd, girl, don't do this just for me! You said you were dead set against joining the dancing, and I understand, I really do...'

Rosalie set her chin stubbornly. 'Sal, how long does Dr Barnard usually take to do his accounts?'

'Oh, ten minutes or so, that's all, then he's eager to mingle with his gents upstairs!'

'Well, I'll go upstairs, too,' declared Rosalie. 'Just long enough to make sure he sees me there, then I'll slip away. Will that do?'

'Won't it, just!' breathed Sal. 'Thanks, gal, for savin' my job here. But...' she patted Rosalie's cheek '...put some rouge on, eh? You got to look as if you mean it!'

Sal hurried off upstairs. Slowly Rosalie dabbed on a little rouge, hating it. Once more, now that she was on her own, she remembered that terrible winter night two months ago, when she'd received the message from Helen. *Rosalie, I'm so sorry, I've found your sister.*

* * *

Memories of a spring morning came back to her unbidden. She had been a small but leggy ten-year-old and Linette just eight. There'd been a storm in the night, with the wind and rain howling around the oak woods that surrounded their village, and at first light she and Linette had raced down to the stream at the bottom of their garden to see how the moorhens' nest they'd been watching for days had fared.

Linette had been entranced by the newly hatched chicks, huddled in their sprawling mound of twigs that was lodged precariously against a small island in the centre of the river. But the morning after the storm Rosalie saw that the high waters had loosened the nest and any minute it might be dragged away, chicks and all, by the muddy brown flow.

Hitching up her skirts and pulling off her shoes, Rosalie had waded in, while little Linette, so pretty even then, had watched from the bank, her hands pressed to her cheeks. Rosalie, up to her knees in water and challenged by the mother moorhen squawking its outrage, steadily placed stones and twigs around the unwieldy nest full of open-beaked chicks until it was firmly anchored again in a cleft of the leafy island.

'Oh, Rosalie! You've saved the babies!' Linette had been ecstatic.

From the top of their garden, Rosalie and Linette's mother, not well even then, had been watching, too. As they ran back up to her, she'd hugged her girls tightly to her. 'My brave darling Rosalie,' she'd said in her broken English. 'And Linette. You are both *mes petits anges*, my little angels!'

That was when Rosalie had noticed the bucket and brush by the wall of the house and realised that their mother had been crying. And then she had seen the words, painted on the side of their outhouse, that her mother must have been trying to scrub away when they came running up from the river. *You don't belong here, French whore.*

Later that morning at the village school Rosalie had shown her new teacher the story she'd written about a bird in its floating nest travelling far downstream and finding a new life.

That young teacher was Helen Fazackerley and she had read Rosalie's story with absorbed attention. 'This is wonderful, Rosalie,' she had said quietly. 'Is this something you would like to do? Travel and discover new places?'

Rosalie had looked steadily up at her teacher. 'If we went somewhere else, would they be kinder to my mother, Miss Fazackerley?'

* * *

On, on flew Rosalie's memories, to the December of last year. A cold evening, a bitter evening, in damp, bleak London. Rosalie had by then been staying with Helen for two months, searching all the daylight hours and more for Linette; asking at the theatres, the opera houses, everywhere she could think of for her sister; following clues that too quickly went cold. *Rosalie, I'm in London. I'm in trouble. Please help me.*

But it was Helen, who regularly went out at night with a group of her church friends to take soup and bread to the hungry in some of the worst districts of London, who found Linette at last.

Rosalie had been reading little Toby his bedtime story when she'd received Helen's message. Biddy, their good young neighbour, had come in to look after Toby, while Rosalie, with one of Biddy's brothers, hurried to meet Helen at the address she'd give her—a rubbish-strewn attic off the Ratcliffe Highway. There, on a dank mattress beneath a broken skylight, lay her nineteen-year-old sister, her once-lovely face pinched with grief and illness, while at her side a beautiful little girl with dark curls gazed up at the newcomers, clutching a battered rag doll and whispering, 'Mama. Mama.'

Rosalie's search for her sister was at an end.

Helen had immediately taken the crying infant to her house in Clerkenwell. In the meantime Rosalie had fought hard to conceal not just her grief, but her overwhelming rage as she'd held her sister in her arms and stroked back her hair from her forehead. 'Take me to him,' Linette had whispered as she clutched her sister's hand.

'Who, Linette?' Rosalie had tried so hard to keep her voice steady, though the pain in her heart had threatened to choke her.

'He has a castle. A wonderful castle. Take me to him, please…' Linette had been struggling to speak by then. Faintly she'd breathed his name—then died, moments later, in Rosalie's arms.

Since then, Rosalie had redoubled her efforts to find Linette's destroyer, working her way round every London theatre, high and low. Not asking outright, for that brought danger; but pretending she was looking for a lost friend. And a few days ago, fast running out of hope, she'd visited a seedy little theatre off the Strand.

The greasy-haired manager, Alfred Marchmont, had said curiously, 'I remember a girl called Linette. Linette Lavalle, that was it—pretty, she was, well spoken, with fair hair…'

For a moment she could hardly breathe. Emotion

twisted her insides. At last she nodded. 'When was she here?'

'Well, she came for an audition—it would be, oh, spring three years ago; I've a good memory for faces and names.' Marchmont looked at her curiously. 'She was pretty, as I said, but she moved on after a couple of months to Dr Barnard's.'

Three years ago. 'Does this Dr Barnard run a theatre, then?'

Marchmont had hesitated. 'He runs a stage show. Of sorts.'

So now, at Dr Barnard's famous Temple of Beauty, Rosalie prepared herself to endure the company of the half-drunken *roués* upstairs. But as soon as Dr Barnard appeared and observed her there, she would slip down to his office to see if his secret book went back to the summer of 1813, when Linette might have worked here—and met Katy's father.

Chapter Four

'Look, lads, it's Captain Stewart! He was one of Wellington's officers at Waterloo!'

Alec Stewart was all set to leave the Temple of Beauty. There was no sign of his brother; Garrett must have been wrong. But now these friends of Lord Harry Nugent's had clustered around him in the smoke-filled bar, blocking his exit.

Alec made a half-hearted effort to answer their eager questions, but he was tired of battle talk. He wanted to point out to these young blades that war was a damnable business, then get the hell out of here. But then Harry himself appeared and accosted Alec with delight.

'So you decided to come after all, Alec! Weren't the girls just wonderful?'

'They were about as I expected, yes,' said Alec steadily. This wasn't the place or time to explain to Harry that actually he thought they looked greedy and desperate. Though not quite *all*. His eyes had been tugged reluctantly back to the stage by just one of the goddesses—Athena—the slender one who tossed her long fair hair and looked almost angry, as though she hated being there amongst those plump, painted courtesans…

For God's sake, man. She has to be a courtesan, too!

'Must go, Harry,' Alec said. But Harry was babbling in his ear, to make himself heard above the general din.

'You're not leaving yet, are you, Alec? You *must* stay for the dancing upstairs.' Harry was pointing eagerly to one of the many winding staircases that threaded through this tall, ancient building. 'You could have your pick, if they knew who you were!'

'Really not my style.' Alec clapped the curly-haired young man lightly on the shoulder. 'I only came because I thought my brother might be here—and he's not. Enjoy the rest of your birthday and don't let yourself be fleeced too badly, will you?' Alec started towards the exit.

'But, Alec, your brother *is* here!'

Alec ground to a halt. 'What?'

'He was too late for the show, but he went straight upstairs to the Inner Temple to take a look at the girls on offer there… Alec? Alec, if you're going up there, too, don't forget you'll have to get a ticket first!'

Alec, already making for the stairs, swung back. 'I'm not going to be paying for my pleasure, believe me.'

'But you need a ticket to get in! Look, you can buy one over there!'

Damn. Alec could see the queue snaking along one of the passageways. But—Stephen was here. And this was a matter—a *family* matter—that could not be put off any longer.

'And so, you see, sir,' Rosalie was saying earnestly, 'that the education of young women is absolutely *vital* to the future of social enlightenment, wouldn't you agree? By education, I mean, of course, not just needlework and a little French, but a full grounding in mathematics, the sciences…'

The young buck who'd waited so eagerly for a dance and possibly more with the extremely striking new blonde goddess was beginning to look distinctly alarmed. He muttered hastily, 'Just remembered. There's this fellow I've got to see…'

With narrowed eyes Rosalie watched the man hurry off across the crowded room towards the door. Five customers had so far bought tickets from the footman at the door to dance with her. Five customers had beaten a rapid retreat as soon as they decently could, thanks to her unexpected—and un-welcome—topics of conversation. Rosalie held up five fingers to Sal and mouthed, 'Enough?'

Sal, busy coping with the attentions of a drunken admirer in a loud plum coat, nodded and whispered back, 'Certainly is—thanks!'

Rosalie heaved a sigh of relief. She'd got Sal out of trouble and had managed to scare all her admirers to death within moments. Now all she had to do was wait for Dr Barnard to appear, then she could change out of this ridiculous outfit, slip down to his office, check his green book and get out of here. Mrs Barnard shouldn't be a problem; the old harridan was still playing the pianoforte with clunking determination, while couples waltzed and groped their way around the floor. Though Rosalie decided to move out of her line of sight, into an alcove away from the light of the candles, just to be on the safe side.

But someone was blocking her way. 'Oh!' Her hand flew to her throat.

For a fleeting moment, some faint physical resemblance made her think of the Captain. But even as her pulse started to race, she realised this man was older and not as tall, with a fleshier face and just a hint of a weak chin. And his clothes were—expensive. His coat was of bottle-green kerseymere, his cuffs were edged with lace and a diamond-studded silver pin nestled in the folds of his cravat. The rather strong scent of citrus cologne clung to him.

'My dear girl,' he said, 'I do apologise if I startled you—that wasn't my intention in the least. I wonder, would you do me the very great honour of dancing with me?'

'As a matter of fact,' she said quickly, 'I was just about to leave.'

A shadow of something—was it anxiety?—crossed his face. 'And I respect your wishes wholeheartedly, but might I mention that there could be a slight problem?'

'A problem?'

'Indeed. You see, I was talking to your Dr Barnard on the stairs only a moment ago. He's just returned to his office for more tickets for his doormen. But he'll be arriving here any minute; since I've paid him personally for a dance with you, he would be a little angry, I fear, to discover that you'd slipped away.'

Rosalie's heart sank. *So it still wasn't safe to get into Dr Barnard's office—bother.* She swallowed. 'Yes. I see…'

'I'll tell you what,' offered the man. 'Instead of dancing, I'll fetch you a glass of wine, shall I?'

'I would prefer lemonade,' she interrupted quickly. 'And I really cannot stay long.'

'I am honoured to be given even a few minutes of your time,' he said softly. 'You can't believe how eager I am for this chance to get to know you.'

Alec frowned as the footman took his ticket and waved him into the Inner Temple. The candle-lit room was filled with gaudy splashes of colour, thanks to the cheap gowns of the women and the scarlet and mauve wall-hangings. In one corner an older woman with red-dyed hair played the piano with more determination than skill and a dozen or more couples moved around the floor in a manner that clearly hinted at more intimate encounters. The odours of stale perfume and tobacco assailed his senses.

And there—Alec's square jaw tightened—there was his brother, Stephen, dressed to the nines as usual and talking to someone Alec couldn't quite see since Stephen's back blocked his view.

Alec walked with deceptive nonchalance across the room. People moved out of his way, as they tended to.

'Stephen,' he said softly at his brother's shoulder.

His brother swung round, the blood leaving his

face. 'You,' he muttered. 'Always *you*. What in hell are you doing here?'

'I've come to speak with *you*, Stephen.' Alec gazed thoughtfully at his brother. 'Since you're too scared to let me into your house, I thought we could have a pleasant little chat right here.'

'This is hardly the place or time to discuss private business!'

'Believe me—' and Alec's voice was suddenly harsher '—I take no pleasure at all in having to step anywhere near the dungheap of your *private business*. But you give me little option.'

Stephen's eyes darted round. Quite a few people were watching; some couples had actually stopped dancing to stare. Stephen turned to the person at his side. 'My dear,' he said, 'I do apologise for this gross intrusion.'

And for the first time, Alec realised who Stephen had been talking to.

He cursed under his breath. He hadn't wanted her to be here. Blue eyes, as he'd thought: turquoise blue. He absorbed the slender delicacy of her figure, the perfect outline of her profile, the way her silver-blonde hair trailed down the silken white column of her graceful neck...

Athena. He felt, for one wild moment, the overwhelming desire to haul her over his shoulder and carry her out of this tawdry place.

Then he realised she was wearing fresh face paint. Rouge, badly applied. Disillusion flooded him. *She is a whore, you fool.* Alec's gaze locked again with his brother's. 'Pay her off,' he said. 'This is just between you and me.'

He saw the girl whiten beneath that rouge as if he'd struck her. But at that very moment Stephen touched her shoulder. 'Listen, my dear,' Alec heard him murmur. 'If you will just wait for me over there, I'll be free in a moment, I promise you…'

'I said—pay her off,' interrupted Alec. 'Or I will.'

Stephen flushed and dipped into his pocket, then thrust some coins in the girl's hand. 'Here,' Alec heard him mutter. 'And there'll be more, if you'll wait for me…' He bent to whisper something.

Alec expected Athena to give Stephen an enticing smile, perhaps, or a curtsy of promise as she left.

But her blue eyes flashed scorn. Two spots of colour burned in her cheeks; then the girl just let those damned coins clatter one by one to the floor as if they scorched her. The noise interrupted the pianist, who stopped playing. And the girl stalked off without a backward glance, blonde head held high. Stephen clenched his fists and looked after her. 'Damn it, I needed to talk to her!'

'Wrong, Stephen,' Alec shot back. 'You need to talk to me.'

'Not here.' Stephen sounded quite feverish. 'For God's sake, not here, in public!'

This time Alec's voice was like a whiplash. 'You make it impossible for me to hold a conversation with you anywhere else. Now, I think you were about to explain to me why you were seen today by the whole of society driving in the park—and you were with her again. Then you come whoring, here. You are—unbelievable.'

'I had my reasons for coming here! A matter of unexpected business—'

'Business? Listen, Stephen. Don't you think it might be a good idea if you suddenly found some unexpected business to take you out of town, for a week, or two, or even longer?'

Stephen moistened dry lips. 'Are you attempting to threaten me?'

'If you think I'm merely attempting it, then I'm obviously not making myself clear enough. Let me put it this way. It would be as well for you, brother— it would be *very much* in your interests—if you disappeared from London for a while.'

'Damn you! You will not interfere like this!' Stephen looked round quickly at the avid onlookers who gathered closer. 'You know, I hold some cards, too, Alec. Push me too far and I'll play them, I swear!'

Alec gave a lethal half-smile. 'Then play them, brother mine. Damn well play them. Unlike you, I have nothing whatsoever to lose.'

'If you think—'

'For our father's sake, Stephen,' broke in Alec warningly, 'I'll expect news of your departure in the next day or so.' He looked around the room and its occupants with scorn. 'Now, my God, I'm out of here.'

'Back to your old soldiers,' muttered Stephen.

Alec swung round on him. 'My old soldiers smell sweeter than this sewer of a place.' And he strode off, the crowd parting to make way for him, the door crashing shut after him as he left.

The murmuring rose to excited chatter. All eyes were now fastened on Stephen, who, still flushed with anger, walked quickly towards the ante-room where refreshments were being served, looking, looking all the time. *That girl*, Stephen swore under his breath. Thanks to his damned brother, that girl, who looked like the other one, had got clean away.

In fact, Rosalie was still there, pressed into a shadowed alcove. She saw that slowly the room was returning to normal. Dr Barnard had arrived and, suspecting there'd been trouble of some kind, he spoke curtly to his wife, who began to play the piano again extremely loudly. Dr Barnard called out that the wine was on the house and a cheer was raised; couples started returning to the dance floor.

But Rosalie's pulse rate showed no sign of calming.

Something had happened to her when the Captain drew near. It wasn't just that he was so handsome. It was because he was so *different* from all these other men. It was as if he was some kind of rebel, walking alone and unarmed into an enemy camp, quite heedless of any consequences. And close up, she'd been able to see even more clearly how his overlong dark hair, his ill-tied neckcloth, the shabby long coat that moulded itself to the powerful muscles of his shoulders and chest, only added to the hint of danger that blazed in those emotion-packed eyes.

He was, quite simply, devastating. And he thought her a whore. *Pay her off—or I will.*

She shivered. She saw that the man Stephen was now talking in a low voice to some footmen at the door. She didn't want to see any more of *him* either, and the sooner she was out of here the better…

'Ros. Ros? Thank God I've found you, girl.' It was Sal, tugging at her sleeve. 'Now listen, you've done me a favour, so I'll do you one, right? Dr Barnard, he's after you. Someone's said to him you've got some connection with a London gossip rag.'

Oh, no. Rosalie caught her breath and tried to laugh. 'Ridiculous—what on earth makes him think that?'

'No use trying flummery with this one, gal. Our Danny-boy's told Dr B. he's seen you out deliverin' news sheets. And soon as he's got everyone back and busy on the dance floor, Dr Barnard is going to be huntin' for you, see?'

Oh, Lord. Rosalie was already on her way, hurrying through the crowd to the back staircase.

Down to the office first, for that all-important book of clients. Then—she'd be on her way.

Alec was walking steadily down the stairs. His brother would do as he'd said and clear out of town for a while, no doubt of that—Stephen's knees had actually been shaking. Though whether Stephen's departure was the solution to a stinking mess or merely a temporary reprieve was another matter altogether.

And Alec was still puzzled as to why Stephen was here. He'd said he had business here—unexpected business. But…with a sweet-faced whore who refused his money almost in disgust?

Alec paused at a branching of the stairs, his brow

dark with thought. When, exactly, had Stephen started hating him? Probably the day Alec was born, unfortunately.

'You. Always you,' Stephen had hissed just now.

Long ago, on his fifth birthday, Alec had been tearing round the estate on a lively pony—his birthday gift—when it stumbled over a fallen branch on a woodland path. Alec had been thrown, breaking his leg.

He'd imagined he saw Stephen, a little ahead of him between the trees, watching him. And days later, lying bed-bound and drowsy with medicines for the pain, he'd heard their father say to their mother, in Alec's bedroom, 'To think that Stephen was capable of such mischief. God help me, but, young though they are, I find myself wishing more and more that Alec were the heir…'

His parents had not seen, as Alec had, his brother lurking outside the half-open door, his eyes venomous with the beginnings of the hatred Alec had noticed just now.

Yes, it was Stephen who'd laid that branch across Alec's path and their father knew it. So did the groom, who warned Alec, grim-faced, when he was getting used to riding again after his leg healed, *You watch out for that brother of yours, Master Alec, sir.*

As he grew up, Alec had never cared that Stephen

was the heir rather than himself. But he knew that Stephen would never forgive him for what their father had said—ever.

He'd barely reached the first-floor landing of the Temple of Beauty when he heard heavy footsteps on the stairs above him. He glanced around. Two of Dr Barnard's footmen, burly brutes both, were heading downwards also and he stepped aside to let them pass.

They didn't.

They came directly towards him. Their faces were twisted with an emotion Alec recognised all too easily. The hunger for a fight. *Damn it.*

The bigger one, a beefy wretch with some missing teeth, went for Alec with his fist, clearly intending a blow straight to the gut. But Alec caught the man a swinging punch to the jaw that made his victim stagger and fall with his hand to his mouth. *More of his teeth gone, hopefully.* In virtually the same moment Alec whipped back his elbow into the stomach of the other brute, driving the wind from his lungs so that he bent double and had to gasp for air.

If they wanted a mill, they'd got it. But Alec knew this would be Stephen's doing. And now—hell, now was going to be difficult, because three more of Dr Barnard's henchmen were coming from the other direction, speeding up as they saw their two felled comrades struggling to their feet…

Not playing fair, Stephen. But then, you never did. With a bit of luck Alec knew he could fling a couple of his opponents down the nearby staircase. But even so, the odds were not good. They were coming for him purposefully, with evil leers on their faces.

'Oh, my brave, brave boys,' said Alec Stewart gently, 'five against one—but even so I'd bet money on me. Do you know why? Because you're a bunch of thick-skulled bastards who would just turn and run at the prospect of any *real* fighting…'

They charged him like enraged bulls, which was Alec's intention. Anger slowed both brains and fists, especially when Alec, moving with light ease, tripped two of them up as they blundered forwards, then sliced another across the throat with the edge of his hand and brought his fist up beneath the fourth one's jaw so the ruffian bit on his own tongue and let out a bloody cry of pain. But Alec knew the odds were against him; it was only a matter of time before he went down.

Suddenly he glimpsed someone else sidling down those damned stairs. A girl looking as if she didn't want to be seen, glancing behind her all the time as if fearing pursuit. But on hearing the noise of the fight, she turned to look down and Alec saw her gasp with shock.

Hell. He flung another punch as one of the brutes ventured too close. It was Athena, in her diaphanous gown. Another enemy. Would the blonde-haired whore stand and gloat at his plight? Or actually join in? The latter at present seemed most likely, because as more of the brutes closed in on him she hurried down the last few steps to the landing where the action was and picked up a small pedestal table that stood in a corner.

Dear God, thought Alec a little faintly, *I'm in for it now.* There was an expression on her face of utter and relentless determination. Alec mentally prepared himself for a final, nasty blow from that small but heavy table.

Shifting her grip to hold it by its base, she swung the table hard against the thighs of his biggest opponent. The man let out a howl of outrage and toppled to his knees. Another man reached out to grab her with an oath—'Come here, you blasted—'—but she dropped the table, slipped neatly from his grasp and kneed him in the groin.

Alec blinked. *Ouch.* Dirty tactics. But he could hear more footsteps, running *up* the stairs this time; then a familiar voice accosted his ears.

'Captain! What ho, Captain Stewart, is that you?'

Not more of Dr Barnard's men, but curly-haired Lord Harry Nugent. Swiftly Harry took in the scene, then gestured his friends forwards with a whoop of delight. 'Come on, lads!' Harry cried. 'Don't like the odds here, against a hero of Waterloo! Let's show 'em a bit of the home-brewed!' Instantly the crowd of young men launched themselves at the footmen, cheering.

The footmen, aghast, tried to flee up the stairs, to the room where the dancing was. But Harry's friends followed and within seconds, Dr Barnard's Inner Temple was more like a rowdy backstreet tavern than a gentlemen's club. As more footmen joined the battle, Harry fought at Alec's side; Alec watched with widening eyes as each of Harry's vigorous punches found its mark—perhaps Harry should take up boxing rather than the foil.

But then Alec began to realise that the girl had disappeared.

Harry caught his eye as the number of assailants dwindled. 'A more exciting night than you thought, Captain!' he called. 'Did you see me draw the stout one's cork?'

Alec shrugged his wide shoulders, laughing. 'Indeed. I underestimated the Temple of Beauty. But do you know what happened to the girl who was here a few moments ago, Harry? The blonde girl who played Athena?'

'She ran past us, on her way down the stairs.' Harry paused to enthusiastically thump a footman who was trying to sneak away. 'Apparently she's in trouble with Dr Barnard's men, too.'

'Is she, by God?' breathed Alec Stewart. 'Is she, now? Look out behind you, Harry!'

Wham. Harry planted a first-class facer. Alec grinned, then turned his back on the battle. He was off, to find Athena.

Chapter Five

Rosalie's heart was sinking fast. Where was she in this labyrinth of passages and stairs? How on earth was she going to find her way to Dr Barnard's office? She needed to see his precious private register, *now*. Because after tonight, returning to the Temple of Beauty just wasn't an option.

Coming to the aid of the Captain had been so stupid! She should have just quietly slipped past all those brawling men while she had the chance! But seeing him there, fighting all those ruffians by himself, had struck her as so unfair...

You fool. He believes you to be a whore. And you're out of your mind to waste precious moments even thinking *about him, when Dr Barnard knows you write for* The Scribbler, *and has sent his men to scour the place for you!*

She stole along yet another dimly lit corridor. The sounds of fighting reverberated round the entire building. What an evening. What a place. And she wasn't out of it yet, because someone else was coming towards her. Someone who reached her before she'd even had a chance to run.

'So here you are, Athena,' said the Captain softly. 'I've a few questions for you.'

Damn. She whipped round and went tearing back the way she'd come, but she heard him striding after her. Swinging past a corner, she pushed at a half-open door into a shadowy room where only a single candle spluttered in a sconce. Charging inside, she flattened herself against the wall, closed her eyes and uttered a fervent prayer that he'd go straight past.

He didn't. He came in. Rosalie dived past him for the still-open door, but he caught her easily by the wrist; when she opened her mouth to utter a scream, she found his other hand clamped firmly across it. She struggled. Yet at the touch of his palm, strong and warm against her lips, a strange tingling sensation started up in all her nerve endings.

'Keep still,' he hissed, kicking the door shut with one booted foot.

She tried to bite his hand. He cursed. Then she froze. More heavy footsteps were coming down the corridor outside. Her chest was so tight she could scarcely breathe. Were they after the Captain? Or—her?

The footsteps went past. She sagged, tension leaving her weak.

The Captain was no longer holding her. But there was no chance of escape, because his broad-shouldered figure completely barred the way.

Something else was just starting to dawn on her. This room was one of *those* rooms that gentlemen paid for. Heavy curtains shrouded the windows and a rather large and obvious velvet couch draped with a shabby silk counterpane filled one corner. The mingled odours of patchouli and tobacco filled the air, and the paintings on the walls—*oh, Lord, those paintings...*

'I understand, Athena,' he said softly, 'that you're in trouble.'

'Trouble?' Rosalie tried to laugh. 'What nonsense. I simply work here, as you've seen...'

He was watching her with inscrutable eyes. 'Then why were you running? Why has Dr Barnard set his men at the main exits to stop you escaping?'

As Sal had said. She sagged again.

'Exactly,' he went on tersely. 'And just for the moment, you're better off—believe it or not—in here. With me.' He tilted his head to indicate the riotous noise of brawling on every floor of this tall house.

The candles flickered, warningly. And oh, how their shadows highlighted the hard slant of his cheekbones, the wicked curl of his sensual mouth. Rosalie swallowed on the dryness in her throat. His dark eyes—she saw now they were velvet-brown, almost black—glowed with golden flecks as he gazed down at her. For a reason she couldn't explain, a sudden lick of heat uncoiled from deep within and suffused every part of her body.

In trouble. Oh, yes.

Suddenly, like an eel—*my God*, thought Alec, *this one's used to fighting her own corner*—she twisted from his grasp and ran for another door she'd spied at the far end of this whore's boudoir. He lunged after her and caught her easily, this time trapping her by planting his hands firmly against the wall on either side of her shoulders. Her small breasts rose and fell in agitation; her amazing turquoise-blue eyes were wide with defiance.

'Steady. Steady, Athena,' warned Alec. 'You know, I'd really like you to explain why you came to my aid in that brawl back there.'

She hadn't the faintest idea. She jerked her head up. 'How about *you* explaining why you're reduced to paying for your pleasure in a place like this?'

And her lips spouted insults. Surprisingly eloquent insults, registered Alec. And the scent of her gleaming blonde hair was quite bewitching. She tried again to wriggle away, knocking a small painting off its hook on the wall so that it crashed to the floor. He stepped back, involuntarily; she swooped to the ground and picked it up.

'Oh!' she cried. 'Look what you made me do, you fool! Luckily it's not damaged...'

Alec looked on, incredulous as she turned her back on him and very carefully replaced the painting on the wall. He said at last, 'You know, you're in all sorts of trouble, Athena. And you're worried about—a *painting*?'

She looked at him furiously. 'It's not just a painting, like the other cheap nonsense in here!' The colour tinged her cheeks as she glanced round at the other works of art, whose content, Alec had noted, was decidedly bawdy. 'Any fool can see that this painting is by Boucher and he's famous for his watercolours! His paintings are masterpieces, though what one of them is doing in *this* dreadful place I cannot imagine!'

Dreadful place. Alec noted that. 'How, Athena, do you know about art?'

Her hands were on her hips again; she tossed back her hair defiantly. 'Why shouldn't I know about art? Anyway, I'm not the only one in trouble—what did *you* do, to make those men attack you?'

'I rather think,' he said, 'that I offended someone here tonight.'

'If you go around speaking to people as you did to that man you called Stephen, then I'm not in the least surprised!' she said tartly. 'Why were you so rude to him?'

He shrugged. 'I don't like him very much,' he said. 'And judging by the way you threw his money back in his face, you didn't take to him either.'

Rosalie caught her breath. Something she'd never experienced before surged warmly through her. She, normally so resistant to men and their various wiles, could not even look this one in the eyes—those dark, glinting eyes—without her stomach turning peculiarly upside down.

Alone in a whore's boudoir. With him.

Outside beyond this room the mayhem continued, with the sounds of men brawling and furniture breaking, followed by the crashing jangle of Mrs Barnard's piano as it went over on its side. Rosalie forced herself to meet his dark eyes. 'Do you have this effect wherever you go?'

'Not my fault. I told you, someone paid those louts to attack me. Though it's true that I attract attention,' he said. His sleepy eyes gazed, unblinking, into hers. 'Yours, for example, Athena. Earlier I saw you watching me. From the stage.'

Her heart juddered. 'Watching you! Ridiculous! I'm short-sighted, I couldn't possibly see that far!'

'Strange, I gained the distinct impression you were watching me quite carefully.'

His hand, unbelievably, was curling round her slender waist. Drawing her close. Even more unbelievably, she was letting him do it. His fingertips were warm and firm through the filmy fabric of this stupid gown… She jerked herself away, the blood racing through her veins. 'Oh, no! You can *stop* this, right now!'

'Stop? But isn't this why you're here?' His expression was innocent, but there was a hint of dark irony in his voice. 'To—make yourself available?'

Damn the man. 'Yes,' she lied, her heart racing, 'yes, of course, but at a time like this—it's absurd—it's like…'

'Fiddling while Rome burns?' he murmured, eyes glinting. 'Deuce—I forgot—we're supposed to be in Grecian mythology tonight, aren't we? Athena, I appeal to your sense of justice. My God, I've had to pay *a lot* for tonight's entertainment!'

She let her eyes rove scornfully over his shabby coat, which had certainly seen better days. 'Too expensive for you?' she said sweetly.

'It's a matter of principle.' He smiled pleasantly

back. 'You see, I normally never have to pay for female company.'

Unbelievable arrogance! She gasped and tried to slap him; a mistake, because he caught hold of her raised wrist, and of course once more she was in his power. She fought hard to free herself. 'Let me go. You *know* that I'm in danger here and need to get out!'

Just then a couple of men tangled in drunken combat blundered through the doorway, grunting and swearing. Releasing her, he moved swiftly to push them back into the hall and kicked the door shut again, hard, before locking it.

And he came slowly back towards her. Dear Lord, this man was dangerous. Hadn't she registered it from the moment she saw him? That velvet couch seemed to fill the blasted room. Even the single candle flickered as if in warning. A coil of something dark, something forbidden, snaked down to her stomach even as she clamped down desperately on the effect this man was having on her pulse rate. Her breathing. Her *existence*.

'A bargain, Athena,' he said quietly. 'I'll get you safely out of here, if you'll tell me why that man Stephen claimed to have business with you.'

She shrugged and moistened her dry lips. 'How

should I know? He just said—he was eager to get to know me better. As they all do,' she supposed.

His dark eyes flashed with incredulity. 'Yet you threw away his money?'

Rosalie glanced towards the locked door. 'Let me go now. Please.'

Still his lithe figure blocked her way. His strong hands were warm on her shoulders again. 'Not before you promise me that you won't throw yourself away, in a place like this. To a brute like Lord Stephen Maybury.'

She breathed in sharply. The touch of his fingers was nothing less than a caress. Gathering her wits to protest, she couldn't help but notice that on one of his hard cheekbones a livid bruise was appearing. And there must be other injuries, all over that lithe and supple body...

'Perhaps you should stay away from here yourself,' she said, tossing her head. 'Those men were trying very hard to kill you.'

He arched one eyebrow. 'And that's why you launched yourself into the fray—*on my side*? Surely you're not telling me that you actually care?'

'No! I mean, you're just another client of Dr Barnard's, your private affairs are no business of mine whatsoever!'

'A true professional,' he was murmuring, in that

husky voice that made her blood pound. 'How much does it cost for a kiss, Athena? And don't try telling me again that you're not for sale.'

He was drawing her closer. She could feel the heat of his body now. See the texture of his skin, his lightly stubbled jaw that her fingers ached to touch…

'Let me tell you,' he was saying softly, 'that on closer inspection I'd have paid twice the usual rate— for *this*.' His eyes never leaving hers, he lowered his head and brushed her lips with his.

It was a fleeting caress, but even so Rosalie had never experienced anything like it. A sweet, melting sensation was pouring through her nerve ends. A moment later his strong arms were cradling her even more securely and he was kissing her properly, his mouth possessing hers, his tongue stroking her soft inner moistness in a sensual dance that stirred the blood in her veins to white heat.

He was masterful. Dangerous. Exquisitely provocative. The worst of it was that she wanted more and he knew it. She felt one of his strong hands slide up to cup the back of her head so his tongue could continue its rhythmic thrust, the slight roughness of his stubbled jaw providing a sensuous counterpoint to the silken sweetness of his mouth. His other hand slid tighter round her waist, pulling her closer against the hardness of his powerful body, his chest, his thighs. The urge to succumb to this dark magic and open herself to his potent masculinity was irresistible. Her hands crept upwards of their own volition to cling to his shoulders, feeling and savouring the vital force of his body.

This should not be happening. She'd sworn to let no man touch her again, yet her body was melting to his every caress.

He let out some sort of sigh and pulled her still closer. Now his right hand was sliding over the thin muslin that covered her breasts and, as her nipples peaked beneath his touch, she shuddered. The liquid warmth in her lower abdomen was like a burning ache of need; her mouth opened wider to his relentless plundering, and for Rosalie, for that space of time, nothing else existed. The fighting, the clattering of furniture up above, the bursts of raucous shouting, all receded into a meaningless background noise. There was no one else in the whole wide world but her and him.

Until he let her go. She felt bereft. Her legs were so weak that she could almost have sunk on to that blasted sofa in the corner.

Alec stepped back. *Damn.* He knew he'd come to his senses a little too late. It was a long time since he'd been so tempted by a woman. *Too* long, if he was feeling like this about one of Dr Barnard's wenches. And he certainly wasn't prepared for what this one's melting pink lips did to him.

Shy. Delicate. God, it was almost as if she'd never experienced a man's kiss! Yet at the same time she was so sweetly, wonderingly responsive that sheer lust had for a moment gripped his loins…

Damn it. She was a bewitching little hoyden, feigning innocence when the rouge was still fresh on her face—hoping, perhaps, to lure him into making some sort of offer for her, because she sure as hell wasn't going to be working *here* again. Gazing down at her, he held up his five-shilling ticket for the dancing that he'd drawn from his pocket and, tearing it into tiny pieces, let it flutter to the floor.

'Well worth it, for that kiss,' he said flatly. 'You're surprisingly good at what you do.'

Rosalie felt, suddenly, as if her heated blood had turned to ice in her veins. Of course. He thought her a whore.

'Do you know,' she said steadily, 'I was a fool to come to your rescue earlier. Doubtless you thoroughly deserved the beating you were about to get. Will you let me past, please?'

'Feel free to go.' He shrugged. 'And I hope you find a new job soon. You'll certainly need to. Remember what I told you. They're watching for you down at the main exits.'

He saw the colour leave her face beneath that rouge. 'The main exits…'

He jerked a finger towards the far door, the one she'd already tried to make a run for. 'One of the first rules of warfare, blue-eyed Athena: always plan your escape before the battle begins. If this house runs true to form, through there is a flight of stairs that leads down to the back of the house, where you should find an unguarded door.'

'And—and you?' *Curse the man*, thought Rosalie. Why did she ask that?

He lifted his eyebrows as if the same thought had struck him. 'You still care? I'll go and check that Harry and his friends aren't doing too much damage. Then I'll leave, too.'

He held the door open to show her the stairwell. Head high, she marched past him.

'Remember,' he called out softly, 'watch out for Maybury.'

She made no acknowledgement. But halfway down, where the staircase turned so he could see her no more, she leaned her back against the wall. Oh—*fiddlesticks*. The man called Lord Stephen Maybury posed no threat whatsoever as far as she was concerned. But dear God, the Captain was another matter altogether.

She felt dazed. She'd been out of her mind, to let him caress her like that. She had been pressed so close to his body that the potent force of his manhood had been all too evident in the heat of their embrace—and *he* had been the one to move away first!

She felt shattered. She felt bereft.

And his kiss had been the most magical moment of her life.

She hurried on down the stairs, ashamed because her legs were shaking. *If those brutes caught her...* But he was right. None of Dr Barnard's men were to be seen in the back room she emerged into.

The dressing room first. No time to get changed, so she thrust the clothes she'd arrived in into a bag, rammed on her cloak and bonnet, and stole into Dr Barnard's silent office. *Back to business, you fool.* Reaching up, she heaved down that heavy tome—*The Myths of Apollodorus*—then laid it on the desk and opened it.

As Helen had said, the pages had been carved away to form a cavity. Inside was a book bound in green morocco, where the names of Dr Barnard's many customers were listed by the dates of their visits, together with their addresses.

But the name her dying sister had whispered was not here. She flicked to and fro, her agitation increasing. She checked all through the spring and early summer of 1813, but there was no sign of it at all. All this effort, all this risk, and she was no nearer in her search. For a few moments the disappointment crushed her.

But towards the back of the book, she found a list of the girls who'd been employed here. *June 1813. Linette Lavalle.* She caught her breath. That was the name Linette had used at Marchmont's theatre. Their mother's maiden name. She read on hurriedly. *From the country... The girl has fancy ideas above her station. Refused to do anything except the stage show—then one day just didn't turn up. Found herself a rich protector, I suspect...*

Her throat aching with sadness, Rosalie carefully replaced the book in its hiding place, then stole from the house, using the door the Captain had told her was unguarded. Outside it was starting to rain, heavily. Rosalie hailed a hackney cab—her one concession to Helen's concern for her safety—and the driver gave her a look indicating what he thought of young women out on their own at this time of night. She tossed her head defiantly as she gave him directions.

But all the way back to Clerkenwell the usual

questions tormented her. When had Linette realised that she was pregnant? Was that when her—*protector* discarded her? Had her poor sister lived for a while in the agonised hope that her seducer might marry her?

Oh, Linette.

Alec Stewart rode back to Two Crows Castle as the rain poured down on London's dark streets. Those damned footmen would have been paid to attack him by his brother, as Stephen's cowardly revenge for Alec's ultimatum tonight.

As revenge on Alec for *existing.*

When Stephen went away to boarding school, distance had temporarily eased their relationship. But Alec's arrival at the same school two years later had sparked off the old jealousy, especially since Alec, as ever, had excelled at sports and had a light-hearted manner that made him friends far more easily than Stephen did.

A crisis came when Stephen, aged fifteen, had set up a secret gambling clique and, when discovery threatened, had slipped the evidence—cards, dice and money—under Alec's dormitory bed.

Alec had silently taken the blame and the beating for it. But since then Alec had not troubled to show his contempt for Stephen on the rare occasions on which they met. A year ago Alec had been utterly disowned by their father—told he was no longer part of the family, in effect—and Alec had thought Stephen would be satisfied. No danger now of Alec supplanting Stephen in the Earl's affections.

Yet still his brother diced with fate.

Why had Stephen come here, to idle away his time in a place like the Temple of Beauty, picking up girls like blonde Athena?

Alec felt his insides clenching again. That girl. The girl who knew about French watercolours, with her exquisite face and her clouds of silver-gold hair and that meltingly slender body… He remembered how, as he drew her close, her warm breath had feathered his cheek and the delicate scent of lavender had risen sweetly from her skin. Remembered how her fingers had almost shyly stolen up to his shoulders, how her lips had parted for his kiss.

But then had come the moment of pure shock. For as he took the kiss deeper, as he prised her lips further apart, she'd registered almost utter innocence. Her exquisite, thick-lashed blue eyes had flown wide open in surprise as he tasted the soft flesh of her mouth and, when he'd cupped her tender breast and felt it peak, he would swear she'd shuddered in his arms and clung to him as if she'd never experienced a man's caress before.

He'd only pursued her because he wanted to know what Stephen's business was with her. That kiss had been part of his strategy to wrongfoot her. Yet he, Alec, had been the one to leave that place with all his convictions shaken.

Be sensible, you fool. The rouge was still fresh on her face. Innocent? Impossible. Yet his body still raged for her.

His mouth set in a hard line. Just a clever act on her part, down to the detail of denying any interest in his rich brother's attentions. And she was in trouble with Dr Barnard—probably for arranging appointments with clients on the side and keeping all the profits for herself, a common trick.

His mind flew on in conjecture. Yes, she had an air of innocence that would draw men to her like moths to a candle flame. But she worked at the Temple of Beauty where she was attracting the likes of Stephen, damned Stephen, who, having spent years of debauchery with professionals like *her*, was now, whenever he could, secretly pleasuring the woman who just happened to be their father the Earl's beautiful young wife.

Chapter Six

By the time that Rosalie let herself into Helen's house in Clerkenwell, it was almost midnight. Lighting the lamp in the kitchen, she made a pot of tea quietly so as not to wake anyone. Then she sat down by the embers of the fire, still huddled in her cloak. Tonight had been a disaster—not least her encounter with the Captain, who'd managed to disturb her peace of mind in a manner that she guessed would cause her more than one sleepless night.

Why was he there?

Be honest with yourself, Rosalie. Why did any men go there? They went, of course, be they lords or tradesmen, to ogle the girls and pick out one for an hour of lechery upstairs. And at a place like that, her sister's seducer would have found it easy to spot Linette, with her head full of fanciful dreams.

She drew some blank paper from a nearby table towards her and by the light of the lamp started writing, assuming the easy-going tones of her *alter ego*, Ro Rowland. Since childhood, she'd found that it helped to write. Her earliest stories had been fantasies, a way of escaping into a place where happy endings existed. Later she'd found that wit was an even more effective weapon against the cruelty of strangers and this was now Ro Rowland's world— a world not one of heartbreak, but of wry, almost cynical humour.

Tonight your fellow about town Ro Rowland took himself to the well-known Temple of Beauty. And there he observed... The Captain. Damn him, damn him. She stared into the distance, her thoughts unravelling once more. A fencing master, Sal had said.

It had been a long time since Rosalie allowed herself to think of any man with anything other than suspicion. Yet the thought of an hour alone with that dark-haired rogue, using the private room in Dr Barnard's house for the purpose it was intended, set off a disturbing wobble somewhere at the pit of her stomach. She could not forget the rough silk of his lips and tongue; the warm, muscle-packed strength of his body—his *aroused* body—moving against hers... Oh, Lord. *You stupid fool.*

Suddenly she heard footsteps out in the hallway and Helen padded in, her long nightshirt covered by a large India shawl. Rosalie jumped to her feet. 'I'm so sorry, Helen. I didn't mean to wake you!'

'I was awake anyway. I heard the hackney and I'm just so glad you're back safely… Rosalie, why are you still wearing your cloak?'

Because I'm wearing next to nothing underneath it! Airily Rosalie replied, 'Oh, I'm a little cold, that's all. Would you like some tea?'

'Yes, please.' Helen pushed her loose brown hair back from her face, adjusted her spectacles and flopped down in a chair. 'How did you get on at the Temple of Beauty? Was it full of fat old *roués*?'

'They weren't all old!'

'But they're all despicable, the men who patronise such entertainments! Oh, I knew that you shouldn't go.'

Rosalie decided there and then that it just wasn't safe to tell her friend any more. 'I was perfectly all right.' *What a terrible lie.* 'It was actually quite boring.' *An even worse lie.* Rosalie quickly poured Helen's tea and curled up on the small settee opposite her. 'Helen, did you manage to get *The Scribbler* out everywhere today?'

Helen immediately looked happier. 'I did. That piece you wrote about the swells in Hyde Park is going down an absolute treat.'

'Good! Though I hope none of the men I described recognises himself; I'd really hate to get you into trouble. Did you take Toby with you to deliver them?'

Helen sipped her tea. 'Yes, but I left Katy with Biddy; she's happy with her.'

Biddy O'Brien was a warm-hearted young Irish neighbour who kept house for her brothers, all in the building trade. She came in every day to clean Helen's home and the children adored her.

'Thank goodness for Biddy,' said Rosalie fervently. 'But, Helen, you really should allow me to pay you for letting Katy and me stay here.' She had offered before, but had always been refused.

Helen chuckled. 'Your Ro Rowland articles are payment enough, believe me. I've never sold so many copies of *The Scribbler*, and people are always asking me who the real Ro Rowland is!' Her face suddenly became more serious. 'We're two sides of the same coin, you and I. You expose the wealthy by making fun of them, whereas I hope to *shame* them by pointing out the truth. Just as in my report the other day about that haughty woman—the wife of an earl, no less!—who had a young maidservant whipped and dismissed, simply because she accidentally dropped a vase. A paltry vase, Rosalie!'

'I know. The poor, poor girl…' Rosalie hesitated.

'Helen, I did just wonder. If this earl or his wife should hear of your article…'

'I mentioned no names. And even if they guess, they'll not dare to take action. That would be as good as admitting their own guilt!' replied Helen crisply. 'You know, it's as if the so-called lower classes aren't *human* to these people! Though it's one thing for me to be as outspoken as I am, but quite another for you, you're so much younger. Sometimes I even wonder if you should be writing your articles for me.'

'What, me stop being Ro Rowland? Dear Helen, I adore writing; if you didn't print my pieces in *The Scribbler*, I'd find someone else to publish them, I assure you! I am twenty-one, after all! I *love* exploring London, and all the fascinating people I meet on its streets…' Her smile faded. 'Well, nearly all of them.'

'Be careful. That's all,' said Helen crisply. 'And, Rosalie dear—' Helen was already delving into a pile of notes on the table '—if you're determined to keep writing as Ro Rowland—'

'Try to stop me!'

'In that case, I thought that *this* might be just up your street, because I know that you were, only the other day, starting to write an article about the rapacious landlords of London who let out hovels for high rents to desperate people!'

Rosalie nodded. The practice known as rack-renting was a subject close to her heart, not least because of that dreadful room off the Ratcliffe Highway where her sister had died.

Helen was adjusting her spectacles and running her finger down a sheet of her own notes. 'As chance would have it, I heard today about a place in—yes, Spitalfields—that takes disgraceful advantage of poor soldiers. It's called Two Crows Castle, and it's not a real castle at all, but a rundown barracks of a place, owned by some ne'er-do-well—I haven't got his name—who lets out rooms at exorbitant rents to unemployed soldiers. I thought you might investigate.'

'Of course! Spitalfields, you said? Where, exactly?'

'The house is in Crispin Street. It's an unsavoury area even by daylight, so I trust you're not even thinking of actually going there, my dear! But what I did hope was that tomorrow you might deliver a bundle of *Scribblers* to the news vendor in Bishopsgate, which is close by. You could take one of Biddy's brothers with you and just ask some of the shopkeepers there—carefully, mind!—about this Two Crows place.'

Building work was slack this time of year and Rosalie knew that one or other of Biddy's burly brothers could usually be relied upon to take on extra jobs for Helen—repair work to Helen's house, errands, or in this case, thought Rosalie wryly, a spot of personal protection.

Rosalie patted Helen's hand. 'It sounds just my sort of story. I'll get your *Scribblers* delivered, and I'll make sure I've got an O'Brien brother with me before I start asking any questions about crooked rackrenters.' She was just getting up to tidy away the tea things when the door opened and two sleepy little figures stood there hand in hand.

'Toby!' cried Helen. 'Katy! What are you doing, out of your beds?'

Toby clung to Katy's hand protectively. 'She was crying,' he explained. 'I thought one of you would hear her, but you didn't. She's upset.'

'Oh, Katy darling.' Rosalie picked up and hugged the tear-stained infant, who was clutching her battered rag doll. 'Poor Katy, what's the matter?'

'Mama,' whispered the child. 'I want Mama.'

Rosalie kissed her, at the same time fighting down the sudden ache in her throat. Taking Katy upstairs to the cot in the corner of the bedroom they shared, she gently sang her to sleep. Tenderness and love she could give in abundance; she would also fight, with all her strength, to make sure Katy was not pointed at, whispered at, as she and her sister used to be as children.

Taking off her cloak at last, she smoothed down her filmy muslin gown and stared into the darkness beyond the candlelight as another memory wrenched her: of her mother dressing both her children carefully for the Christmas service at the nearby church. It had been their second winter in England and snow lay thickly. 'Mama,' Rosalie had said, 'do we *have* to go? I don't think they like us there...'

'Christmas is different, *ma chère*,' had said her mother, wrapping Rosalie's scarf tightly against the winter chill. 'It is the season of goodwill to all.'

But not to the Frenchwoman and her family. The vicar had turned them away. And her mother's stricken face, as they trudged home through the snow, would stay with Rosalie for ever.

That same night Rosalie had written a story for Linette, about a party at a magical castle. Linette's face had lit up as she read it. 'Will I ever go inside a *real* castle?'

'Some day, why not? There'll be food, and dancing, and—oh, we shall wear such pretty dresses, Linette!'

'There might be a prince!' Linette's eyes shone.

'And he will dance with me, and I will be a princess… Won't I, Rosalie? Won't I?'

Now Linette was dead, along with all her dreams. As Helen bustled around downstairs putting out the lamps, and Katy slept, Rosalie vowed anew that she would never rest, until she'd found the man who'd destroyed her sister's life.

Lord Stephen Maybury was sitting alone in the candlelit library of his fine house in Brook Street. And the more he pondered on the events of the evening, the darker grew his thoughts. *The girl.* The girl with impossibly fair hair and turquoise eyes, at the Temple of Beauty tonight… Who in hell was she?

When Markin, his serving man, had informed him earlier about the new one who'd joined Dr Barnard's troupe of so-called actresses, and how she resembled the other, Stephen had put it down to Markin's imagination.

But Markin, whose visage was made sinister by a pale scar, had been, in his way, adamant. Markin had spies everywhere; that was what Stephen paid him for. Markin had seen her himself, he'd told his master, entering the building early this evening to get ready for her first night on stage with the other women. Looking nervous.

'This new one, my lord,' he told Stephen, 'no one could say she's the exact image. She's older, for a start. But I could see something…'

Could she be family? God forbid. The other one had been gently born, a virgin, a mistake in other words, and Stephen wanted no past scandal rearing its ugly head. So he'd gone to look for himself. And the new girl was not at all what he'd expected. There was a physical similarity, yes. But this one was spirited. Defiant. His lip curled. My God, he'd have enjoyed breaking that spirit.

But if there *was* a connection, it could mean danger. And his questioning of the girl tonight had been wrecked by damned Alec, who even after Stephen had paid those footmen to give him a beating, had friends running to defend him from all corners of the building!

More than ever Stephen wanted his younger brother destroyed. Alec had been a torment to him since childhood—taking Stephen's place in their father's affections, parading himself in his army uniform all around town. Then last year Alec had fortuitously sealed his own fate and got himself disinherited.

But his brother could still be a threat. Best for now to do what he suggested and leave town for a while. Just in case Alec was tempted to do anything rash.

As he cursed his brother anew, Stephen's eye fell on a cheap news sheet he had picked up earlier. *The Scribbler*, it was called. Idly, he flicked through it. And he froze.

Why Lady A. feels she has the right to so viciously punish a poor young maid for a minor accident—to inflict such suffering over a mere broken vase!—is, dear reader, beyond the average citizen's comprehension...

Stephen's blood boiled. He called Markin, who was dressed in black as usual, and thrust the news sheet at him. 'Find out where this sordid scandal-sheet is published, will you? And check out the Temple of Beauty, for more about that fair-haired whore!'

There must be a way to find some weakness in his brother's armour. And bring Alec to his damned knees—for good.

Rosalie got up purposefully the next morning. Last night she had been a scantily-clad Greek goddess, publicly on display. This morning—well, plump Biddy O'Brien, Helen's cheerful housemaid, had put it best as she settled Katy in her chair and gave her warm milk and toast. 'Oh, Miss Ros,' Biddy cried, 'you look ready to convert the heathen!'

And Helen added drily, 'My dear. You appear

not only dressed for church, but set to preach the sermon.'

Rosalie smiled and poured herself tea. 'Hardly. Are any of your brothers at home this morning, Biddy?'

'They are, Miss Rosalie. They've got a roofing job this afternoon, but they've got the morning free, so they'll probably just lie around waiting for me to feed them, the great lummocks!'

Helen was looking puzzled. Rosalie quickly drew her aside and whispered, 'You remember? This morning I'm going to investigate the place called Two Crows Castle.'

'Oh, dear.' Helen looked anxious. 'Perhaps I shouldn't have mentioned it…'

'Of course you should,' soothed Rosalie. 'You can see I'm dressed as a drab little widow…' she pointed to the cheap ring she wore '…and I'm going to take Biddy's brother Matt with me, just as you suggested. I'll deliver your *Scribblers* to Bishopsgate, as well. Don't look so worried, Helen. It's broad daylight, and with big Matt O'Brien at my side no one will come near me!'

But Rosalie's plans went awry almost immediately, because Matt and his older brother had been called at short notice to another job that morning, according to little Joe, the youngest of the family, who at only ten was not much use as a protector.

Rosalie hesitated for only a moment. Then, heaving up her canvas bag of news sheets, she walked down to Clerkenwell Green to hire a hackney cab.

At busy Bishopsgate, the driver softly grumbled as he lifted her heavy bag out of the cab for her. 'You deliverin' the Bible or some such round 'ere, missy? Best make sure you're well away before the alehouses get crowded at noon. And don't say I didn't warn yer!'

Rosalie took charge of her bagful of *Scribblers*. 'Consider me warned,' she said lightly.

A slight breeze lifted the concealing veil of her severe bonnet. The driver looked at her curiously, then his eyes fastened on the plain wedding band on her finger. 'Why, yer only young. Quite a fetching little thing…' She snatched her veil down again. 'Well, well,' he sighed. 'You take care now, missy.'

Bishopsgate was busy. First she delivered the copies of *The Scribbler* to the news vendor, who took them eagerly. 'These should go like hot cakes, miss!' he said. ''Specially if there's a piece in by that fellow Ro Rowland—my gents are fond of them!'

Rosalie smiled. 'I do believe there is.' And, her

bag now much lighter, she walked on towards Crispin Street.

Thank goodness Helen and Biddy didn't know she'd ventured here, alone.

Immediately she found herself in a different world. The ancient buildings leaned in over the street, three, sometimes four storeys high; they were unkempt, with broken windows, and in the roughly paved lane dogs nosed amongst heaps of rubbish. Ragged children gathered by doorways, even their attempts at play half-hearted in this oppressive neighbourhood.

As she hesitated, an urchin came up boldly to stare at her and Rosalie asked the grubby child, 'Can you tell me which house is Two Crows Castle?'

'It's the big 'un, see.' The child pointed. 'Can't miss it. All the soldiers live there.'

Rosalie swallowed and nodded. It was a huge old house set back from the road, with a bunch of men slouching outside, defying the freezing February drizzle that had just started to fall. It must once have been a grand mansion, but grand was no longer the word that applied to it. The broken crenellations resembled nothing more than gapped teeth; the stuccoed façade was cracked and stained. Clearly, as the district had sunk into poverty during the last fifty years, so had this place. And the man who charged the homeless ex-soldiers to live in such squalor was once an army officer. Shameful.

She became conscious of rough-looking people assessing her from open doors, of the smells of greasy cooking and ale from the various taverns. Her heart missed a beat. Time, most definitely, to go. She turned to head back to Bishopsgate, where the street would be busy with shoppers and the atmosphere less menacing. Suddenly, she heard footsteps coming up behind her. And a hand grabbed her arm.

'Now, what may you be wantin'?' a rough male voice demanded. 'Some kind of charity lady, are yer?'

She spun round to see a small but fierce-looking individual in a tattered soldier's uniform, his whole demeanour made even more sinister by the black eyepatch he wore. A big golden dog hovered close to him, growling softly. And soon there were more men looking her suspiciously up and down, men who'd been loitering outside the ominous building known as Two Crows Castle.

Despite her apprehension, she couldn't help but gasp, 'How many of you are there in that place?'

'None of your damned business, pardon my French,' Eyepatch said tersely. 'I'll let you off with

a piece of advice—don't go stickin' yer ladylike little nose into other folks' affairs. Now, be off with
you!' The dog barked in agreement.

In the circumstances, it seemed sensible to do
precisely what he said, but at least a dozen ragged
men had come to crowd round her in a distinctly
menacing sort of manner. They were big. They were
blocking her path. Rosalie's heart was thumping
hard. *You idiot, coming here alone...*

'I'll be on my way just as soon as you let me pass!'
she said, rather faintly.

She felt acute relief as the men slowly stepped
aside.

Then Eyepatch said, 'Wait. What've you got in
that bag of yours?'

Rosalie swallowed. 'It's empty. I've just been de-
livering something, and now I really must go.'

'Empty, eh? Let's just have a little look-see.'

Eyepatch was drawing closer. Rosalie looked
round desperately for help that clearly wasn't going
to arrive. She'd remembered that her bag wasn't
quite empty, after all. Grasping it tightly, she turned
to run. But her long cloak hampered her and suddenly Crispin Street was alive with scowling ruffians, appearing from every doorway, every alley,
from the walls themselves, it seemed. Could things
get any worse?

They could, and they did. She dropped her bag and saw it fall open. Oh, *fiddlesticks*. Yet more men gathered, and Rosalie whirled round, her heart pounding painfully. The lethal piece of paper that had fluttered from her bag was drifting towards the gutter; one of the men snatched at it and gave it to Eyepatch.

Rosalie, feeling a little faint, saw Eyepatch scowling at it. Not *The Scribbler*, but a few notes she'd been jotting down in the cab—ideas for her next article. Something not intended for public scrutiny *anywhere*, let alone here. What a tumble, as Ro Rowland would say.

'Please give that to me,' she said rather weakly. She was fervently hoping the ruffian wouldn't be able to read.

'No, hold on,' said Eyepatch, 'this looks interesting.' And slowly he began to decipher her scrawled notes, while his companions gathered round.

'Your fellow about town wants today to draw your attention to the scandalous practice of rackrenting. Rackrenting?' He lifted his head to glare at her. 'Who wrote this?'

'Just somebody—well, it's me! I—I amuse myself, during carriage rides, by writing things down, silly things—' She tried to grab the sheet back, to no avail.

He hung on to it grimly. Started again. *'Scandalous practice of rackrenting. What is truly—truly—'* Eyepatch broke off. 'Can't read the rest of this flummery.'

Thank God for that.

But there was no reprieve. For someone else—a big, redheaded man—was announcing, in a broad Scottish accent, 'Awa' with ye, Garrett, I can read the rest. It says, *"What is truly shameful is that many of those who are thus exploited are former soldiers, forced to live in squalor at a place called Two Crows Castle..."'*

The dog barked. They were all pressing around her again. Eyepatch looked at her with his one eye. 'Exploited? By God, we ain't exploited here at Two Crows Castle. We don't like people who write filthy lies about our Captain, do you hear? As he'll tell you himself—'cos he's on his way right now!'

Her heart, she was sure, had stopped beating. The Captain?

Don't be a fool, Rosalie. There must be dozens of ex-army Captains in town. Nevertheless she pulled down her veil as far as it would go, until she felt like a blinkered horse with a fly-gauze over its face.

Just in time.

For at that very moment, the crowd was parting to let someone through. A man who was saying, 'What

in the devil's name is going on, Garrett? And—
what's that damned dog still doing here?'

At the sound of that husky male voice, her heart
sank to the soles of her little laced boots. *No. No.
It can't be...*

Eyepatch had for some reason shoved the dog out
of sight. 'This woman, Captain,' he was saying importantly, 'she's come 'ere bold as brass, with a pack
of filth about this place, and about you!'

The bruise on his cheek had darkened since last
night. Otherwise he looked just the same, in that
loose grey overcoat that hung carelessly open over
his tight buckskin breeches and dusty riding boots.
And, hands on his lean hips, he was just watching
her, with those hard eyes in which, today, there was
no hint of the humour or kindness that he had allowed her to glimpse last night. He took the sheet
Eyepatch thrust at him, absorbing her brief but lethal jottings swiftly; then he said levelly to Rosalie,
'Well, madam? Are you or are you not responsible
for this pack of lies?'

She prayed fervently for the ground to open up
and swallow her. *He* must be the rackrenter. The
owner of Two Crows Castle. The man whom she'd
allowed, to her eternal shame, to kiss her last night.
All she could hope was that, in her spinsterly garb,
he would continue not to recognise her. And it was

too late, now, for denial; she just had to brazen this out.

'Lies?' She lifted her veiled face to boldly meet his dark gaze. 'Perhaps you just cannot stomach *the truth*!'

Eyepatch gave a nasty leer. 'Oh, you're a brave 'un, to challenge the honour of Alec Stewart, the best swordsman in town!'

Oh, my God. This time she really did feel the blood freeze in her veins. 'Did you say—Alec Stewart?'

The Captain surveyed her, still clearly puzzled by her veiled visage. 'That's me all right,' he said narrowly.

And horror—*nausea*—shook her.

For the name Linette had breathed as she lay dying was—Alec Stewart.

Chapter Seven

Alec had been up and about early, for he'd had appointments to keep. But he'd arrived back at Two Crows Castle to find the place in utter uproar, because of some sanctimonious lady do-gooder. Alec read those scribbled notes Garrett had handed him with dawning disbelief. *'The scandalous practice of rackrenting...rapacious landlords...Two Crows Castle...'*

Hell and damnation!

Well, the charity lady who'd penned this heap of lies had made one mighty bad mistake. She hadn't run fast enough. Alec's men were holding her tight; as he tried to scan her face, which was all but hidden by a truly hideous bonnet and veil, Alec began to feel sheer shock coursing through his veins.

'Take off that bonnet,' he grated at her.

'No! I won't!' The slender captive was struggling again in Garrett and Ackroyd's strong grip.

Alec walked up to her and pulled the repulsive thing off himself. Swathes of long, silver-blonde hair fell around her face. His men gasped. One or two of them whistled softly and clicked their tongues in lewd sounds of appreciation. 'God's blood, Captain, she's a ripe little piece!' 'Take off her cloak, then we can all 'ave a good look…'

'Shut up,' Alec told his men. And he grimly readjusted to this new reality.

Yesterday this *do-gooder* had been parading her delectable wares on stage at the Temple of Beauty. Last night the taste of her softly parted pink lips had disturbed his dreams. All through the hours of darkness he'd been haunted by images of her long fair hair cascading around her breasts, her naked limbs entwined with his between silken sheets… Yet this morning, she was dressed like a church mouse—a very defiant church mouse—and was in possession of some hideously insulting notes about himself and his men. Who the hell was she? What was she playing at?

He rapped out to her, 'Who wrote this filth? And why is it in your possession?'

She tossed her lovely wild hair back from her face. 'Why should I tell you anything?'

He registered the swiftly concealed fear in those blue eyes, along with something else that was almost hatred. But then it was gone again, replaced by steadfast defiance. 'Take her inside,' he ordered Garrett. 'We'll keep her here until she changes her mind.'

'No!' She started struggling again. 'You cannot do this!'

'Try me,' was Alec Stewart's terse answer.

Two of his men led her down a stone staircase and locked her in the basement, where the only light came in through a high-up single window. Rosalie had fought them all the way, but now she simply stood and shivered with cold and fear as her faith in her own judgement came crashing down around her.

Alec Stewart. Last night, he'd seemed—different. He'd assumed she was a whore and that hurt, but otherwise he'd seemed totally unlike the rest of the men at that hateful Temple of Beauty—so much so that she, Rosalie, whose defences against men she'd considered bullet-proof, had let him kiss her. And had felt her insides melt with a strange, sweet sensation she'd never experienced before.

Could he be Linette's seducer? Yet there must be many more men of that name! Wildly she clutched at straws. His name had not, after all, been listed in Dr Barnard's secret book as having visited the Temple that fateful June nearly three years ago!

Her heart sank again. He might have given a false name to the doorman. And it might have taken only one night for him to cast his spell on Linette and whisk her away. For heaven's sake, she, Rosalie, had submitted to his charms swiftly enough! Captain Alec Stewart. *He has a castle, Rosalie. A wonderful castle...*

Clearly he'd never brought her sister to this crumbling heap. Her stomach cramped in torment. If it *was* him, he probably didn't know or care that Linette was dead. Probably didn't even remember her.

Rosalie would never, ever have guessed. But then, neither had Linette. *You idiot, Rosalie. You thought Linette was so stupid, thought yourself so clever...* She paced the floor. She lacerated herself with reproach.

Suddenly she thought she heard low voices out in the passageway. She'd been in here how long? An hour? It felt like for ever. She heard a bolt being drawn back and, as the door opened, she sprang round to face it.

Alec Stewart walked slowly into the room, loosening his necktie with his right hand. There was an unreadable look in his hard dark eyes, and somehow the sheer physicality of him, the extremity of male power emanating from that rangy, muscular body, slammed the breath from her lungs. She was reminded, in a surge of excruciating emotion, of the sweet knowingness of his kiss. The melting ache of his fingers on her breasts.

Then she realised he was holding that piece of paper.

He kicked the door shut with his booted foot and just *looked* at her. Rosalie hitched up her chin. 'Locking up women now,' she declared with scorn. 'What right have you to keep me here against my will—Captain Stewart?'

He ignored her question. 'I've been making enquiries,' he said. 'About who you are. You're versatile, aren't you, Athena?' He stepped closer and pointed at the finger on which she wore the cheap little wedding band. 'You weren't wearing *that* last night. Does your husband know you were playing the whore at the Temple of Beauty?'

Fiddlesticks. She should have taken the stupid thing off. She jutted her chin. 'I'm a widow, as it happens!'

'My condolences.' His sympathy was short-lived. 'And your *real* name is…?'

'R-Rosalie.'

'Rosalie,' he echoed thoughtfully. 'And do you by any chance pen scurrilous articles for a rag called *The Scribbler*?'

Oh, Lord. 'I don't see why you should—'

He waved the sheet at her. '*Fellow about town.* That's how the journalist Ro Rowland describes himself—or should I say *herself*? I wasn't born yesterday; I am acquainted with London's gutter press.'

The colour drained from her face. That meant Helen was being dragged into this! This was just what Rosalie had wanted to avoid; this was one reason why Rosalie had never told Helen or *anybody* the name of Linette's seducer, even though she'd realised it might have hastened her search… *Helen, I'm so sorry.*

She squared her slender shoulders. 'Sometimes, I've written pieces for *The Scribbler*. But often I just make notes—like the ones your men stole from me!—for my own interest. And what I'm doing isn't against the law!'

'It is if you're intending to print lies. Defame my reputation.'

'*Reputation!* Oh, believe me, I could write so much more about you that you wouldn't like, Captain Stewart!'

She saw the gleam in his steely eyes and dragged air into her tight lungs. *Too far. Too dangerous, Rosalie. You cannot possibly tackle him right here in his stronghold.*

He was still staring thoughtfully down at her. 'Is

that so? Might I suggest you can hardly afford to take the high moral ground, Mrs Rowland, since I could retaliate by asking—what the hell were you doing last night, parading on that stage half-naked?'

'I really don't think that's any of your business!'

'Unfortunately it is, since you've set yourself in judgement on *my* affairs. You were putting your-self up for sale at Dr Barnard's—why? To dig up filth for your news rag? Is that why Dr Barnard was after you?'

Rather too close to the truth, that. 'I was not for sale!'

'All right, I correct myself.' One dark eyebrow arched. 'You were, in my case at least, offering it for free.'

She gasped and struck out at him. But he caught her hand in an iron-hard grip.

Blue eyes, turquoise-blue eyes, whose bed did you sleep in last night? Yesterday Alec Stewart had found himself rather hoping that there was some reason—and not the obvious one—for this girl to be appearing on stage at the Temple of Beauty.

Well, perhaps he'd found that reason and he didn't like it one bit. She made money out of digging up prurient details of other people's lives. Hence her appearance at Dr Barnard's, hunting, he guessed, for lurid gossip about the visitors to that seedy place. Hence her temerity in coming here, to cast her blue eyes boldly over Two Crows Castle, while carrying in that bag of hers some nasty notes about the crimes of a so-called rackrenter. Yet—how stunned she'd looked when she realised *he* was the owner of Two Crows Castle! And why was it that everything she did, or said, challenged all his preconceptions of her?

He remembered the way she'd reacted to his kiss last night. Even now he caught his breath at the way her silvery-blonde hair tumbled like a silken waterfall around her shoulders, at the way her drab cloak had fallen apart to allow him a distracting glimpse of the small but ripe breasts that were prominent beneath her shabby gown.

Very pretty, and very professional. Get a grip, man. Not only is she a courtesan, but she writes for a news rag. She's damned dangerous.

As if to confirm his every suspicion, she made a dart for the door. He grabbed her easily with one outstretched arm. Still she struggled, panting to get away. He pulled her closer and his physical desire reared inevitably at the sensation of her warm body agitating against his. 'Little fool,' he uttered. 'Little fool, stop that. Or I won't be held responsible for my actions, do you understand?'

That quietened her. Her turquoise eyes flew up to his in shock and she went very still. Then she tossed back her glorious hair. 'You need not think, Captain Stewart,' she shot up at him, 'that I'm afraid of you and men like you!'

'Then you damn well ought to be,' he said dispassionately. 'Though to be fair, you dealt with Dr Barnard's customers—myself included—most *professionally* last night.'

She gasped. 'Last night was a mistake! If I'd *known* everything about you...'

'Known what, exactly?' he drawled.

'Do you deny that you pack this—this hideous old ruin with impoverished ex-soldiers?'

Frowning, he let her go. But now his broad shoulders and back were planted solidly against the door and he made a formidable barrier indeed to any thought of escape. 'My friends know the truth.' His eyes blazed danger. 'Write what you like, Mrs Rowland, and be damned to you.'

'I will, if I choose! And I could also write about the way you expect young women to just *melt* at your feet! How you promise them—promise them...'

His eyes gleamed. 'Promise them what, exactly?'

'Nothing,' she muttered. *Oh, Lord.* She should not have *said* that.

He was drawing nearer. 'Promise them what, Mrs

Rowland? I want to know.' Now a truly wicked smile was curving his lips. 'Money? Pleasure? Perhaps you're more tempted than you care to admit by what you think our encounter last night promised?'

She gazed up at him, speechless. It was impossible. It was incredible. Yet—desire, raw and primitive, flooded her veins. Her breasts ached traitorously for his knowing touch. Her eyes were locked with his as she wildly sought inspiration that didn't come. And he was drawing nearer, a wicked light in his gaze. 'Playing coy, are you, Mrs Rowland? Who knows—if you promise to be…*generous*, I might consider letting you go, with no more questions asked.'

'Generous?' Her heart shrivelled. 'Exactly what—?'

'You were only too happy,' he silkily prompted, 'to allow me a sample of your wares last night. Now, what's the price of your freedom, I wonder?' He'd reached out, to touch her cheek. *This woman*, thought Alec grimly, *was testing his self-control with her dangerous games.* Desire was licking hungrily at his loins; his manhood was thickening, and though he had no desire to lower himself to her level of trickery, he most certainly wanted to teach her a lesson.

The realisation of what he was suggesting hit Rosalie like a hammer blow. The brush of his hand across her delicate cheek scorched her. 'You wouldn't. You can't…'

'I really cannot think of a more enjoyable way of bargaining,' he said softly. 'Can you?'

Her world spun. All she could feel were his hands, splayed across her back, his fingertips firm and warm through her clothing. All she could see, when she jerked her head up, was his hard face, lit with an emotion she could not name as he drew her relentlessly into his arms.

His dark eyes raked her. 'I think the price of your freedom, Athena,' he breathed, 'should be—this.' He lowered his head and pressed his lips to hers.

She meant to resist. She had no intention of letting him *do* this. But as he clasped her close, heat uncoiled from deep within and flooded her veins, awakening each and every pleasure point in her body. This time there was no gentleness whatsoever in his touch, but his mouth was wildly sensual as he took hard possession, parting her lips with ruthlessness. His tongue was thrusting, at the same time caressing; she felt her legs giving way, felt herself longing to surrender to more, much more, as he hauled her against him and she felt the lean length of his muscular body, felt the hard intrusion of his arousal pressing against her abdomen.

Her breasts were peaking painfully, demanding his touch; between her thighs was liquid longing. His kiss was slow, erotic and powerful, tasting faintly of brandy and the very essence of male domination. She'd thought she hated men and their ways. Yet she was powerless to resist this one.

Linette. Her sister's name tore through her. With all her strength she thrust him away. 'You are—you are *vile* to treat me in this way!'

He stepped back, his hard face bleached of every emotion. 'I thought it was maybe what you wanted. You are, it strikes me, a deceptive and muddle-headed young woman, Mrs Rowland. This gossip sheet you write for—if anything at all should appear in it about Two Crows Castle, then I warn you, I'll take strong action. Because there are people who depend on me and I won't let them suffer for the sake of your cheap scandal-raking, do you understand?'

Just then there was a knock on the door, which opened to reveal Eyepatch. Rosalie found herself shuddering at the scornful look he cast her way. He said, 'A word, Captain?'

Alec joined him in the doorway, bending his dark head to the other's in a brief exchange. Eyepatch left and Alec Stewart came back in, slowly.

Alec had to admit that this woman—Rosalie— confounded him at every turn. What was she? *Who* was she? A whore at the Temple of Beauty, who knew rather a lot about art? A pretty little widow and a digger-up of scandals, who had no idea of the effect she had on men?

And now Garrett brought still more news about his treacherous captive. Alec folded his arms and gazed down at her. 'Well, Mrs Rowland, investigative reporter amongst other things, it seems you've got certain obligations that you've neglected in order to come on your little jaunt this morning.' He pointed to the open door. 'You'd better be on your way.'

Obligations? What…? She glared up at him. 'You mean I'm free to go?'

'We made a bargain, remember?' He shrugged. 'That kiss was payment for your freedom. I've no desire to hold you captive.'

'You already *have*!' she flared. 'I've been here against my will for at least an hour! I could press charges on you.'

'That's a novel idea.' His dark eyes gleamed. 'Though I would, of course, be forced to press charges in return. Of robbery, perhaps.'

'I—impossible!'

He raised his eyebrows. 'Think about it, Mrs Rowland. It would be more than easy for me to say there are valuables missing from this place. After all…' he looked at his pocket watch coolly '…you've been here for quite a while on your own.'

'But I've been *locked in a bare room*!'

Again he shrugged those wide, powerful shoulders. 'Your word against mine. And I could produce plenty of witnesses who'd remember you from the Temple of Beauty. Do you really think you'd be taken seriously at the magistrates' court?'

She tilted her stubborn chin. 'Would *you* be taken seriously, Captain Stewart?'

'I'm a war hero,' he responded tonelessly. 'Though it means little in financial terms, my word would carry more weight than that of a courtesan who writes for a gossip rag.'

He saw the colour stinging her creamy cheeks. Saw her fighting to find words of resistance and failing.

He was almost disappointed. Almost felt his heart softening for the defiant little widow. But he clamped down hard on any errant feeling like pity. His face as stone, he went to open the door and pointed the way. 'As I was saying, you've clearly been missed. There are three people outside, looking for you. Including—' his eyes narrowed '—your daughter.'

Chapter Eight

Katy was outside, clinging to Biddy. As soon as she saw Rosalie, she reached out to her. 'Mama? I want Mama...'

'Oh, darling...' Rosalie hurried to hold her tight in her arms. Alec Stewart was looking at them both, sharply, knowingly. Naturally, Rosalie thought with scorn, that *devil* of a man had assumed Katy was hers. Well, let him. She realised Matt was there, too, looking rather warily at Captain Stewart and his crew.

'Biddy. Matt,' she said quickly. 'What are you doing here?'

'Miss Helen sent me after you, miss, and told me to bring Matt, too. She was really cross when she realised you'd not taken him, like you'd said.' Biddy glanced wide-eyed at the formidable figure of Alec Stewart, who had gone to say something to one of his men. 'She told me,' went on Biddy, 'to say you must come home, because you ought not to be on these streets alone! I brought little Katy, too, 'cos she was missing you bad, weren't you, chick?'

Katy, in Rosalie's arms, seemed quite happy now, and in fact had wriggled round to stare at Alec, who was strolling back towards them. She was clearly intrigued by the gleaming gold curb-chain of his pocket watch and her little fingers reached out to it.

'Katy, *don't*!' Rosalie backed away with her quickly. She feared that he would use this as an opportunity to castigate her still further. Accuse her of rearing a future child-thief, perhaps.

But Alec had forestalled her. He pulled out his gold watch so Katy could see it. 'This is all it is, sweetheart,' he told the infant softly. 'Something to remind me that I'm a busy man and I should have been somewhere else half an hour ago at least.'

'Tick-tock.' Katy looked up at him with her wide, dark-lashed green eyes. 'Tick-tock man.' She reached out to touch it, then gurgled in merriment.

Rosalie saw Alec's mouth curl into a brief but devastating smile as he patted Katy's chubby fist and put his watch away. Her heart jumped. So handsome. So beguiling. *So false.* As if to prove her point, he turned to Rosalie and the smile was quite gone. 'It appears to me that your duties lie elsewhere, Mrs Rowland. I warn you—and I assure you I mean it—that there'll be no writing about me or Two Crows Castle. My men will escort you and your companions as far as the hackney stand on Bishopsgate.'

Matt O'Brien was still watching him almost with awe; much use *he* was in protecting her from Captain Stewart, Rosalie thought in despair. Her chin lifted an inch. 'We will make our own way, thank you!'

'You won't,' he broke in icily. 'I want you well clear of this place.' He swung round and raised his voice. 'Sergeant McGrath!' The villainous-looking Scotsman with red hair came up. 'Find Mrs Rowland and her companions a hackney cab, will you? And make damned sure they get into it.' Without a further glance at her, he turned and strode off while McGrath led the way along Crispin Street, with Matt O'Brien at his side, eagerly asking questions.

'I hear your Captain fought like the very devil against the French at Waterloo,' Matt was saying to McGrath.

You traitor, Matt. Rosalie, holding Katy tight, walked furiously behind, with Biddy chattering away beside her. And she herself was a fool. Today, as Ro Rowland, roving reporter, she'd blundered straight into that man's stronghold. Twice now she had let him kiss her. She'd twice melted in his strong arms, and, even worse, had wanted more. She shivered at the memory of that powerful body, moulded hard against hers; dear Lord, she had not even *tried* to resist him!

Her cheeks burned at the recollection of her astonishing stupidity. If Alec Stewart truly was Linette's seducer—how on earth was she going to tackle him now?

McGrath beckoned a hackney, spoke to the driver, then strolled off. Biddy's brother said he'd walk, since his next job of work was close by in Fenchurch Street. So just Biddy, Rosalie and Katy got into the cab.

'Where to, miss?' asked the cab driver.

'Clerkenwell. St John's Church,' she answered distractedly, fumbling for her purse.

'No need for that,' said the cabbie. 'Your fare's bin paid.'

'No! I won't allow it!' she exploded with renewed fury. Captain Stewart must have given the necessary coins to McGrath. How *dare* he…?

'Suit yerself,' shrugged the cabbie. 'Pay me twice over if you wants to throw your money away.'

Rosalie slumped inside the carriage. Biddy was excited by the novelty of the trip and pointed the sights out to Katy through the window. 'There's St

Paul's, Katy, see? And there's the Smithfield market...'

But Rosalie could see nothing except Alec Stewart's hard, mocking face. She remembered his mouth and how it had branded her with the kind of kiss she hadn't even known existed.

Katy had become fretful by the time they reached Clerkenwell. As they climbed out, the clock of the nearby church was chiming one, and Katy, in Rosalie's arms, was crooning softly to herself, 'Ticktock man. Tick-tock man.'

Thus Rosalie would always remember the exact time that she realised what her enemy was capable of. Would always remember, as she held little Katy tight, the moment when Biddy cried out, 'Lord have mercy, what on earth's happened *here*?'

Rosalie swung round to thrust Katy into Biddy's arms. 'Look after her,' she breathed. She was already hurrying towards the house.

The door was wide open. Helen was standing on the steps surrounded by neighbours and little Toby was clinging tearfully to her.

'Helen.' Rosalie pushed her way through. 'Helen, what's happened?'

'Oh, *Rosalie*... Come and see.'

A horrible sick feeling tore at Rosalie's gut as she followed her friend inside. In the front room the little square-built printing press, Helen's pride and joy, had been viciously attacked with what could only have been a strong hammer or a pick-axe. Leaden type and pieces of wooden frame were scattered all over the floor.

'Someone broke in while I was out. They picked the lock. Then—my printing press…' Helen's voice broke. 'Look at this.'

She handed Rosalie a note scrawled in ink. *Gossip-raking bitch.*

Rosalie felt quite faint. 'Did no one see anything?'

Helen shook her head. 'Mrs Lucas over the road went for the constables when she heard the noise, but whoever it was had run off by the time they arrived. Oh, Rosalie, I—I knew I had enemies, but—*this*? Who could have done something so malicious? How am I going to start, all over again?'

Rosalie was reeling, because *she* knew somebody who was capable of such a ruthless revenge. Someone who had, quite possibly, kept her locked in his basement to give his men time to do this. Would such a person feel any regret whatsoever for seducing and abandoning an innocent girl? The answer, surely, was no.

She felt physically sick. *I'm afraid I've found him, Linette.*

And, oh, Lord, he was going to be a powerful adversary.

Some hours later Alec was pacing the landing outside the main bedchamber of his father's magnificent Belgrave Square house.

As soon as he'd seen his unwelcome visitor—Mrs Rowland—off his premises, he'd ridden to give a fencing lesson in Piccadilly, then he had an appointment down at the Limehouse docks with a warehouse owner who wanted to hire a dozen men. Alec always tried to find work for his ex-soldiers if they were fit for it.

He'd got back to Two Crows Castle to find a message for him, written by the Earl's steward, Jarvis. *Master Alec. I'm afraid that your father has been taken ill. The doctor is with him. Please come.*

A thousand thoughts had raced through Alec's brain as he'd urged his horse westwards through London's busy streets to Mayfair. A thousand regrets. How serious was this? Had his father's bout of illness been brought on, perhaps, by the shock of evil knowledge? Would his father even want to see the son he'd disowned a year ago?

Jarvis, a loyal old retainer, came out of the bedchamber now, bearing a tray laden with medicinal beakers. 'Your father will see you now, Master Alec, sir.'

That was something. 'Is the doctor still with him?'

'He's gone, but he'll call back within the hour. He said there are no physical signs of illness, but your father needs to rest.'

Alec felt a great release of tension throughout his body. But— *No wonder he needs to rest, with a young wife who pleads to be taken to every party of the Season. With a young wife who...*

No. You must forget that, for now.

Alec went swiftly up to the lavishly furnished chamber. His father lay against the pillows of the four-poster in the half-light, for the curtains of the big room were already drawn against the early February dusk and only the coals in the fire lightened the gloom.

'Alec.' Slowly his father turned towards him. His gaunt hands twisted the bedcovers fretfully. 'It's been so long, Alec. So long since I've seen you...'

When you told me you'd no desire to see me ever again.

'Sir. If there's anything I can do, you have only to say the word. How are you?'

'Oh, the doctor says I'll live.' His voice rasped.

'Your brother—he was here the moment he heard I was ill.'

I'll bet he was. Alec merely nodded. 'Jarvis told me what the doctor said. That your affliction is thankfully nothing serious.'

'Yes,' muttered his father. 'Damned quack poked and prodded everywhere. But he said it would do me good to get away from London.'

Away from London. *Yes.* But… 'What does Lady Aldchester think of that, sir?' Susanna adored London life. She'd once said that she would die in the country.

The Earl shuffled against his pillows and coughed. 'I don't know, I don't know; she's been out shopping with friends all afternoon, she won't even be aware that I've had this damned turn. But she'll come with me, she's devoted, Alec, despite what you said! And so is Stephen. Would you believe it, he's just told me he was setting off for Carrfields himself today, to see that everything was in good order!'

Alec's fists tightened at that. So his brother had taken heed of him then, last night.

'But now,' went on his father, 'he needn't go, of course. Because I'll travel there myself, with my dear Susanna.'

I would die in the country.

'And,' went on his father, 'no doubt Stephen will escort us there and visit us regularly.'

Alec exploded. 'The hell he will!' He dragged his hand through his hair, said in a quieter voice, 'I do beg your pardon, sir.'

His father was silent a moment, kneading the bed-cover with his fingers. 'Do you remember the times we used to have, when you were home on leave? We used to sit up till late into the night, didn't we, and you'd tell me, oh, such tales, about the battles, and the sieges in Spain…'

'I've never forgotten it, sir.'

'But now…' and his father's voice was growing fretful '…now, all I hear about you is that you avoid civilised company, you avoid your brother, except to fight with him. And my wife has told me, reluctantly mind, that it's you, always you, stirring things up…'

'I suppose she would,' said Alec bitterly.

'What? What did you say? Do you take heed of me, Alec? Your mother died so long ago—am I never to be allowed happiness again? Will you make your peace with your brother and your stepmother?'

Alec stood ramrod straight. 'You ask the impossible, sir.'

The Earl stared at him. Then he waved a tired hand. 'Go back to your soldiers' drinking dens. Go on, go. And once I'm at Carrfields, I want you to clear out everything of yours that's left in this house. Your old army journals, your maps of Spain—all the paraphernalia that clutters up your room and my study. It hurts me to see them all, to remember… Take them away, do you hear?'

'Everything will be removed. Though I hope you know that if you ever need me, I'm here for you—'

'Leave. Just *leave.*'

And Alec turned, with a heavy heart, to go.

He found Stephen in the first-floor drawing room, gazing with narrowed eyes at the paintings on the walls—some of them inherited, some acquired from auction houses—and worth, like everything in this palatial house, a small fortune.

'So, little brother.' Stephen, on observing Alec's entry, turned from staring at a French landscape to sink on to a sofa, where he tapped his fingers rather nervously on its satin upholstery. 'Come in hopes of taking advantage of the family drama, have you? Planning, perhaps, to weasel your way back into our father's affections?'

Alec gazed at him calmly. 'You've had a respite, Stephen. Last night I suggested you leave London. Now there's no need. Because our father's going to Carrfields with his wife.'

'No! Has he just told you that?' Stephen was on his feet again, his face flushed. 'Susanna will die of boredom there!'

'Perhaps. But if you do anything other than tell her she must accompany our father, then your game is at an end.'

'You wouldn't...'

'Oh, I would. Believe me, I would.'

'She's young, Alec! Younger than me, younger than you. And Carrfields—it's like a prison for her!'

'She should have thought of that before she married him,' rapped back Alec. 'Obviously his wealth distracted her from the practical realities of playing wife to a much older man.'

Stephen drew in a hissed breath. 'Now, look. As far as London society is concerned, I'm merely being the dutiful stepson by escorting her to her various engagements...'

His voice faltered, because of the way Alec was gazing at him. 'You won't be escorting her *anywhere* in the foreseeable future—' Alec pointed a finger at him, casually '—because she's going to Hampshire with our father.'

Stephen opened his mouth, then shut it again.

'Oh, and there's one more thing,' went on Alec. 'Why were you talking last night to the blonde whore who played Athena?'

'Why? The usual reasons.' Stephen's lip curled. 'So *you* noticed her, too, did you? Are you going back there tonight to tup the wench? I'd be interested to know what bedroom tricks she employs—'

Stephen broke off, because his brother's bunched fist was suddenly in front of his face. 'Oh, Stephen,' Alec said softly, 'I've no intention of paying for anyone's services. But I've another question. You paid those men to attack me last night at the Temple of Beauty, didn't you? Why?'

'I really don't know what the hell you're—'

'Don't waste your breath trying to deny it. Because I'm just longing for an excuse to give you the beating you deserve.'

Stephen cowered away. 'Not here. Not in our father's house!'

Then the door opened. And Susanna was there.

Lady Aldchester, the former Contessa di Ascoli, was exquisite, everyone was agreed on that. Her origins were obscure—she had been born in England to an Italian mother and had married a Milanese count, considerably older than she.

When he died in Italy two years ago his widow had decided to come to live in London, where she had made her entrance in considerable style. She had rented a fine house where she held glittering soirées with her mother, and soon half of London's gentry were in love with her.

Including his father.

Now she looked from one to the other, lovely as ever, with her clouds of raven curls and her sultry dark-blue eyes. She was younger than both of them. Then she said, in her silken voice that bore the allure of her Italian heritage, 'Stephen. Alec. I've just been told that your father is ill.'

'It's nothing serious,' said Stephen. 'Rest assured.'

'I will go up, then, to see him…'

Stephen strode forwards. 'I will come with you.'

'No. Best if I see him by myself.'

Alec had already turned to go. But he became aware that she was following him out on to the palatial landing above the staircase, where they were, momentarily, alone. The faint scent of gardenias clung to her skin and hair.

'Alec,' she said, 'my dear, please will you speak with me one moment before I go up to your father?' Her delicate gloved fingers were touching his arm. 'It's been so long since we spoke. I'm sad, because you used to be at every society gathering. You are missed,' she added softly.

'Do you know,' he said in a curt voice, 'I find that London society doesn't appeal to me very much at the moment. Susanna, my father wants to go to Carrfields.'

The colour left her cheeks. 'Carrfields! But he promised me—'

'I take it,' Alec cut in, 'that you'll go with him? Stephen, by the way, is staying in London.'

She hesitated. Then, 'Of course I will go.'

With a tight bow, he turned to leave, but she caught again at his arm. 'My dear, I so wish we could be friends again! And I'm sorry about the Bedford Street house. I told your father that my mother wished for a residence in London. But I didn't realise you would be made homeless!'

'Didn't you?' This time he couldn't help the bitterness showing through. 'Believe me, that's the least of my worries.'

Her eyes were clouded. 'What can I do, to redeem myself?' she murmured. 'Alec, I am not happy, you must know that. I am not, if it's of any consolation to you, in the slightest bit proud of myself.'

'I think you know, Susanna, what you ought to do. Whether you do it or not is entirely up to you. You have a better side. Use it.' Alec gave a curt bow and left.

She watched him go down the vast staircase that swept to the entrance hall below. Stephen had come out of the drawing room and was looking at her.

'Carrfields,' he said. 'How will you bear it?'

'It seems,' she answered, 'as if I must.'

And she went upstairs, to visit her husband.

Shortly afterwards, Lord Stephen Maybury went back to his house in Brook Street and spoke to the man with the scarred forehead. 'Well, Markin? Did you do as I ordered?'

'Hire a couple of ruffians to wreck the printing press that produced that foul stuff about Lady Aldchester? Aye, my lord. And there's more. The fair-haired piece from the Temple of Beauty that you asked me to follow last night—turns out *she* lives there, as well! She's some kind of writer!'

And Stephen's narrow green eyes widened.

He had been absolutely enraged to see the way Susanna looked at Alec out there on the landing. The way she had agreed, in spite of all her earlier protestations about hating the country, to go with his father to Carrfields.

Was she tiring of her secret games with Stephen?

Now, though, the blonde girl from the Temple of Beauty drove everything from his mind. If there was a connection, with the other one from three years ago, he needed to shut the girl up. And fast.

Chapter Nine

The next two weeks were blighted by the blustery rain of late March and the leaden skies reflected Helen's mood of despair. 'I'll never feel safe again. Oh, Rosalie, who could have done such a thing?'

'The constables are hunting the culprits,' Rosalie soothed her as she brought her a cup of tea. 'Why not start writing again? You have a gift for it and for teaching. I'll never forget how you inspired us in the village school, about art and history. You opened up a new world to me, Helen.'

Helen gave a glimmer of a smile. 'You had a hunger for learning anyway. Every book I brought to you, you used to devour. When I took you all to that art gallery in Oxford, I could hardly tear you away!'

'My father was an artist, remember?' Rosalie sat down next to her on the little sofa. 'I think I hoped there might be some paintings there by him. Of course, there weren't. But I looked, and looked—so foolish of me!'

Helen gazed at her. 'Oh, I'd no *idea*... Rosalie, you must have missed him so!'

'Always,' said Rosalie quietly. 'I was so young when he died. But I never forgot him.' She tried to smile again. 'Do you remember how on the way back from Oxford, I wouldn't stop asking you questions about everything we'd seen? How you put up with me, I can't imagine. Seriously, Helen, I know you feel dreadful, but how about writing again? Stories, poetry, anything!'

Helen shook her head. 'I worry far too much to write. I still feel as though I'm being watched.'

Rosalie shivered, because sometimes she felt the same. But aloud she said resolutely, 'Nonsense! Biddy's brothers are close by, remember—and you have such loyal friends. Do please try to stop worrying.'

'Oh, Rosalie. You are being so good to me.'

'Not as good as you've been to me, Helen,' answered Rosalie quietly.

And she felt a liar and a hypocrite. *All of this is my fault. I drew down the wrath of Alec Stewart upon you.*

The constables, she privately thought, would be doing very little about Helen's wrecked press; you needed money and influence to stir the forces of law into action. Who else but Alec Stewart would have set his men to do this vile deed? He had left that note to warn Rosalie to be quiet about his exploitation of those poor soldiers. What would he do if he knew that Linette had whispered his name as she lay dying?

It was up to her to confront him. But how could she, secure as he was in his castle of rogues?

At least Rosalie had been right to assure Helen that she did indeed have friends, because Francis Wheeldon, the kind churchwarden who lived in nearby St John's Square, called round almost daily; one afternoon he asked Helen if she would write some articles about the history of Clerkenwell for the parish magazine.

Rosalie had seen Helen's face brighten with interest, and tactfully she had left them alone, taking Katy and Toby to the Green to play in the spring sunshine. She liked Francis. Quite a few years older than Helen, he lived with his spinster sister and was a scholarly, gentle man.

Indeed, when Rosalie got back, Helen was looking almost happy and was already sitting at her writing desk.

'So you managed to get rid of Mr Wheeldon at last?' teased Rosalie gently.

Helen turned with a smile. 'Oh, yes. It's a little embarrassing really, the way he fusses over me.'

'He's sweet. And he thinks a lot of you, Helen.'

'Nonsense!' Helen was brisk again. 'But, well, writing these articles about Clerkenwell will be interesting. Francis is so *knowledgeable*. And that reminds me, Rosalie—I hadn't realised before, but Francis knows such a great deal about French history. So I mentioned your mother's family—they owned property south of Paris, didn't they?'

Rosalie swallowed the lump in her throat. 'They used to, but they lost everything in the Revolution and were scattered far and wide, my mother said.'

'That's what I told him. But Francis corresponds with a friend in Paris and he said he'd ask for any news. Isn't that kind of him?'

'Incredibly kind, yes.' Rosalie was anxious not to dampen Helen's enthusiasm. 'And it's so good to see you writing again!'

Helen clapped her hand to her forehead. 'Oh, Rosalie, that reminds me—will you do me a very big favour? I was asked to a poetry reading above Hatchard's bookshop in Piccadilly tonight—they wanted me to write a review. But now I'd much rather get on with this, for Mr Wheeldon. I wonder, will you go instead?'

Rosalie hesitated. Amateur poets did not always make for the jolliest of evenings.

'Please,' urged Helen. 'I'd be so grateful!'

'Of course I'll go,' Rosalie said swiftly. She owed Helen so very much.

But later, as she was upstairs preparing herself for a night of would-be versifiers communing effusively with nature, she was disturbed by a knock at the front door. She knew Biddy was in the kitchen giving the children their supper, and of Helen there was no sign; doubtless she was engrossed in her writing and deaf to the world. So Rosalie hurried downstairs to answer it—and found Sal, from the Temple of Beauty, wrapped in a hooded mantle against the cool March night. Rosalie flinched inwardly. The Temple of Beauty could only mean trouble. 'Sal,' she said. 'This is a surprise. How did you find me?'

'Caught sight of you earlier, gal, at the market in Cheapside!' grinned Sal, hands on hips. 'Then I simply asked around and tracked you down—a neighbourly visit, that's all!'

Rosalie nodded. 'How is the Temple of Beauty?'

'Put it this way, it's not been the same since the

night *you* were there. Remember that fight? Dr B.'s still got a black eye from it and Mrs B.'s given Charlotte the push, 'cos she realised that same night what the pair of them was up to between the sheets! So the place has had a right old turning-over, though that wretched piano's busted to bits, so it's not *all* bad news.'

Rosalie shivered slightly. 'Dr Barnard's not still after me, is he?'

'For bein' some sort of writer? Lord, no, he forgot that in all the trouble over Charlotte.'

'And—you've not seen the Captain in there again?'

She tried to make her question casual, but Sal arched one painted eyebrow. 'Still hankering after him, gal? No, no sign of *him*. Forget his handsome face, that's my advice.' She peered inside the hallway. 'Nice-lookin' place. Stayin' with family, are you? I remember you mentioned a sister to me.'

Rosalie was puzzled. She didn't think she'd mentioned Linette to anyone there. 'I did have a sister, but she died.'

'I'm sorry, gal, real sorry. Your only sister, was she?'

'That's right.'

'Well…' Sal looked up and down the street and shrugged her shoulders '…just thought I'd call to see how you was and everything. You look mighty smart. All dressed up for something, or someone?'

Rosalie glanced down at her serviceable blue gown and managed a smile. 'Oh, it's a poetry reading in Piccadilly, though to be honest, I'd much prefer to be indoors on a night like this.'

Sal laughed. 'Poetry. La-di-dah! Walkin' there by yourself?'

'I'll take a hackney cab. But once I'm there I'm sure I'll be perfectly safe among the poets!'

'Well, I'm one of the Three Graces tonight at Dr B.'s, so I'll be dressing up, too, but I shan't be wearin' as much as you. Just thought I'd see how you are, you know?'

'Yes. Of course. My thanks for calling.'

Rosalie watched Sal hurrying away as the cold wind whipped some rubbish down the street. With a catch in her throat, she remembered seeing Alec Stewart for the first time, lounging at the back of Dr Barnard's hall. He'd quite simply taken her breath away. So stupid of her. She knew now that her judgement had been most terribly awry.

Alec Stewart would be unaware that Linette had whispered his name to Rosalie as she lay dying. But surely, surely he realised she would guess instantly that he was the one behind the destruction of Helen's press?

No doubt he dismissed her as powerless, she thought bitterly. As he'd said, no magistrate would take seriously the word of a woman who'd appeared on stage at the Temple of Beauty. But she wouldn't, she *couldn't* let him get away with his crimes!

Meanwhile—oh, Lord, she was going to be late for the poets.

Sal pulled up her hood and hurried round the corner to where the man waited for her. She looked up at him defiantly. 'She *did* have a sister. But she's dead. That's what you wanted to know, ain't it?'

'Dead! Are you quite sure?'

'Sure as I'm standin' here—look, am I gettin' paid, or what?'

'When you've earned it, slut,' snarled the man. 'Did you find out if she has any plans for the next few days?'

Sal hesitated, then muttered, 'She'll be at some sort of poetry affair in Piccadilly tonight.'

'Tonight...'

'Remember, mister, you swore to me she'd come to no harm!'

The man with the scar on his forehead pushed some coins into her palm with contempt. 'Take your money, slut. And get out of here.'

Sal gave a shudder of revulsion and ran off into

the dark night. She could only pray that the girl would come to no harm…

Rosalie smothered a yawn as she listened to yet another soulful poet describing in verse, to a hushed audience, the joys and agonies of the sensitive heart.

Deciding that Lord Byron—whose *Childe Harold* she adored—would have given the fellow a crushing set-down, she edged her way to another part of the big reception room above the Piccadilly bookshop where food was being served. Heaping a plate with several small but delicious savoury patties, she found herself a chair in a quiet corner, pulled out her notebook and pencil and began to write.

Tonight your fellow about town Ro Rowland took himself to a literary reception. Who, dear reader, would have guessed that so many London citizens long to express their innermost thoughts in verse? Who would dare to tell these would-be poets that their innermost thoughts are better kept precisely where they are?

She chewed the end of her pencil, frowning as her mood darkened once more. Even if Helen were miraculously to get hold of another printing press, there would be no more *Scribblers* until Alec Stewart was dealt with…

'I don't believe it! My dear girl, what on earth are

you doing here?' The voice came from behind her and she jumped up, quickly slipping her book and pencil into her reticule.

It was Lord Stephen Maybury. Last time she'd seen him, at Dr Barnard's, he'd had a heated argument with Alec Stewart. And of course Lord Maybury must still think she was one of Dr Barnard's girls. *Fiddlesticks.* She swiftly composed herself. 'Poetry happens to be an interest of mine, my lord!' she answered lightly.

He drew a little closer. 'You don't write the stuff, do you?'

He was wearing a fine blue kerseymere tailcoat with a striped-silk waistcoat and a shirt with a high, starched collar. Rosalie stifled her instinctive dislike of fashionable men. 'No, no,' she said, 'I have no such talent.'

'Thank God for that. But—' she saw Lord Maybury was taking in her plain gown with its long sleeves and high neck '—this is rather a different setting from the place where we last met.' He raised one questioning eyebrow.

She ventured a smile. 'I can see I must confess to you, my lord. In fact, I was only at Dr Barnard's for one night…'

'Ah.' He was pulling up a chair and beckoned her to sit again. 'Some kind of challenge?'

She seized on that. 'Yes. Yes, a challenge! We ladies like to wager occasionally, you know! Although—' she leaned a fraction closer '—some of my more timid friends would be just a little shocked were they to hear of it, so I do hope that it will remain our secret!'

His eyes had fastened on her wedding ring. 'What about your husband? Would he be shocked, too?'

She'd got into the habit of wearing the ring. So many people assumed Katy was hers that her story of widowhood protected them both. She pretended to dab at her eyes. 'My husband sadly died some time ago, my lord.'

'My dear,' he said sympathetically, 'you look scarcely old enough to be married, let alone bereaved. Tragic. Well, my lips are sealed about your little adventure at Dr Barnard's. Indeed, I would not normally visit such a place myself, but certain—circumstances demanded it.' He looked around. 'I was, to be honest, about to leave here. Can't stand much more of this drivel. However—if *you* were to keep me company for a while, it might be just tolerable. Would you care for a drink? Lemonade is your preference, I believe?'

Before she could reply, he was snapping his fingers for a waiter and murmuring his order.

Then he shifted his chair closer. 'Do you know,'

he confided, 'I shall always think of you as Athena, goddess of wisdom. But I would be truly honoured to know your real name.'

'It's Rosalie,' she said.

'Charming. And here are our drinks.' He was putting money on the waiter's tray and passing her a chilled glass. 'Now, I am so glad,' he went on with fervour, 'to learn that you were only at that place for one night! Indeed, my own visit was, as you no doubt noticed, sadly curtailed.'

In the background, the chatter of all the guests rose and fell; her pulse was racing because here, perhaps, was a heaven-sent chance. 'I noticed you seemed dismayed, my lord, to meet Captain Stewart there. May I ask why you dislike him so very much?'

She saw a shadow cross his features. 'Do we really have to talk about that dissipated wretch? Couldn't I just advise you to keep as far away from him as possible? The man is a disgrace.'

Her pulse thudded. *A disgrace...* 'I'm aware, of course,' she said steadily, 'that he extorts money from former soldiers.'

He'd been sipping his wine, but now he spluttered a little. 'What?'

'I know he's a rackrenter,' Rosalie explained. 'Letting out squalid accommodation.'

'*Ah.* You've heard all about that.' He ordered fresh drinks from the same waiter, then leaned closer, bringing with him the strong scent of his citrus cologne. 'You'll realise, then,' he went on, 'that it's no wonder I and other men of decency cannot tolerate the sight of him! There's also—no, I really mustn't talk of it.'

'Please.' Rosalie gulped too much lemonade in hope that it would ease the sudden dryness of her throat. 'Please tell me.'

He pursed his lips. 'Very well, since I see you have no illusions about the scoundrel. I'm afraid that Alec Stewart is an utter reprobate. Ex-soldiers, ladies of the night—he keeps company with the lowest of the low.'

Ladies of the night. *Oh, no.* If she'd had any doubts, they were banished in that instant. She put her hand to her forehead, which throbbed with the beginnings of a headache. *Linette...*

'I'm extremely sorry,' said Lord Maybury with concern. 'I do not mean to offend you, Rosalie, but you are a woman of intelligence and you saw him yourself, at the Temple of Beauty.'

'You were there also,' said Rosalie.

Something—some alertness—flickered across his smooth face. 'I had certain enquiries to make. That was all. I was *not* there to watch the show—

you might have noticed. But I believe Captain Stewart was.'

Yes. Yes, he was. She was going to say so, but her throat was still horribly dry and now her head was starting to swim. 'I'm sorry,' she said, 'so stupid of me, but I really am beginning to feel rather unwell.'

Lord Maybury leaned over her, concerned. 'Indeed, you look quite pale. I hope I haven't upset you by speaking of that unpleasant man, Captain Stewart. You were most spirited to fulfil your wager by appearing there and now we will say no more of it. Finish that drink and I'll take you home.'

She got to her feet and was horrified at how unsteady she felt. 'I really will be quite all right, I assure you…'

'Do you have someone here who can take you home?'

'No, I will find a cab…'

She'd dropped her reticule under the table; he bent to retrieve it for her. 'Correction—*I* will fetch you a cab. No arguments, please, Rosalie.'

He escorted her down to the entrance hall, where he brought her cloak to her and left her while he went outside to find her a hackney. She saw a seat and rested there with her hands to her throbbing temples.

How could she even for one minute have been

taken in that night at Dr Barnard's by Alec Stewart's façade of integrity? How ever was she going to deal with him? Why did she feel so ill? *This is ridiculous. I will be all right soon. I must simply be tired.*

Chapter Ten

Lord Maybury came frowning back into the hall. 'No sign of any hackneys at all and it's started to rain, so it could be some time before we find one. Now, I will brook no argument, my dear Rosalie; my own driver will take you home.'

'No, really.' Everything seemed to be getting worse and worse. She shook her head, but he was already adjusting her cloak around her shoulders as he led her outside.

'I absolutely insist,' he said firmly. It had begun to rain hard and Piccadilly was crowded with pedestrians and vehicles. 'My carriage should be just down the road. Stay here, will you, while I tell the driver to bring it round?'

She watched him stride off. Then she blinked. Of all people, there was Biddy, hurrying towards her along the wet, crowded street, with her brother

Matt at her heels. *What on earth...?* And Biddy was holding Katy in her arms.

'Biddy! Matt! Oh, Katy darling!'

The small child, wrapped up in a cloak against the rain and clutching her rag doll, looked fretful. 'Want Mama. Want Mama.'

Quickly Rosalie gathered Katy close. 'Poor lamb, hush now... Biddy, what are you doing here with Katy, at this hour?'

Biddy looked breathless and terrified. 'There's been a fire! At Miss Helen's house!'

'A fire!'

'Yes,' said Matt grimly. 'Started deliberately, the constables reckon!'

Oh, no. 'Tell me everything.'

'Miss Helen and the children got out in time,' Biddy went on in a trembling voice. 'My brothers Matt and Dickon and little Joe did everything they could to put it out, but by the time the fire engine arrived, the place was a ruin! Mr Francis, he came straight away, and she and little Toby have gone to stay with him and his sister. But little Katy was crying so hard for you, Miss Rosalie, that Helen said to take her to you and to tell you to join her at Mr Francis's house in St John's Square, see.'

No. Rosalie's stomach clenched in anguish. Not possible—for this fire must be the work of Alec

Stewart, continuing to wreak revenge for her allegations about his rackrenting. And if he started to guess that she knew about him and Linette, he would be even more dangerous. Rosalie could not abuse Helen's friendship still further by endangering her in her new-found place of safety with Mr Wheeldon.

Then Biddy was curtsying wide-eyed, because Lord Maybury was back, his gaze immediately fastening on Katy in Rosalie's arms. He didn't look pleased. 'What's this?' he said rather abruptly.

'Some bad news,' breathed Rosalie. 'There's been a fire at the house where I live.'

He stepped back in shock. 'I'm so sorry. How terrible.'

Rosalie said quickly to Biddy, 'Please tell Helen I'll be all right. Tell her to look after herself and Toby; I'll send word to her in the morning.'

Matt was stepping forwards, squaring his broad shoulders. 'Now, Miss Helen said we was to see you safe to Mr Francis's house, isn't that so, Biddy? Or you could stay with us.'

Rosalie summoned the last of her strength. 'Thank you, but my mind's quite made up. I'll find lodgings close by.' There were several small, respectable hotels round here and she and Katy would be safe enough, for one night at least. But what next? Her head was reeling.

'I'll be off, then, and tell Miss Helen you're fine.' But Biddy still looked worried. 'Oh...' and she reached inside her cloak '...Miss Helen sent this for you.' She handed over a folded note, which Rosalie pushed in her pocket; then, darting one last shy glance at Stephen, Biddy hurried away with Matt.

'Rosalie,' Stephen was saying, 'what dreadful news about this fire! For the sake of your child, you must allow me to take you straight to my house in Brook Street, where my staff will see that you have everything you need, both of you.' He reached out to touch Katy's hand, but Katy started crying.

Rosalie was shaking her head. 'No. I cannot accept. My intention is to find lodgings.' She was already reaching in her reticule for her purse. But cold fingers of dread, as well as nausea, were stealing down her spine. It had gone. Her purse, with all her money, had gone.

Just then, a fast-moving hackney cab splashed through a puddle close to the kerb and sent water flying up to soak Rosalie's cloak and boots. Katy was crying bitterly in her arms.

Stephen put his hand on Rosalie's shoulder. 'This is no time to go looking for lodgings with the child. Surely you realise she could catch a dangerous chill if she's out in this rain for much longer. Look, there's my coach.' He was already guiding her towards an elegant vehicle with a coat of arms emblazoned on its doors.

What he said was all too true; Katy was shivering and sobbing, 'Mama, Mama.' Rosalie was feeling dizzy now, as well as sick.

Stephen was calling curtly to his driver. 'Take us to Brook Street.'

And he climbed in after her, watching her from the corner of his eye as the carriage rolled away.

This was his chance. His chance to investigate this girl who looked like the other one. This girl who, even in her drab, damp-stained clothes, was a tempting little beauty. The gin he'd paid the waiter to slip in her drink had achieved its purpose swiftly in fuddling her wits. His man Markin had done well, too, in getting information from the slut Sal that the girl had a sister who was dead. Markin had also got the fire started at exactly the right time.

There was just one problem. No one, unfortunately, had made any mention of this woman Rosalie having a child—Stephen detested children. But that was a minor issue. He had her in his power, and now was his chance to find out exactly what mischief she might be about to stir up.

* * *

Alec Stewart had spent the afternoon at his father's house, gathering up the possessions the Earl had ordered him to remove.

The Earl had gone to Carrfields with his young wife and the big house was quiet as Alec sorted through his various maps and campaign diaries, his bound volumes of war sketches done by talented comrades and some books about eighteenth-century art that he'd inherited from his mother. She'd died in a hunting accident when Alec was ten and the whole house, for Alec, still bore the stamp of her loving devotion to her family. Many of the paintings around the house had been hers.

Jarvis, his father's loyal steward, had helped him to pack up some biographies of the commanders Alec had idolised in his youth. 'A pity we see you here so rarely nowadays, sir,' Jarvis had said gravely.

'My father's got a new wife, Jarvis. Things were bound to change.'

Jarvis's silence was telling.

'Have you heard from Carrfields yet?' Alec asked.

'Indeed, sir, they arrived safely. And the longer they stay there, the better.'

Another enigmatic remark. 'The country air will certainly do my father's health good,' agreed Alec.

But he reckoned that wasn't what loyal old Jarvis meant.

He'd filled up three packing crates and Jarvis had promised to have them sent over to Two Crows Castle the next morning. 'My thanks.' Alec nodded. 'I'll be back for more in a day or so.' He was already on his way to the door, when something in the entrance hall caught his eye. He halted. 'Do you see that painting, Jarvis?'

'Which one, sir?'

'The oil, of the British troops at Blenheim.' Alec stepped closer. 'It looks different. Brighter. Or has it always been like that?'

'Lord Stephen's been telling your father he ought to get some of those old paintings cleaned, sir. In fact, Lord Stephen's been seeing to it himself over the last few months, taking them off to be restored. That one's just come back.'

Alec frowned. *Restored?* But his father had always declared that he liked the patina of the old oils...

'You'll realise, Master Alec, that I had no choice but to agree,' Jarvis was saying anxiously.

That evening Alec had had a fencing lesson and was tidying away his equipment when Garrett came in. 'One of the lads has got some news of a poetry reading in Piccadilly, Captain.'

Alec almost laughed. 'Poetry! God's teeth, why should that be any concern of mine? And confound it, Garrett, didn't I tell you to get rid of that dog weeks ago?' The big golden mongrel bounded happily up to Alec, wagging its tail.

'His name's Ajax, Captain. And I keep tellin' him to go, but he won't.'

'He'll eat us out of house and home!'

'I'm payin' for his food myself, Captain.'

'Anyone ever told you you're a fool, Garrett?'

'I know that, Captain.'

Sighing, Alec continued putting away his foils. 'This poetry reading you mentioned. I can only assume there was some purpose in your raising that unlikely subject?'

'Well, yes, Captain. The girl's there, you see—the one that was writin' those lies about you and this place, the other week.'

Alec went still. 'Mrs Rowland?'

'Aye, Mrs Rowland. You ordered us to keep an eye on her, since we told you about that printing press of her friend's bein' all busted.'

'Indeed,' muttered Alec. '*Busted*, as you put it, by some enemy Mrs Rowland's made with her scurrilous writing, no doubt.'

For God's sake, she looked for trouble! She'd been blatantly on stage at the Temple of Beauty, half-clad, then she'd written some vile stuff directed at him and confronted him with a whole pack of lies in his own home. Yet she was so young, so vulnerable, despite her bold defiance… The dog came up to him, wagging its tail, and Alec absently stroked its head. 'So you've discovered she's at a poetry reading. Is that the sum of your information, Garrett?'

'Not quite, Captain. We've got an informer there—a cousin of McGrath's—who was hired as a waiter, 'cos there was refreshments, see. And he's told us that someone else you know is at this lit'rary faradiddle. *Your brother.* He and the girl seem pretty friendly.'

Alec's hand went very still on the rapier he held. Despite her defiant words to him, the little widow knew Stephen!

'What do you expect me to do, Garrett? My opinion of her is already pretty low,' he answered, sliding the rapier back into the wall rack. 'Finding out that she's a friend of Stephen's does nothing to alter that.'

Red-haired Sergeant McGrath had come in also. 'There was somethin' odd, Captain, if they're friends,' McGrath offered. 'My cousin told me your brother ordered some gin to be put in the girl's lemonade. And she was startin' to look a bit sick, apparently.'

Damn it. Alec gave up hope of a quiet evening. 'Saddle up my horse, Garrett. This place is in Piccadilly, you say?'

'You will remember she ain't no friend of yours, won't you, Captain?' Garrett warned. 'Remember that nasty stuff she wrote about you…'

'I'll not forget it, never fear,' Alec gritted, heading for the door. 'That's why I'm going to see what they're both up to. Oh, and saddle a horse for yourself, too.'

'Why's that, Captain?'

'You're coming with me.'

Pulling on his greatcoat, Alec left. And Garrett muttered to McGrath, 'I hope, I do hope, that our Captain's not laying himself open to the tricks of another sweet-faced whore.'

'Now you know and I know, my lad,' replied McGrath, 'that our Captain's no fool in dealing with the muslin company…unless you're talkin' about that society lassie with all the money who ditched him just before Waterloo?'

Garrett snorted. '*Her?* The bird-witted little Lady Emilia? He was well rid of *her* and he knew it. No. It was someone else I was thinkin' of. Someone who's a real bundle of wickedness and is out to make more, unless I'm very much mistaken.'

'Who—?'

But Garrett had hurried on after Alec, leaving Sergeant McGrath scratching his head in bewilderment.

'Wait,' Rosalie said urgently to Stephen as his carriage turned into Holborn. She clutched Katy tighter. 'Can we stop? *Please?* I—I don't feel well.' Thanks to the lurching of this heavy coach, she was actually feeling desperately sick.

'You're just cold, my dear,' Stephen said soothingly to Rosalie. Solicitously he placed a plaid rug across her knees. 'We'll soon be at my house, you and your little daughter.'

Katy hid her face from him. Rosalie tried to say, 'She's not my daughter.' But something choked in her throat and her head was swimming. 'I need fresh air *now*. I must get out…'

Suddenly she realised that the carriage had indeed come to a juddering halt, but not at Stephen's bidding. As Stephen exclaimed, 'What in God's name—?' Rosalie was already on her feet and heading unsteadily for the door with Katy in her arms. It was opened before she could reach it by a tall, rain-soaked man who looked blazingly angry.

Alec Stewart was here. Alec Stewart, from Two Crows Castle, had stopped the coach. She saw suddenly that his horse was close by, held by none other than Eyepatch, who looked at her balefully. Stephen's driver up on his box was swearing, but Alec rapped out a few choice words that silenced him utterly.

Rosalie's stomach was roiling. With Katy still in her arms, she stumbled down, swaying. Alec grabbed the child and held her very tight as Rosalie leaned her hand against the side of the carriage and vomited into the gutter.

The gin, thought Alec. He cursed under his breath. Garrett had warned him that Stephen had doctored her drink. But no one had warned Alec that she had the child with her. At a poetry reading? What the hell was going on? He held the infant close, protecting her from the distressing sight of her mother being sick. She reacted by reaching up her chubby fists to his cheek, instantly smiling through her fretful tears. 'Tick-tock man,' she said.

And now his damned brother was climbing out of the carriage, his face livid with rage and, yes, fear as he growled out, 'Alec. What the hell do you think you're doing here?'

'I've come to see what *you're* up to, Stephen.' Alec's voice was harsh. 'It's not your usual style to be conveying a sick woman and her infant in your carriage.'

'Do you know,' breathed Stephen, 'it's absolutely none of your business. Now, I know you fancied this little blonde slut that night at the Temple of Beauty...' he glanced swiftly at Rosalie, who, still leaning against the carriage with her head bowed, was beyond hearing anything '...but if you've come to try to blacken my name with her, don't expect her to believe a word you say!'

Alec didn't, especially as last time they had met, he'd locked Rosalie in the basement of Two Crows Castle. She was an interferer. A troublemaker. But she didn't deserve *this*.

She was turning towards him, white but resolute. 'Give me the child, Captain Stewart!' she declared rather desperately.

Dark rings shadowed her eyes. Dear God, she was scarcely fit to stand, but still defiant! 'No!' he snapped back. 'Not until you can show you're fit to be in charge of her.'

She wasn't. She knew that and he knew it. Alec Stewart, her enemy. He looked vitally, frighteningly male, in his greatcoat and boots, his white shirt all crumpled, his neckcloth loose. His over-long hair, almost black in the rain, was all askew. His lean jaw was already dark with stubble, and his eyes were narrowed to angry slits.

The man Linette denounced on her death bed, thought Rosalie with a shudder. The man who was most likely responsible for the destruction of Helen's house. Why was he here, with Eyepatch? Somehow she summoned up the last of her strength and lifted her head to blaze resistance. 'How dare you *interfere* like this? Give me the child!'

Stephen smirked. 'Well, well, Alec. Think you've really overstepped the mark this time.'

Alec, ignoring him, said curtly to Rosalie, 'Did you let this man buy you a drink?'

'Yes! But it was only lemonade!'

'Only lemonade. You surely don't intend, considering the state you're in, to let him take you and your child to his house?' Alec knew Stephen's acquaintances. Their ways of passing the night-time hours made the Temple of Beauty look like a haven of respectability.

She was gazing fiercely up at him, but her face was white as a sheet. 'I—I had no alternative.'

'You could have made him take you to your home!'

'I couldn't!' She clenched her hands. 'The house where I stay has been burned to the ground!'

He was stunned. 'Burned to the ground... Deliberately?'

But she'd bent over to be sick again. Alec held Katy tight—'Mama?' the child was saying uncertainly. Dear God, this woman's home had just been burned down. And now she was going to Stephen's house, with her child—when Stephen had as good as poisoned her!

He couldn't stand seeing her there, so wretched. So damned foolish as to trust his brother. Alec swung round, Katy still in his arms, to fix Stephen with a steady, burning gaze of contempt. 'That's it, Stephen. Take your fancy carriage and leave—*now.*'

Stephen glanced angrily at Rosalie. 'You forget. Rosalie and her child are under my protection. Give me the infant—' He reached for Katy, who began to scream and clung to Alec even tighter.

'Your protection! That's a joke,' breathed Alec. 'Do you value your inheritance, Stephen? Do you value your *life*? If so, then you'd best get the devil out of here!'

Stephen paled. Then he squared his shoulders and turned to a trembling Rosalie, murmuring, 'My dear, you'll observe that the matter is out of my hands. But I suggest you think carefully about believing anything this man says, especially if it relates to me. I'll see you again soon, I hope. And as for you, Alec—I hope to see *you* in hell.'

With that Stephen barked orders to his driver, climbed back into his carriage and it rattled away down the street.

Chapter Eleven

Rosalie moved quickly. Snatching Katy from Alec, she began to march off in the rain, her mudsoaked clothes clinging coldly to her legs. She didn't know where she was or where she was heading. She felt sick and desperate. Katy was crying again.

Alec charged after her while Eyepatch, face set, held the two horses. '*Stop*, Rosalie. Where are you going?'

'I don't care! Anywhere!' she cried. The rain was pouring down; they were all wet through.

'*Rosalie.*' Urgently he caught her by the shoulder and swung her round. 'You surely didn't believe that Lord Maybury intended to *help* you!'

'I think he'd have found us better accommodation than his basement!' She tilted her chin defiantly. 'Why do you hate him so? What *is* he to you?'

It was a timely reminder for Alec that she didn't even know Stephen was his brother. And now was perhaps not the moment to tell her. 'Sorry,' he grated, 'sorry, there was I forgetting that you had an appointment with him, back in Piccadilly.'

'I did *not* have an appointment with him!'

'So you believe he was at the same place as you by chance, do you?'

'Of course! Why else?'

'He bought your drinks. And now you're sick as a dog… Yet you were going back with him, in his *carriage*?'

She clutched Katy tighter, her face blazing defiance again. 'I had nowhere else to go! And you, of all people, should know why, since you are responsible!'

Alec drew a deep breath. Light was just beginning to dawn. 'I take it you're talking about that fire again.'

'Yes, and don't insult me by pretending you don't know! My friend Helen's home was burnt to the ground tonight, because you took exception to my comments about your way of life, that day at Two Crows Castle! And I know you also set your men two weeks ago to destroy my friend's printing press—her *livelihood*!'

Oh, devil take it. The smashed press, the fire. She thought it was *him*. He clenched his jaw. 'Certainly I did not like the garbage you spouted that day you came to my home, chiefly because it in no way resembled the truth. But to think I would take such squalid and petty revenge…' Alec took a deep breath. 'Listen to me. I was *not* responsible for the damage done to your friend's printing press. I did not set fire to your friend's home tonight.'

She lifted her chin, in defiance and disbelief. 'You have plenty of men to do your dirty work, though, haven't you?'

'You are insulting them,' he snapped. 'I thought you as Ro Rowland pretended to be on the side of former soldiers. Now you're assuming, as so many others do, that they're all common criminals. Well, *don't*. And your friend with her printing press has no doubt made countless enemies if she regularly publishes vitriol-filled, inaccurate pieces like the one *you* were starting to write about Two Crows Castle that day you came to visit.'

She swallowed hard. Either he was an extremely good liar, or he was telling the truth. *Impossible*. But…

He was reaching into his pocket, pulling out a folded sheet of paper. 'Here,' he said tiredly. 'You dropped this.'

It was the letter Biddy had brought to her, from Helen. She had forgotten all about it. Still clutching Katy, she unwrapped it with fingers that were numb with cold.

Dear Rosalie, we are all safe, though the house is a burned-out shell. I am sending Katy to you with Biddy, because the child was inconsolable and wanted you badly. As Biddy will tell you, you must make haste, both of you, to Mr Wheeldon's house.

I have more idea now, Rosalie, who our enemy is. Because shortly before the fire another note was delivered, just like the first—on the same notepaper, in the same handwriting—saying, 'If you write one more word about Lady A., then you and those close to you will be the target next, not just the house.' *I fear I have made a vicious enemy, Rosalie. But Mr Wheeldon and his sister and their servants here make me feel most secure...*

Rosalie felt the world tilt around her. An enemy Helen had made, then, not her. So the finger of blame was no longer pointing at Alec Stewart... Oh, Lord. She tried to shove the letter back into her pocket, impeded because Katy, upset, was fighting to get free.

'Hush, sweetheart,' Alec was saying softly to the little girl. He'd picked up the tattered rag doll she'd dropped and gave it to her.

Katy gazed up at him, her crying hiccuping to a stop. 'Polly-doll,' she said.

Decisively Alec took her in his arms. 'News?' He nodded curtly towards Helen's letter.

The colour crept hotly up Rosalie's throat to her cheeks. 'It seems I might have been mistaken. In the matter of what happened to my friend, and the fire at her house. I—apologise.'

His expression remained iron hard. 'You make rather a lot of mistakes, don't you, Mrs Rowland?'

'I've said I'm sorry!' she flashed. 'Let me have Katy back.'

'You're not fit to look after yourself, let alone a child!'

Katy stared up at Alec, wide-eyed, interested. 'It's all right,' he said soothingly to her. 'It's all right, sweetheart.' He gazed narrowly at Rosalie. 'You've nowhere to go, you're not well and you have the child to think of. You're what I'd call in trouble.'

'Lord Maybury would have helped me!'

His lips thinned. 'If you believe that, you're even more foolish than I'd thought. And as Lord May-bury's gone on his sweet way, I'd say you've actually no choice but to let me take you both to my house for the night.'

Fear jolted through Rosalie. She'd always intended to tackle this man. To enter his lair somehow, and find out all she could about Linette's enemy. But, oh, Lord, not like this. Not with her legs shaking, and her stomach heaving, and her brain a woolly mess. And with—Katy.

Yet what else could she do? She had no money. No means now of even getting safely to Mr Wheeldon's house. 'Wonderful,' she said bitterly. She pushed back her hair. 'So it's your basement again, is it?'

Her legs wobbled and he saw it. 'Take hold of my arm,' he ordered. 'I've got the child safe. And this time, we'll try to do better than my basement. Garrett!' He was turning to call out to Eyepatch.

'Captain?'

'I want you to take the horses home. But first find me a hackney, quickly. I'm bringing Mrs Rowland and her child to Two Crows Castle.'

Garrett's face was a picture of dismay. 'My God, Captain, have you lost your wits?'

'Button it, Garrett. Just do as I say, will you?' Glancing down, Alec saw that Rosalie looked white as death.

The child looked anxious. 'Mama?'

'She's all right,' Alec said gently. 'Your mother will be all right, Katy.'

Alec realised he was getting himself into a fine pickle. No wonder Garrett had looked aghast. But when Alec had seen her struggling to get out of Stephen's carriage, he'd wanted to punch his brother into the gutter. She looked so defenceless in her drab wet cloak, with her rain-soaked hair clinging to her face. Yet not only had she paraded her wares at the Temple of Beauty, but she'd been with Stephen tonight. *She's no innocent, you fool. Young though she is, she's a widow and has a child. What's more, she's a gossip-raking troublemaker who's wrongly accused you of all sorts of rubbish...*

The hackney summoned by Garrett rumbled to a halt close by. He thought he could see tears misting her eyes as she turned to him and whispered, 'You promise me the child will be safe?'

'I promise,' he said, tight-lipped. *God, she could barely stand.* Grimly he climbed after her into the dingy hackney with Katy still secure in his arms and cursed himself for a fool all the way back to Two Crows Castle. His men would be far from delighted to see her after her last visit. But he couldn't leave her out on the street. *'Why not?'* loyal Garrett would say. *'She deserves no better.'*

Alec sighed. The trouble was that even now, bedraggled and sick and hostile as she was, she was still so eminently desirable that his loins ached. Dear God, she was prey to *anyone* like this, let alone his evil brother. She was clearly of gentle birth and educated. So what the hell was she doing, getting involved not only with the gutter press, but with Dr

Barnard's place and with Stephen? She could be big trouble. Could? She already *was*, damn it. Nowhere to go, apparently. No one to turn to except him.

The child slept in his arms. If he'd not tried to warn his father off his new wife, and if he himself had married that heiress as he was supposed to, he might have had a child of his own by now...

A hell of a lot of *ifs*. The coach was pulling up. They were there.

Rosalie's heart plummeted as they pulled up outside Two Crows Castle. The smoky lanterns that hung on either side of the big front door did little to relieve the gloom. She insisted on holding Katy herself as soon as she was out of the cab. *For one night. One night only.*

'What've you got there, Captain Alec?' That big red-haired Scotsman—oh, she remembered *him*—was drawing closer, frowning suspiciously. 'Och, now, you're not forgettin' she's the one that accused you of all those bad things the other week?'

'That was a misunderstanding,' said Alec curtly, guiding Rosalie towards the door. 'And she's here to stay, Sergeant McGrath, just for a day or two.'

More men were gathering round. Rosalie clutched Katy tighter. 'A child,' they were muttering. 'He's brought in a child and that woman.' Eyepatch was there, too; he must have stabled the horses, and his frown was equally dour.

Panic-stricken, Rosalie swung round to Alec. 'Look. I've changed my mind. Katy and I will find somewhere else.' *Anywhere else.*

'We've been through this,' Alec answered tightly. 'Where else, exactly, would you find shelter at this time of night?'

Nowhere. She shrank back from all their cold stares.

'Don't worry, Mrs Rowland.' Alec sighed. 'You and the child will have a room of your own, with a key on your side of the door—not that you'll need it. This place is far from luxurious, but at least we're all honest.'

Suddenly Katy opened her eyes and reached out to Alec, who touched her chubby hand very lightly. And when just the smallest of smiles crinkled his sombre eyes, the result was so devastating that Rosalie felt her insides lurch again. He said to her, more gently, 'Garrett will show you to your room. We'll discuss what's to be done in the morning.'

Already McGrath was trying to draw Alec to one side. 'Captain, there's more fellows needin' rooms tonight. They're waiting in the Rising Sun for you…'

She watched Alec's tall, rangy figure disappearing from view, with red-haired McGrath at his side. And she felt as if her one pillar of safety was abandoning her.

Safety? Was she insane? Was this how Linette had felt? Still feeling sick, she held Katy close and struggled to gather her disarrayed thoughts as Eyepatch—oh, Lord, she must remember his name was Garrett—led her surlily up the stairs.

The accommodation she and Katy were to share consisted in fact of one small room. Garrett had lit a lamp before he left; as she looked around, she felt a tiny but welcome sense of relief. There was just enough space for two narrow beds; the blankets, though threadbare, looked clean and the floor was swept, with a closet for clothes and even a small mirror nailed to the wall over a washstand.

A middle-aged woman knocked on the door a few minutes later. 'My name's Mary, ma'am, and I've brought you both clothes, 'cos the Captain said yours were soaked and here's some milk and bread for your little one. You'll be sure to let me know, won't you, if there's anything else you want? Bless her, isn't she sweet! My little granddaughters, now—'

'Thank you, that will be all,' Rosalie cut in. Unable to find the promised key, she jammed the door shut with a chair after the woman had gone. On the one hand, she rebuked herself for being abominably rude. On the other hand—she was in the domain of her enemy.

And she was so tired, all she wanted to do was sleep. But first she changed Katy into those dry clothes, then took the plate of bread and, after hesitating—*they wouldn't stoop to poisoning an infant, don't be a fool*—she sat Katy on her lap and fed her.

That was when she heard the noise of men talking somewhere outside. Going over to the window with Katy still in her arms, she pulled back the faded curtain to gaze out.

'Tick-tock man. There,' Katy announced with satisfaction.

The window overlooked a large, overgrown garden at the back of the house. A flagged terrace was lit by the glow of a brazier, and gathered around it, with tankards of ale in their hands, were a dozen or so rough-looking men—and two young women, with whom the men were clearly on familiar terms. In their midst was Alec, laughing and joking with them. One of the women, who had dyed black hair and upthrust breasts on full display, had her hand possessively on his arm.

What had Lord Maybury said? *I'm afraid that Alec Stewart keeps company with the lowest of the low...*

Shivering with dismay, Rosalie turned away from the window, freshly appalled at the situation in which she'd landed herself. Katy was nodding off in her arms; Rosalie wiped her face and fingers clean and put her in the spare bed with her rag doll next to her. She remembered, with a wrench at her insides, how in the cab Katy had slumbered in Alec Stewart's arms, her thumb in her mouth, her dark curls tousled around her angelic face. *I envied her, in those strong arms... Don't be stupid! Don't be so utterly idiotic!* She blinked away her own hot tears of weariness and despair.

No matter how much she tried to tell herself that this was her heaven-sent opportunity to find out more about the dangerous master of Two Crows Castle, she was in a mess, she acknowledged bitterly, an almighty mess. She changed into the nightdress Mary had provided and settled herself awkwardly on the bed, preparing herself for a sleepless night. Why did Alec Stewart and Lord Maybury hate each other so? There was so much that she couldn't make sense of...

But suddenly something that should have been obvious struck her with a dreadful jolt. *No wonder Katy was so happy in Alec Stewart's arms. She had, after all, most likely found her father.*

* * *

Alec didn't reach his bed until late. Tonight he knew he'd vastly added to his problems by taking in Rosalie—Mrs Rowland—and her child.

Why had he done it, when she so clearly hated him? When she was preparing to go off for the night with Stephen?

It was because Rosalie still struck him as Stephen's *victim*, rather than his whore. And—though he despised himself for this—because he found her irresistible. He'd been fool enough to kiss her twice and both those kisses had been delicious. She was sweet, tenderly responsive, yet almost innocent… Impossible! For God's sake, she'd been selling herself at the Temple of Beauty! Displaying herself, on stage, looking for the highest bidder!

His raging doubts were succinctly echoed by Garrett, as the two of them went as usual round the big place one last time, to check all was well before locking up for the night.

'You've let yourself in for a whole heap of trouble, taking that one in, Captain, if you don't mind my saying,' warned Garrett softly. 'A whole heap.'

Alec was awake early the next morning as ever and went down to breakfast, brushing aside that damned great dog, who'd jumped up to greet him from a warm spot by Mary's cooking range. Quite a few men were already at the big table, eating. The newcomers were especially hungry and shovelled down the food as if they couldn't believe their luck, while the two new women Garrett had hired to help out were cheerfully dishing out the plain but hearty food.

They all greeted him warmly. 'Mornin', Captain!' He nodded in reply. The dark-haired wench who'd tried her luck with him last night lifted her face for a kiss, but he'd already made it plain she was hired to work and nothing else. He couldn't see Mary, though he knew she couldn't be far away, because only she could have got so many pans full of sizzling fried bread and bacon on the big cooking range.

He went to pour himself some coffee, then saw Mary coming through from the breakfast room—with Katy in her arms.

'Where's the child's mother, Mary? Isn't she down yet?'

Kind Mary, a mother and grandmother herself, looked anxious. 'She's still a-bed, Captain. The little one was heard cryin', so I went up to fetch her. Took her clothes to freshen up, as well. The mother, she didn't wake!'

Garrett entered just then. 'Doubtless she's not used to keeping early hours, Captain,' he said pointedly.

Alec whipped round on him. 'She has a *child*. No mother normally sleeps when her child's crying!'

'This one does.'

Alec said grimly, 'In that case, I'm going up to her. She cannot be well.'

But first, Garrett handed him the note.

Hell's teeth.

Chapter Twelve

Rosalie was in an old dark castle, where every room was full of sneering soldiers and gaudily dressed whores. She was running along endless passageways in search of Linette, for ever glimpsing her, but unable to reach her; then she was faced with a door which turned out to be not a door, but a mirror. In it she saw herself wearing nothing but a silken underslip, through which her hips and her breasts were outlined. Her hair was tangled, her cheeks flushed, and Alec Stewart was coming up behind her, lithe and dangerous, pulling her to him, kissing her, plundering her mouth with his lips and tongue…

Linette's destroyer. A rackrenter, who sought out the company of loose women.

Darkness enveloped her again. Flames were burning her. She could hear Katy crying, *Mama, Mama,* and Rosalie was struggling to get to her, but was powerless to save her. *There is no hope*, someone was saying, *there is no hope.*

Tears were streaming down her cheeks. Weakly she hauled herself up against the pillows, still light-headed, still nauseous. Daylight poured into the room. And she saw that Katy's bed was empty.

She began to scream.

The door opened and Alec Stewart was there. Instantly he strode to her bedside. 'Rosalie. You're having nightmares—my God, you look as though you're burning up!'

'Katy.' The tears were still rolling down her cheeks. 'What have you done with Katy?'

'She's safe. Do you hear me?'

'I must go to her. I must…'

He sat quickly on the chair by her bed and gripped her hands. 'She's downstairs, having breakfast. Mary is looking after her; she's quite safe. *You're* safe.' He touched her forehead. 'But you have a fever. You're not fit to go anywhere.'

She was trying to pull away. 'I must get up, I must get out of here.'

'And go where precisely, damn it?'

She sank back, pulse thudding. She had no money. Helen's house had been destroyed. And she was clad only in a loose nightgown—*where were her clothes*?

Alec had gone over to the dressing table and was pouring something from a jug into a cup. 'Here,' he said, coming back to her, his face strangely shadowed. 'Drink this. It's Mary's barley water.' He sat on a chair next to the bed, supporting her shoulders with one hand and holding the cup for her with the other hand. She felt as weak as a kitten. Her throat was parched, and the barley water was cold and pure. His hand was unnervingly comforting against her back. But—

'You will be *all right* here,' he emphasised softly. 'Katy will be all right. Mary has her two young grandchildren here nearly every day while her daughter works at a bakery in Bishopsgate. The little girls are playing with Katy now and Katy is perfectly happy. I'm going to send for the doctor.'

'*No.*'

'I know that you hate this place, and me,' he said quietly. 'But unless you can tell me of somewhere else you can go—somewhere *safe*—you really have no option.'

She hesitated, her stomach pitching. 'I will find *somewhere...*'

He shrugged his wide shoulders. 'If you insist. But I take it you're going with a bodyguard to accompany you?'

The blood pounded through her veins. 'What—what nonsense is this?'

'Not nonsense, unfortunately. *This* was delivered at the house this morning.' He passed the crudely written note to her. She took it with trembling fingers.

Stop asking questions, whore. Your friend has already suffered the consequences, and you're next.

The writing. The notepaper... Her stomach lurched.

He said, 'Do you know who it's from?'

'I think—I think it could be from the same person who has been threatening my friend Helen. The same writing. The same notepaper.'

He drew in a sharp breath. She went on, in a voice that shook despite all her efforts to control it, 'This is ridiculous! I cannot be threatened like this; I will go to the constables, or a magistrate—they will help me!'

'Save yourself the trouble,' he said.

He didn't need to explain. He'd told her before that no magistrate would take the trouble to listen to her. *A courtesan who writes for a gossip rag.* That was how he'd described her. 'Then I am even more determined that we will leave here!' she cried. 'Katy and I, we will find somewhere...' She was trying to push back the bedclothes.

'No!' he rasped, flinging out his arm to stop her. 'Whoever it is, they'll follow you—you and the child!' Then, a little gentler, 'I don't make a habit of throwing women and children out on the street. Stay here.'

He must have seen the downright fear shoot through her. 'I realise the idea doesn't immediately appeal,' he said. His eyes darkened. 'But believe me, as soon as word goes around that you're under my protection, you'll be far safer than anywhere else in London. And rest assured I will require nothing of you at all. Except, perhaps, obedience.'

She swallowed, hard. 'Then—you truly think I'm in danger?'

He pointed at the note. 'Don't *you*?'

She sank back against the pillows. Oh, Lord. Where else could she go? But how could she possibly think herself safe *here*, of all places?

Alec was mentally cursing himself. If he hadn't gone to Dr Barnard's to tackle Stephen, he would never have seen her. She'd have been left to deal with her own problems, which she'd surely brought upon herself. But—was she really used to earning her living on her back, as well as with her vitriolic pen?

She was trouble. Even in that voluminous nightgown, she was treacherously alluring. He remembered her slender waist, the sweet curve of her hips, the warm scent of her skin as he'd hauled her against him in that kiss, the last time she'd paid a visit to Two Crows Castle. The memory sent a nagging ache of need throbbing through his veins.

You fool, Stewart.

'Have you decided?' he asked curtly.

Her eyes looked bruised with distress. 'Will you truly promise me Katy is safe here?'

'Of course she is,' he said. *Safer than she was with you last night, since you were dragging her around the town.* No. He wouldn't rebuke her—yet—for her idiotic trust in his brother.

She drew herself up and said, with that air of defiant dignity that so confounded all his preconceptions of her, 'Very well. For as long as the danger stands, I will—accept your protection.'

He nodded, as if it were a matter of as little importance to him as the hiring of a hackney cab. 'I am overwhelmed by your gratitude,' he said.

'Some day you must let me pay you!'

He shrugged. 'Why? Nobody else does.'

Her eyes flashed. 'Only those poor soldiers!'

'My soldiers?' He looked coldly angry now. 'I'd like to make it quite clear that none of them pays me a penny.'

Oh, God. She bit her lip. For some reason she believed him. 'I'm sorry. Oh, I'm sorry. I thought you were a—a...'

'A rackrenter,' he said tightly. 'Indeed. As you implied in those scribblings of yours—wait! Where in hell are you *going*?'

She'd suddenly slid to the side of the bed away from him. Was trying to heave herself out, but was instead doubled up and starting to retch helplessly.

In a couple of strides Alec had pushed the porcelain bowl from the washstand on to the floor beside her. 'I'll send Mary up. I'm going for the doctor.'

'No—'

'This time,' he said, 'I'm giving you no choice.'

Exhausted with sickness and with Mary quietly tidying up around her, Rosalie sagged back against the pillows in despair. *Oh, no.* She'd made so many dreadful mistakes. She'd been wrong about Helen's printing press, and the fire, and about his rackrenting. In return he despised her as a cheap little widow, a courtesan. And even though Alec Stewart might be a despicable seducer—*my own sister denounced him to me!*—just now she'd found comfort and something even more disturbing in his calm voice, his very presence...

You are mad. You are ill, Rosalie.

Ill indeed, because during the course of that

morning the fever took her more firmly in its grip. Bed rest, the doctor ordered.

The next few days for Rosalie passed in a haze. She was sometimes aware of Mary serving her with the powders the doctor had prescribed, or bringing her a fresh cotton nightgown. Of Katy being brought up to see her, her little thumb in her mouth, sometimes with Mary, sometimes in Alec's strong arms, which Rosalie found almost unbearable.

Sometimes, she would hear the physician's grave voice. 'The fever lingers… She must have caught a chill on the night you found her.'

Then Alec's low tones. 'Mrs Rowland was drenched that night, in the rain. And I've reason to believe she was served drinks that had been tampered with.'

'That would not have helped. Rest is what she needs; a little light food, plenty of liquids…'

That threat, that note Alec had shown her, hung over her all the time. *Stop asking questions, whore. Your friend has already suffered the consequences, and you're next.*

Who could it be from?

One morning—Rosalie guessed her fourth day here—Alec knocked and came in after the doctor's daily visit. She had tried getting up earlier, but her legs were as shaky as a newborn colt's.

'I've brought you a letter,' he said. Her pulse began to race. 'It's from your friend Helen.'

Helen. Oh, poor Helen would have been so worried, so angry... 'How did she know I was here?'

'I told her,' Alec said quietly. 'I went to see her at Mr Wheeldon's house two days ago to explain that you were ill and had taken shelter at my home. She—expressed her disapproval quite strongly.'

Rosalie could imagine. She opened the letter quickly. *Rosalie, my dear. What can you be thinking of, staying at that place? You know you are welcome here, with Francis and his sister! I have news. But first please write, to let me know you and Katy are safe.*

'She wanted to visit you,' Alec said. 'More than that, I think she wanted to drag you and your child away from here and tear me limb from limb. Her friend Mr Wheeldon was more reasonable. Do you wish her to visit?'

'No, I don't. Because that threat was directed to her, too, wasn't it, Captain Stewart?' Rosalie managed to sound calm. 'So at the moment I imagine it's best if she has as little as possible to do with me.'

'Then I'll tell her that the doctor still advises you

to rest. And if you wish to write to her, I'll see that your letter's delivered.'

So Rosalie wrote to her.

A reply came the next day from Helen. Alec waited while she read it. *Rosalie. I am disappointed that you have chosen to place any trust in that man. Since you don't wish me to visit, I am obliged to write with my news. Francis has asked Toby and me to travel to Oxford with him for two weeks, because he has been approached to set up a church school in a village there and wants me to help. Just think, it's not far—ten miles or less—from where you used to live, and I used to teach! I am considering making a permanent move— I don't think I can be happy in London again. I hope you know, Rosalie, that I will be there whenever you want me. Yours, Helen.*

Alec was watching her. 'Are you all right, Mrs Rowland?'

She pushed some loose strands of hair back from her cheeks. 'Helen is leaving London for a little while. I—I think she feels I've rejected her.'

'You did so for very good reasons,' he reminded her quietly. 'Unselfish reasons. Some day, you'll be able to tell her so.' He hesitated. 'I'll leave you to rest.'

She lay back against the pillows.
Now, she really was on her own.

Whenever she was by herself she would get up from her bed and try to walk a little further around the room, but Rosalie was frightened by how weak she was after these days of illness. Katy was brought up to her regularly, but was always happy to return to her new friends.

Time for Rosalie hung heavily, until she noticed some books on a shelf by the window. She was surprised by their quality. Several of them, she realised, were sketchbooks that must have belonged to someone in the army. Quickly she became captivated by the swiftly but skilfully drawn portraits of soldiers at rest, or marching, the deft watercolours of mountains and villages, in Spain, she guessed. There were also other, heavier volumes containing reproductions of the work of more famous artists.

Mary had brought her some spare clothes, and on her seventh morning there Rosalie took off her nightgown and pulled on a sleeveless cotton chemise, intending to wear the plain rose-pink cambric dress that lay over the foot of the bed. But it was warm in here with the sun pouring through the window, so she decided to continue reading the book on

Boucher she had found while sitting curled on the bed. The doctor had been and there was no danger of any other visitors just yet.

She was fast learning the rhythms of the household. She'd heard from Mary, always willing to chatter, that the soldiers were usually up and about early. Some went off to local places of work, at building sites or timber yards. Others were organised by Sergeant McGrath into doing repair work around this ungainly great building. Alec was often out until his fencing lessons began in the early evening.

But now, as Rosalie sat cross-legged on the bed in that flimsy chemise, engrossed in her book, Alec Stewart walked in, carrying a tray laden with a steaming teapot, china cups and a plate of bread and butter. He almost dropped everything. He clutched the tray and steadied it with a clatter of crockery, but not before one of the cups had rolled off and smashed on the floor.

He said, 'My God.'

She dropped the book and jumped off the bed, putting it between herself and him. With his tousled dark hair, his rumpled white shirt, black boots and breeches that clung to every inch of his muscular thighs, he looked utterly devastating.

Her pulse was hammering. 'If you'd knocked

first,' she declared, 'you might have saved yourself a broken cup! How dare you just march in?'

'It's my damned house,' he pointed out reasonably. 'And Mary asked me to bring your tea. Normally you're hiding under the sheets. I had no idea you'd be putting on such a display.' To be truthful, Alec was flummoxed. He knew he should leave. But— he was entranced. He felt lust stroking his loins. In that simple white chemise, she looked exquisite.

Already she was tugging on the rather faded rose-pink gown.

But that was hardly any better at concealing her charms either, thought Alec, cursing under his breath as he picked up pieces of the broken cup, because the soft fabric had moulded itself tightly to her small but rounded breasts. Earlier she must have tied back her hair, but now some blonde tendrils had escaped to cling enchantingly round her face. And as she gazed up at him with those defiant turquoise-blue eyes, he saw that they were shadowed with fear.

He sighed. He poured her some tea. 'Please sit down again. How are you feeling? I see you were looking at one of my books.'

The big book still lay outspread by her pillow. She struggled to fasten the last button and sat on the edge of the bed because her legs were suddenly unsteady again. 'I'm feeling a good deal better, thank you. I'm sorry, I shouldn't have looked at them without your permission…'

'Permission? Don't be ridiculous! What were you looking at?' He'd pulled up a stool by the bed and was reaching to examine the open pages. 'These paintings are French, aren't they? By François Boucher. You told me about Boucher at the Temple of Beauty, remember?'

Rosalie swallowed. *Be prim. Be polite.* But as she watched his lean brown hand gently lifting and turning the corners of the pages, some sort of inner turmoil set her blood racing.

'I remember,' she said as steadily as she could. Oh, Lord, how could she forget? *Just before that kiss.* 'And they're in Boucher's early style,' she went on, pointing. 'In fact, he served his apprenticeship as an engraver, but moved on to historical paintings and portraits—' She broke off. 'I'm sorry, I sound as if I'm giving a lecture.'

'You're knowledgeable.'

'Only because my father was an artist. He painted watercolours and studied the French artists of the seventeenth and eighteenth centuries.'

'Why French artists?'

'Because he lived for some years in Paris and married my mother there.'

'She was French?'

'Yes. My father died when I was seven.'

There is no hope. No hope at all, I'm afraid, madame…

Memories. The doctor, talking to her mother in Paris, at her father's sickbed. Her father, holding Rosalie close with what little strength he had. *'Be a brave, good girl, my Rosalie. Look after your mother and your little sister for me…'*

Alec said, 'Was that when you came to England?'

'Yes. My father had told my mother, often, about a cottage he owned in Oxfordshire.'

'And is your mother still there?'

She gazed up at him, her blue eyes wide with loss. 'She is dead, too.'

Alec tried not to look at the slenderness of her neck. The faint pulse beating there. *What had happened to her life next?* he wondered. An impulsive early marriage, he supposed, and pregnancy followed by her husband's early demise, leaving her penniless with a child to support. So she'd decided to come to London to seek her fortune—as a writer? As a courtesan? Whatever, somehow she'd made bad enemies.

Yet he found it so damned hard to believe she was capable of selling herself. She'd looked so innocent when he'd come in just now, wearing that pure white bit of nothingness and intently poring over that book…

He forced himself to remember how she'd been parading on stage at Dr Barnard's—for sale, or as good as. Unfortunately, the memory did nothing to quell the nagging of harsh desire between his thighs. *A French mother*—perhaps that explained her grace, her allure, her *beauty*, damn it all.

'Being left alone with a child to take care of can't be easy,' he said. 'But you must admit you've made some rash decisions.'

She closed the book rather abruptly. 'I have always paid my own way, I assure you, Captain Stewart. And I have never before been forced to stay in a place like this!'

He was angry now. 'No one is forcing you. And considering you were dragging a small child round London with nowhere to go except Lord Maybury's on the night I found you, you can hardly claim to be a model parent!'

She'd risen shakily to her feet, her colour high. 'I've done what I could for Katy. How *dare* you criticise, when you've no *idea*!'

He stood up, too, to make her sit down again. 'Hush. Hush, I'm sorry. Everyone can see that you adore her.'

'Everyone can…?' His warm hands on her shoulders made her fury melt into something far more disturbing. She was struggling for breath.

'Of course.' His eyes, she saw, were concerned, Almost—*tender*.

'I'm sorry,' she whispered, 'it's just...' she swallowed and rubbed her hand across her eyes '...it's just that sometimes I think I will go mad if I have to stay trapped in here another day!'

'You have been ill. Don't be so hard on yourself, Mrs Rowland.' He sat next to her and smiled quizzically down at her. 'Now, I'm going to tell you a secret. Actually, I used to rather enjoy your Ro Rowland articles.'

'You—*you did*?'

'Yes. You have talent and wit. You have—courage.'

'No. No. I've been stupid, I've made a mess of everything!' Bitterly she looked up at him. 'Oh, if only I had not been *ill*.'

'Poor Rosalie. Taking the whole world on your shoulders.'

'I can look after myself!' she flared. 'I—I am in temporary difficulties, that is all.'

He tilted her chin up with his fingers, frowning. Temporary difficulties? The sight of her struggling defiantly against the troubles that life had thrown her way had touched some part of him that he'd long buried. That belonged to a better part of him, perhaps.

But it wasn't the better part of him that made him ache to kiss her. To feel the softness of her tender body in his arms…

'Stop fighting the whole world,' he said quietly. 'Stop fighting *me*.'

And he kissed her. My God, he knew he'd regret it, but—he kissed her.

Rosalie went very still at the first brush of his lips against hers. But as his warm mouth cherished hers, her lips parted instinctively, her heart thudded and she felt that in the whole world there was only this man. Only the heady, floating sensation of his slow, deliberate kiss. Only the need to feel his hands, his lips, caressing her body, arousing, promising…

It was as if he *cared*. 'Forget it, gal,' Sal would warn bitterly, 'forget them all. Once a feller's got what he wants, he'll throw you away like rubbish.'

But Rosalie was beginning not to care what Sal had said. This was where she wanted to be, in his arms. It was so good to breathe in his clean male scent and all that mattered now was his mouth on hers, his tongue delicately probing, deliberately possessing her with a skill that was utterly devastating. Her heart was beating quite wildly.

Then she gasped, because he had unbuttoned her dress and slipped aside the shoulder of her chemise and was cupping one breast with his sword-calloused palm, caressing it deliberately, wickedly until the sensitive peak leapt to his touch. She felt an answering pulse at her very core, full of liquid warmth as she realised it would be so easy just to melt into his strong arms. So easy to let him bed her...

A sharp knock, at the door.

Garrett's voice. 'You've got a visitor, Captain.'

Alec drew slowly back from Rosalie and swore under his breath. 'Whoever it is, tell him it's not convenient.'

A pause. Then—'I think you'll want to see him. Captain. Sir.'

Alec turned to Rosalie, his jaw set. Once more he was tough Captain Stewart, master of a lowlife soldiers' hostel. 'I must go. Don't do anything stupid. Don't even *think* of leaving.'

He was gone. And she felt desolate. She clutched the bedpost, white-faced. Once more she'd succumbed to this dangerous man—she was surely losing her wits. She pushed herself up from the bed. Despite what he said, she had to get out of here! But—that threat. *Stop asking questions, whore...*

Talk about being trapped between the devil and

the deep blue sea. She tried again to get up and walk around the room, but within a few moments she had to sink back on the bed, because her legs felt like cotton wool.

She closed her eyes and surrendered briefly to despair. And the worst thing was—she was just starting to realise how very much she *wanted* to be wrong about Alec Stewart and Linette.

Garrett was waiting for Alec out on the landing. 'Listening at keyholes, Garrett?' queried Alec caustically.

'No!' Garrett looked hurt. 'No, God's truth… Captain, Lord Conistone's waitin' in the fencing hall for you!'

Lucas. Indeed, this was the first good news Alec had had for a long time. And his friend had called at the right moment, because a few more minutes with Mrs Rosalie Rowland and he'd have been hard put to stop himself seducing her there and then. My God, whether she intended it or not, everything about her was an erotic enticement: the defiant flash of her eyes; the way she tossed her hair to face up to him; the stubborn pout of her full, rosy lips.

Alec was no stranger to female enticements and he'd enjoyed many a willing bed companion. Yet something about her was so damned *vulnerable*. If she was playing games, she excelled at them, because she was driving him wild.

He'd longed, how he'd longed just then to caress her into submission with his lips and hands. He was possessed by an image of her naked, her slender legs wrapping around his as he sheathed himself in her again and again...

God, Alec, don't. She's dangerous. A whore and a scandalmonger. A dousing of cold water for you, man.

That threatening note had been nasty. Someone vicious was after her—the same person doubtless who'd made her homeless through the fire. She would make enemies easily, with the mixed messages she sent out. One minute all erotic allure, the next, prim as a young school miss...

You can't take her as your mistress. You mustn't.

Physical pleasure for a man of Alec's station was easy to come by, but intimacy of any other sort he'd sworn to avoid for good. His mind wandered back to the painful memories of a spell of home leave when he'd become betrothed to a pretty young heiress who thought herself in love with him. She'd been an innocent, of course, well chaperoned because of all that money. She'd kept asking about the battlefields of the Peninsula, but she'd not wanted to know the harsh reality, so he kept it from her. Kept *him-*

self from her, until in a fit of petulance she'd broken their betrothal last spring. Which was as well, considering the dark secrets already unfolding at the heart of his family.

Now Alec's thoughts ran riot as he made his way to the fencing hall. What the hell was he to do with Rosalie Rowland? He cursed anew when he saw that some of the plaster-and-lath ceiling had fallen in overnight thanks to a spell of heavy rain; cursed again when he had to push aside that great mutt of a dog who leapt up eagerly to greet him. 'Garrett, I thought I said—'

'Aye, Captain. I'll find a new home for him soon enough.'

Alec sighed and went to greet his oldest, his truest friend.

Lucas Conistone, Earl of Stancliffe, looked just the same as ever: effortlessly elegant, his clothes exquisite. Alec clasped his hand. 'Lucas, by God! I thought you'd become a rustic, never to grace the city again. When did you arrive in town?'

'Late yesterday.' Lucas smiled. 'Even Verena felt it was time to catch up on the gossip of the *ton*.'

Alec noted how his friend's handsome features lit up as he spoke his wife's name. 'How are Verena and the children?'

'Well, all well; the children cannot wait to see Hyde Park, and the Tower, and so on. Verena—oh, she pretends, you know, to take an interest in clothes and balls and such, but really…'

'Really, she's just happy wherever you are, Lucas, admit it!'

'Indeed.' Lucas's elegant drawl softened. 'I'm a lucky man, Alec.'

Garrett came in, grinning all over his face because he thought the world of Lucas Conistone. He carried freshly polished glasses and a bottle of burgundy. Alec glanced at the label and whistled.

'Brought by his lordship, Captain,' explained Garrett, expertly wielding the corkscrew.

'Are we celebrating something?'

Lucas nodded. 'Remind him, Garrett. And pour yourself a drink also, man. You were there, too.'

Garrett lifted his head proudly. 'Two years ago to the day, the garrison at Bordeaux surrendered to Lord Wellington! There was still Toulouse and Waterloo to come, of course. But Bordeaux was the beginning of the end for Mister Nap!'

'Indeed,' affirmed Lucas, lifting his glass. 'Here's to victory.'

'And here's to those who didn't make it back,' added Alec softly. Suddenly serious, all three raised their glasses, thinking of the dead and wounded.

Then Garrett, a broad smile once more splitting his face to see these old friends together again, left them with the wine.

They talked for a while about the war and mutual acquaintances. Then Alec wryly indicated Lucas's fine clothes. 'You said you were a lucky man, Lucas. You're also a damned expensively dressed one—now, let me guess—boots by Hoby, coat tailored by Weston? I wonder what it's worth to keep quiet about the filthy clothes you wore to play the spy in Portugal? My God, you used to go unwashed for days on end!'

Lucas pointed at him, laughing. 'You, too, Alec— you were with me on some of my most dangerous adventures, remember? We were ragamuffins, both of us! But that's all behind us. And your father's not well, I hear.'

'My father's not well and I've got a brother I wouldn't wish on my worst enemy.' Alec finished off his wine. 'My father's gone to Carrfields, though that's not the solution. Lucas, I'd do anything for him—you know how close we used to be. But he won't have me near!'

'Then he's his own worst enemy,' said Lucas levelly. 'Look, Alec, you need a change of scene. We're opening up our Mayfair house and we want you to visit us—in fact, we'll be offended if you *don't*. Though you seem to have your hands pretty full here, from what I've seen…'

They talked on, about Two Crows Castle and a parliamentary bill that was going forwards to secure better rights for the injured soldiers. Then it was time for Lucas to leave, but out in the hallway he paused.

'Alec, tell me if this is none of my business, but I was in Rundell's yesterday—you know, the art dealers on Ludgate Hill? And I noticed two rather fine oil paintings there that I'd swear I'd last seen in your father's drawing room. Were you aware that he was putting some of his collection on the market?'

'No,' breathed Alec, suddenly tensing. 'No, by God, I wasn't. And I wonder if my father is!'

As soon as Lucas had gone, Alec clenched his fists. That painting, of Blenheim. Sent to specialists, to be cleaned? His suspicions ran riot. But how to go about this? How to tackle this new, damnable problem without letting the whole world—especially his father—know?

His mind flew to Rosalie Rowland.

He'd been a fool to kiss her again; that had helped nothing. If he'd been hoping to breach her defences, he'd learned not a fragment more about the enigmatic little widow from the Temple of Beauty—except that she knew rather a lot about art.

Then Garrett came in. 'You know you told the lads to ask round careful-like about Mrs Rowland, Captain? Well, they've found out that when she arrived in London last autumn, she stayed with that printer friend of hers, in Clerkenwell.'

Alec nodded tiredly. Helen Fazackerley.

'And she spent most of her time,' went on Garrett, 'goin' round theatres.'

'Going round *theatres*! With her infant?'

'She didn't have the infant with her then, see?' said Garrett patiently. 'The little 'un—Katy—seemed to turn up some time in December. Mrs Rowland left 'er then for an hour or two at a time with her printer friend, or a neighbour of theirs. And she carried on traipsing each day from one playhouse to another. Askin' about someone called—Linette.'

With that, Garrett nodded and left.

Alec frowned, rubbing the tension from the back of his neck.

Who the deuce was Linette?

He'd gone easy on the questions so far, because of Rosalie's sickness. But now, perhaps, the time for soft-footing it was over.

She'd just told him that she was going mad, confined to her room, hadn't she? Well, he'd thought of rather an interesting outing for her—*and* a way to put her secretly to the test.

Chapter Thirteen

By the time Alec got back upstairs, Rosalie was sitting by the window, with a drab shawl over her gown and her hair pinned up, and—

'What exactly are you doing, Mrs Rowland?'

She stiffened. 'Mending some shirts. Mary came up after you'd gone and I asked her if there was anything I could do.'

'Mary had no business giving you servants' work!'

Her blue eyes flashed. 'Captain Stewart, I'm aware that I've been taking up a room, and your time and your servants' time. That you've been feeding both myself and Katy for *days* now—'

'And neither of you eats enough to keep a bird alive,' he retorted, glancing at her slender frame, which was a big mistake, because he remembered with a jolt just how it had felt, spanning that tiny waist with his hands, feeling the feminine swell of her hips, the sweet warmth of those lips…

Damnation. He clamped down hard on the sudden surge of desire.

He went on, in a voice he strove to make less abrasive, 'I take it you're feeling considerably better. Would you care to come out for a while with me?'

'Out...?'

'Yes. To look at some paintings. They're at a private house, to the west of the city. It will take us perhaps half an hour to get there.'

She hesitated. 'You think I'll be safe?'

'I don't think the coward who sent that note would dare to do anything in broad daylight, not while you're with me.'

She nodded tightly. 'But Katy...'

'Your daughter has already been in Mary's care for days, with my men watching the house—and her—constantly. I thought you might like a change of scene, since earlier you told me you feared you would go mad, trapped in here.'

Rosalie bit her lip. *And then she'd let him kiss her.* What a fool he must think her. For all her protests and defiance, she'd surrendered to him yet again, so very easily! No wonder he didn't question her role as a whore at the Temple of Beauty—she played the part so well. Heat unfurled in her insides just at the thought of his lips once more caressing hers.

It was time, finally, to confront him, but not here.

Not in this place where he was master. 'An outing to look at some paintings?' she said pleasantly. 'That sounds—*delightful*, Captain Stewart!'

He gave her twenty minutes to get ready, then came to lead her downstairs. 'Why not go and see your daughter first?' he suggested. 'She's out in the garden. I'll let you know when we're ready to leave.'

He'd pointed to an open door and she blinked to find herself in the bright sunlight. The garden was larger than she'd thought, a walled quarter of an acre or so of trees and tangled shrubs that ran quite wild. The sound of children's laughter drew her around the corner to a flagged terrace, where Mary sat sewing in the sun and watching over the children.

Mary beamed a welcome. 'It's so good that you're up and about, my dear! You'll see for yourself how happy your little girl is with my granddaughters— there's Jenny, she's three, and Amy with the pink dress, she's four...'

Indeed, Katy seemed engrossed in the game she was playing with two merry girls. And nearby at another table were two old soldiers, playing cards idly; but Rosalie remembered what Alec had said— that his men were watching the house and Katy constantly. Again, a pang of warning clamped her ribs.

Who to trust? Who to believe?

'I need to thank you,' said Rosalie quietly, 'for taking such good care of her while I've been ill.'

'Bless you, she's no trouble at all.'

Just then Katy saw her and ran up to her; Rosalie hugged her tightly. 'I'm going out for just a little while, Katy, sweetheart!'

Katy gave her a kiss, then ran off to her game again. She was happy here, as Mary said. Had settled as quickly as she'd settled into Helen's house, with Rosalie.

She realised Alec had come out and was watching. 'She makes friends easily,' he commented.

Rosalie nodded. 'She's always been adaptable.'

'How old was she when her father died?'

The question made her catch her breath, sharply. 'She was—only a baby.' She stumbled over the words. 'Really, she never knew him.'

Was there doubt in his dark eyes? If so, he let it go. 'I've just got to attend to the horses. I'll see you in the entrance hall.'

She went back to the house, her apprehension rising again. But then a great big golden dog with woebegone eyes ambled up to her and seemed to be leading her into the kitchen, where a tray of freshly baked biscuits sat on a high shelf.

He was wagging his tail so eagerly that Rosalie

just had to reach for two of them, which he wolfed down as if he hadn't eaten for days. As she petted and fussed him, she didn't notice that Garrett had come in.

'Like dogs, do yer, ma'am?'

His voice made her jump out of her skin. 'Oh! Not always, to be honest. But this one—he's gorgeous! What's his name?'

'Ajax. He's a good lad, Ajax is.' Garrett was actually looking at her with something approaching friendliness. 'Been giving him some of my wife's biscuits, have you? That's good, she'd have my hide if she caught me doing it, but 'cos it's you, it's all right, see?'

Rosalie struggled with the logic of all this, but Garrett was already pointing to the door. 'The Captain says he's ready for you outside now, ma'am.'

Indeed, Alec had obtained a curricle from somewhere, harnessed to two passable greys, and Garrett rode at the back like a rich man's tiger, so private conversation was impossible.

But—she enjoyed it. She enjoyed sitting at Alec's side, wrapped up against the fresh spring breeze, looking round at London's crowds, at the shops and other carriages. She enjoyed Alec's steady presence beside her, his skilful hands so sure on the reins.

The admiring glances he got from passing women, their looks of envy at her...

Pretending. That was what she was doing. Just pretending, she reminded herself. And she found talking to him easier than she'd thought, for she had a neutral topic of conversation: that garden. 'Such a beautiful place,' she said warmly. 'Or at least it must have been, once!'

He nodded. 'I'm afraid my priority is in keeping the actual house in one piece. But you're right, it was once beautiful. Don't tell me—you know something about gardens also, Mrs Rowland?'

She hesitated. 'We had a garden with the cottage in Oxfordshire. My—my mother loved it.'

Her voice faded away. Her mother had planted it with such care, to remind her of the man she'd loved. It bloomed with the English flowers: roses, hollyhocks, heart's-ease. When Linette had gone, their mother used to sit out there day after day, hoping that her lost daughter might return....

'Mrs Rowland, are you all right?'

Rosalie quickly dabbed her handkerchief to her eyes, pretending that a little dust had blown in them. 'Yes. Yes, thank you—perfectly.'

Impossible that he could have guessed at her grief—and yet it was as though he did, because Alec went on to distract her, as he drove the curricle expertly through London's streets, with descriptions of the wonderful gardens—many of them sadly ruined by war—that he'd seen in Spain and Portugal. Then he became silent, concentrating on the busy traffic, and she felt her spine tingle in renewed warning. *You have to ask him about Linette.*

But then what? If he was guilty, what did she expect him to do? What did she *want* him to do?

She wanted him to say he was sorry, perhaps. But most of all—she wanted to be wrong.

When he told her they'd arrived, she was bewildered. She'd taken little notice of their surroundings for the last ten minutes or so, being too absorbed in her own thoughts. Now, she was speechless.

They'd stopped in a street where huge mansions with white-stuccoed façades gazed benevolently down on a square filled with trees and well-tended shrubs. Liveried carriages with bewigged footmen put Alec's equipage to shame. This was Mayfair, she realised with a jolt of alarm. About as different from Two Crows Castle as a palace from a pauper's hovel. Yet Garrett was marching up to the big front door and lifting the glittering brass doorknocker as if he *knew* the place! Rosalie turned white-faced to Alec. 'Is this some kind of joke?'

'No, indeed.' Alec was watching her, with a

strange expression on his face. 'We're here to look at some paintings, Mrs Rowland—remember?'

'Why, Master Alec!' cried Jarvis, brushing aside the footman who'd opened the door.

Alec returned the greeting. 'Just a quick visit, Jarvis. Is everything all right? Has my brother been?'

Jarvis frowned and lowered his voice. 'He has, sir. He came for more paintings. And he said it was all on your father's orders, Master Alec!'

'Did he, now?' Alec's voice was lethally soft.

'Most of them are back. But take a look round, do. And I see you have a companion.' Rosalie had followed Alec up the steps and stood frozen in the doorway.

'An acquaintance of mine, Jarvis,' said Alec. 'Perhaps you could find us something to eat, in an hour or so?'

'If you're hungry, Master Alec, there's plenty of food, all delivered by Berry Brothers an hour ago. A feast laid ready, in fact.'

'Food? But the house is closed up, surely!'

'Indeed, sir. And your father's cook has gone with him to Carrfields.' The old steward's face had darkened and he lowered his voice. 'But you'll guess, I think, who ordered it—all in your father's name. Some kind of party's planned here tonight. And were we, the staff, informed in advance? No!' He shook his head. 'If you ask me, it would be justice indeed, if you and the young lady were to partake of just a little of it! And there's clothes, sir—' he pursed his lips '—clothes we were told to dispose of, because they're *no longer the fashion.*'

Alec nodded thoughtfully. Then he turned to Rosalie, who was still staring around, stunned. 'Come inside,' he said and she followed mutely as he led the way to the main hall, from which a vast double staircase rose in gilded splendour.

'This,' he said, 'at least gives you the chance to look around and see what a change of fortune has been mine.'

'Change of—?'

'All in good time. But first—I want you to tell me about some paintings.'

He saw her draw her hand across her forehead. 'Indeed, I promised to do so. But I don't understand…'

'It's quite simple. I'd like the benefit of your expertise. Take a look round here, for instance. My particular favourite was always that Poussin, by the stairs—'

'I noticed that one straight away,' she broke in, 'because it's not a Poussin!'

Well. Ro Rowland was continuing to surprise him. 'Pray continue,' Alec said softly.

'It's a good likeness,' she persisted, swiftly walking over to it, 'any art lover would know that. But of course the brushwork, let alone the balance of opaque and transparent colours, is not typical of Poussin in the least.'

He blinked. 'But of course.'

'As for that pair of portraits by Le Brun—' she swung round and pointed to another wall '—the varnish on them is quite wrong. It's too new.' She walked across to peer more closely; he tried not to notice the way her slender hips swayed as she moved. 'And the signature is,' she went on, swinging round and almost catching his too-appreciative stare, 'a forgery!'

That concentrated his wandering mind. *Those were his mother's, damn it.* 'You're quite certain?'

'I am indeed! But if you're doubting my knowledge, Captain Stewart…!'

'Not at all,' he breathed. 'Not at all, Mrs Rowland.' He bowed his head. 'I am—grateful.'

Grateful, and stunned. By her knowledge, by her damned allure—and by Stephen's damned treachery. He led her onwards.

Rosalie was bemused by this house. By the wonderful treasures within it where he was so clearly at home. But, oh, what game was he playing with her *this* time?

Her mind struggled for answers. Perhaps he was an impoverished cousin, who'd been occasionally allowed to stay. For goodness' sake, he certainly knew the vast place backwards! And he knew the paintings, too, which made up a fabulous collection. Indeed, in every salon, every chamber to which he so coolly led her, wonderful works of art adorned the walls.

But she was growing more and more concerned about them, because she considered that at least one in ten were careful forgeries. She pointed them out to him without emotion, and Alec nodded and wrote down the details in a notebook he carried.

But Rosalie failed to see what business it was of his.

In inner bewilderment, she followed him through all the ground-floor rooms, then up to other grand chambers. 'You need not worry about us being interrupted,' he said as she hesitated outside one fine room. 'The owner is away, in the country.'

Well. If that was supposed to make her more comfortable about this intrusion into another's home, it had the opposite effect. But Alec, unfazed, led her onwards, this time to the bedrooms and dressing rooms, where the paintings were smaller, daintier.

One by one she examined each work of art and reported her conclusion.

'This is the final room,' said Alec gravely, flinging open the door to a beautiful dressing chamber and adjoining bedroom. 'And by the way, I'm extremely grateful to you.'

She nodded tightly. 'As long as you or I don't end up in gaol.'

'Not us,' he said. 'Believe me, not us. What about those?'

She turned to examine one last set of exquisite French figure drawings in black-and-red chalk. 'These are not counterfeit, I'm sure. They're by Watteau. They must be very valuable.'

'Good,' he breathed. 'He always loved those pictures.'

'He?'

But Alec was already putting his notebook in his pocket. 'And that's the last of them, thank God. Rosalie, would you like some new clothes?'

Again he saw apprehension glitter in her eyes. 'Not at all. I already have those you gave me, at Two Crows Castle!'

She was pointing to the plain gown she wore, but Alec's lip curled in an ironic smile. 'All women *always* need more clothes, surely. Come and take a look in here.' He led her through to another large dressing room, and she caught her breath at the gowns, pelisses and walking dresses that were simply scattered on couches at either end of the room like jewels from a treasure trove.

'Help yourself,' he drawled.

She whipped round. 'I cannot *possibly*!'

'Let me assure you—*they will not be missed*. I'm grateful to you for examining the paintings. You can take whatever you want as your reward.' His eyes impassively assessed her figure in a way that made her skin tingle. 'Put one of these gowns on now, why not? They should all fit you.'

She was still utterly bewildered. She wanted to ask so many questions, but he was already turning to go. 'I'll see you downstairs when you've made your choice,' he said. 'Then we may as well eat. The dining room is just off the main hall. Ring the bell for a maid if you need anything.'

And he'd gone. She sat down rather suddenly on the edge of the bed. Who did these wonderful clothes belong to? Who did this mansion belong to? What was Alec Stewart doing to her brain, her existence?

He was her enemy. She'd only gone with him that dreadful night after the poetry reading because she'd had no choice; only stayed with him because she'd been so ill. He *had* to be her enemy. But why, then, did he offer to protect her against the writer of that abominable note?

I don't know. I don't know.

He thought her a whore and the knowledge seared her. He thought she'd be delighted with this treasure trove of clothes. Sick at heart, she lifted the extravagant garments one by one, until she found a modest muslin gown in midnight blue, with three-quarter-length sleeves and a fichu to cover her bosom. Then she tidied her hair, using the silver-backed brush that lay on the mirrored dressing table, and dragged it back into a ribbon.

There! Most women of the *ton* would require the assistance of two maids to adorn themselves, but not her. And if he hoped she might betray her vanity, or her—her *availability* by her choice of clothes—he'd be disappointed.

She rang the bell for a servant—she had no hope of finding her way round this palatial house by herself—and the maid, arriving, curtsied with a smile. 'You ready to go downstairs, ma'am? Master Alec said to show you the way!'

Master Alec. Another servant who knew the renegade Captain rather well. Rosalie seized a filmy cashmere shawl to drape across her arms and followed the maid downstairs, nervous again. The afternoon dusk was gathering, but wax candles had been lit throughout the house. Expense was clearly of no account here. The maid opened a door off the main hall. 'There you are, ma'am.'

Rosalie blinked in fresh amazement. This was the dining room—a room Alec hadn't yet shown her—and on a vast linen-draped table were laid out smoked hams, cold joints of beef, pies and whole cheeses, surrounded by a glittering array of porcelain and silverware. This table was set for twenty people. Bottles of wine adorned the sideboard. *'We may as well eat,'* Alec had casually said—but this was a feast!

She suddenly became aware of Alec as he entered the room behind her. 'What's this?' she breathed, turning to face him. 'Is the owner giving a party tonight?'

'It certainly looks like it. Doesn't it? And I see you found yourself something to wear.'

His dark eyes were fastened on her, in a way that somehow made her lungs ache with the need for air. The colour flared in her cheeks. 'I chose the simplest gown I could find!'

'Indeed. And it suits you.'

Rather too well, thought Alec, *damn it all*. Indeed, his pulse rate had started hammering away the minute he saw her standing there, looking so lost and so alone. She'd picked a garment that was downright plain, perhaps hoping to deter him, perhaps not.

For the clinging fabric hugged her sweet curves like blue gossamer, moving whenever she moved, clinging to her gently swelling bosom and hips, her slim thighs... As for her hair, again she had confounded him. As far as Alec was aware women spent hours over their hair, crimping it, styling it. But hers was done so artlessly—pulled up into a ribbon, yet with those few trailing locks that looked delicious enough to run through in his fingers. Devil take it, did she truly not realise how beautiful she looked? And didn't she realise—he noted it and gritted his teeth—how the fichu of her gown, too loose for her slender form, hung away from her bosom whenever she moved, so that if he gazed down at her he could see...

Don't go there. She is cleverer than you think. Alec dragged his eyes away and wished the rest of his body could be as effectively controlled.

Rosalie, too, was in turmoil, because Alec looked different. Stunningly different. He'd changed into formal attire—a black tailcoat that fitted his broad shoulders to perfection, cream skintight kerseymere breeches that clung rather too well to his strong thighs, and highly-polished Hessian boots. Sudden heat surged through her insides. Although his jaw was starting to look darkly unshaven and his thick black hair was rumpled and ungroomed, he looked quite heartbreakingly handsome.

A ripple of warning, of danger, was squeezing at her chest.

She gazed round, rather wildly looking for something to fill her thoughts other than *him*. 'Alec,' she said, 'this is not right. These clothes. The food. We are *stealing*.'

Alec regarded her with speculative dark eyes. 'Hardly,' he said. 'The food was an oversight; we have every right to help ourselves. And my clothes are my own.'

'Your—'

'Indeed. After all, this is the house I grew up in.' Her heart had juddered completely to a halt.

'I was trying to tell you earlier,' he went on. 'But you didn't believe me, did you?'

'I thought, perhaps…'

'You thought, perhaps, that I was some impoverished relative, kept hidden below stairs when the *ton* came to call?'

She flushed. Alec could tell those were her exact suspicions.

And yet in all other ways this woman was again confounding all his expectations. Damn it all, most females would exclaim avidly over this wonderful house and any hint of a connection to such wealth. Would cry out in delight over the clothes and dress themselves, if offered the chance, in the most showy, the most expensive. *Especially* a woman who'd worked at the Temple of Beauty.

Instead, she'd chosen the simplest gown there was, which showed off her slender yet gorgeous figure to absolute perfection. She was either utterly naïve or she was playing him at his own game very cleverly.

This whole visit was intended to test her—yet it was *he* who was being wrong-footed at every turn.

Sighing inwardly at the mystery that was Rosalie Rowland, he drew out a chair for her. 'Yes, I grew up here,' he said softly. 'My father—who is away at present—is a peer of the realm—an earl, no less. And as for me—I, Mrs Rowland, am his younger son.'

Chapter Fourteen

Oh, no. Why hadn't she guessed? The way he carried himself. The way he spoke. His natural air of authority. *His father—an earl...* She dragged in a ragged breath. 'I see. And for what reason, Captain Stewart, did you decide it wasn't worth telling me this earlier?'

'I suppose I never considered it important.' Alec pulled out a chair for her, his steady eyes never leaving her face. 'And anyway, I thought we were both being selective about the truth.'

Yes. She made a tiny gesture of despair and sat down slowly. Yes, indeed. 'But how can you turn your back on all this, to live in—?'

'A wreck like Two Crows Castle?' He pulled up a chair for himself at the table, next to her. 'Simple—my father and I are not on the best of terms.' His tone was dismissive. 'And before your eyes widen at the thought of my incredible wealth, let me just point out that I'm due to inherit not one penny.'

'Do you really think I'm interested in your *wealth*? I simply don't understand why you had to deceive me, and—and...'

She stopped. He leaned across the table to put just the tip of his forefinger on her lips. And her words dried in her throat.

'Deception? Now, I thought *you* were the master of that, Mrs Rowland,' he said quietly.

At just one touch of his fingers, she found herself racked with stomach-clenching uncertainty. He was handsome. He was formidable. He was utterly dangerous. *And soon she must ask him why her dying sister had breathed his name.*

She forced herself to appear calm. 'Where is your father?'

'He's at his estate in the country, with his wife— my stepmother.' He was unfolding his napkin. 'The clothes from which you had your choice up there are about to become my stepmother's cast-offs. She feels that all fashions are sadly outmoded after three months.'

'So your mother...'

'Died long ago, in a hunting accident.'

Rosalie's cheeks flushed. 'I'm so sorry, I didn't

realise.' She hesitated. 'But this…this place, this food! Who…?'

'I told you, my father is away. The food is an error.' He was watching her quizzically as he began to carve a slice of ham for her. 'And do you know, I think I've had enough of your questions for the time being, Ro Rowland. You're not an investigative reporter now.'

She shivered at the sting in his calm voice. But— Alec Stewart, the black sheep of an extremely wealthy family. In those clothes, she could believe it. So different from his usual attire, yet still so rawly masculine. She tossed her head. He'd put them on to impress on her, no doubt, that he was an earl's son! In case she started getting ideas above her station, perhaps.

'Why don't you eat?' he asked almost languidly. 'Take your pick. Chicken *gélatine*. Buttered lobster. Veal pie…'

'I—I can't. I'm worried about Katy.'

'I've told you—Katy is quite safe at Two Crows Castle with my men guarding her. Happy, too. And you're no use to her at all if you're half-dead from hunger. Eat. Drink. You've been ill— you need to build up your strength.' He'd already filled her glass with a fine white wine.

'You are rather taking my breath away with all these surprises,' she said as steadily as she could.

He was cutting some pie to put on her plate. 'Then get your revenge. Tell me more about your childhood. You've already informed me your mother was French and your father an English painter. But wasn't it a strange decision for your mother to move to England when he died?'

'My mother had no family left in Paris. And I think my parents had always planned to move back to England some day. So she decided to take us—'

'Us,' he broke in. 'Do you have brothers? Sisters?'

Oh, a blunder there. 'A sister. One sister.'

He drank his wine, still carefully watching her. 'And did your little family find a friendly welcome at this cottage in Oxfordshire?'

This time she met his brooding gaze steadily. 'Thanks to the war, my mother's nationality was regarded as little short of a crime. And the cottage turned out to be almost a ruin. Yet my mother would not leave—partly because she had nowhere else to go, but also because it had been my father's dying wish that she come to the place he'd loved...' She paused to fight back the ache rising in her throat.

'And now your mother is dead. Your husband, too.' His voice was soft.

Oh, Lord, her lies. 'Yes, indeed!' She drank some wine—she certainly needed it.

He met her eyes calmly. The light from the candles defined anew the sculpted planes and angles of his lean, square-jawed face. He continued, 'So you decided to come to London. As a writer of scandal-broth, or as a prostitute at the Temple of Beauty?'

She should have expected it. She should not have let it wound her so. But it did, oh, it did.

She tossed her head in defiance. 'Well, both, of course! I really do not see why I should not make extra money out of my experiences with the gentlemen of the town, by writing a piece or two!'

'I can see why not,' he broke in flatly. 'It could be damned dangerous. Men don't like their secret lives exposed.'

She gripped her wineglass. Was he warning her not to dig too deeply into *his* private life? 'Oh, I make sure everything I write is completely anonymous!'

She laughed, as if it were all very amusing, but she could see he wasn't amused in the slightest, because he cut in, '*Somebody* is worried about you saying too much, clearly.' His eyes were fixed, darkly, at some place below her throat, and she realised that her fichu had fallen to display a disgraceful amount of bosom. Colouring hotly, she snatched it back up.

'You're thinking of that threat,' she whispered.

'Naturally. And there's not only the threat, Mrs Rowland.' His features were sombre. 'My men have been offered money, to turn you and the child in.'

'They've—' The food she'd just taken stuck in her throat.

'That's right. There's an underworld reward out for you. The usual sort of thing, all done anonymously. The word has gone round the lowlife drinking dens that if you and your child are delivered up at a certain time and place, the money will be handed over, no questions asked.' He paused while the shock surged through her. 'I know, by the way,' he went on, 'that Katy is not yours.'

This time she had to grip the table for support. Her stomach knotted. 'What makes you think…?'

'How do I know you're lying? First: you seem to have no idea when her father died—indeed, you're not even certain of the child's age. Second: I've noticed that whenever Katy sees you she says, *'Mama?'*—but she's looking for someone else. Three: she was not with you when you first arrived in London.'

She stared at him, stricken.

'Enough, enough,' he said with a gesture of dismissal. 'I have no right to question you so, and I assume you are looking after Katy for the best of reasons. Now it's your turn—ah, how your writer's mind must be whirling with curiosity. "What was it like being born into a rich family, Alec? And how, for God's sake, did you manage to make such an almighty mess of it all?" Admit it, you're just longing to know!'

'I think perhaps you've already told me,' she said tightly. 'That you and your father are estranged.'

'Indeed. And of course it's the custom of the aristocracy anyway to leave everything to the oldest.' He drank more wine.

'But surely you could have married…'

'Married into wealth? Ah, yes, once I was betrothed to the granddaughter of a duke. But she was in love with a make-believe hero—and, by God, she must count herself lucky to have broken it off, now she sees that I run a damned seedy fencing school in Spitalfields packed to the rafters with destitute ex-soldiers—out of whom I make absolutely nothing.'

A reminder of yet another of her errors. She bit her lip. 'But surely,' she began, 'you would have had other choices! There can be no need for you to—to…'

'To live as I do? Mingle with men of the lower class?' His voice had become softly lethal. 'For a courtesan and a pedlar of news sheets, you're rather pompous, aren't you, Mrs Rowland? Perhaps it's your mother's French blood showing through—'

He broke off, because she'd put her knife and fork down suddenly. There were small spots of colour burning in her cheeks. 'Please do not insult my mother. You may say what you like about me—but not her!'

Alec looked at her, just for a moment. Curse it, this had been a stupid idea to bring her here. Doomed from the start. Furious with himself, he pushed back his chair and stood. 'Come,' he said. His dark eyes were shuttered. 'I'll take you back. Time we were leaving.'

She tilted her chin. 'Very well. But I will get changed first. I do not wish to wear this gown a moment longer.'

'As you wish.' Swiftly he came round to draw back her chair and help her to her feet.

But the sudden warmth of his hand on her slender arm unsettled her so badly that she tripped as she rose and stumbled against the table, and worse was to come, for she realised in horror that the cursed fichu had slipped down, almost baring her breasts. Even as she dragged it up again she saw the look of scorn in his eyes. *He thought she'd done it deliberately.*

'Well, Mrs Rowland,' he drawled, 'you're playing dangerous games today.'

She whirled on him. 'A gentleman, Captain Stewart, would have turned his eyes away!'

'Oh, did you want me to?' he asked softly. 'I rather thought all that was part of your plan.'

She tried to push past him, head held high. He stood in her way. Her voice shook slightly. 'Please let me pass. I just want to go and get out of this—garment. And return to Katy.'

He captured her shoulders, his long fingers warm and sensuous through the fabric of her gown. 'Playing games,' he repeated softly.

'I think,' she said steadily, 'that *you* are the one playing games. And aren't you enjoying them?'

'Very much. Aren't you?'

The air around them changed. Tightened.

'Alec,' she began, her insides suddenly lurching, but she had no idea what she meant to say. All she knew was that his arms were around her, his chest like a wall against her soft breasts. All she could see when she looked up was his hard face, burning with an emotion she did not dare to name.

Fight him. You have to fight him.

Yet his lips were wicked temptation. His hard-muscled body was a challenge and an enticement. Sal had told her it was easy to deal with men—*Re-*

member, they're all ruled by one rather vital part of their anatomy—but Sal hadn't told her how very difficult it would be to resist her own primal urges.

He fitted his mouth to hers and her world spun.

There was nothing gentle about his kiss. And Alec didn't mean it to be gentle. His hands had snaked round her waist, pulling her close; her face was lifted to his, her eyes wide and flaring, her lips full—with doubt?—with desire? He claimed her mouth with the savage hunger he'd been feeling for hours. For days, damn it.

So had she, to judge by the way her hands had stolen up to cling round the nape of his neck, the way her slender body was moulding itself to his, as she surrendered to the fierce hunger of his lips and tongue. Heat consumed him as her hands swept his shoulders and he in turn let his own palms sweep down over the flimsy muslin to caress the curve of her hips, to splay his fingers and haul her against his hardening desire...

Dear God, swore Alec. She was *inviting* his ravishment. His sure hand caressed the column of her throat, sliding down to rest for a moment on the swelling curve of her breast, then slipping beneath the filmy fabric to caress one soft nipple with the pad of his thumb.

Rosalie felt the coral peak tingle and harden, tightening a cord of desire that reached to her womb, while his sensual wide mouth coaxed her lips apart and his tongue stroked hers with relentless, exquisite pleasure. His hand closed round her breast—warm, hard, erotic. Then he had her in his arms again and his kiss possessed her utterly.

Lost in a delicious haze of wine and longing, she was only faintly aware that he'd moved towards a sturdy chair and was guiding her on to his lap, still kissing her, as her arms clasped him instinctively.

And now, somehow, he'd eased her breast from her bodice. She let out a low cry of loss as he abandoned her mouth, but it changed to a cry of delight as his lips claimed one nipple. She gasped with amazement as his tongue, swirling round the stiffened peak, sent waves of rapture rippling through her entire body.

She clung to him as if he were her pillar of safety, when he was anything but; she was throwing her head back and gasping as his teeth nipped lightly, aware now that his hand was sliding up her leg, caressing the silken skin above her stocking top, stealing up to the juncture of her thighs, then seeking—and finding—the moist warmth at her feminine core.

She was damp, shaking, enraptured. Her hands

digging into his hard-muscled back were her only anchor on reality. With devastating skill he swept his strong, knowing fingers across the swollen bud again and again, watching her with smouldering eyes as she arched herself against him, all restraint forgotten, and cried his name aloud as the sweet, unfurling spasms of her climax shook her body.

Her eyes had fluttered shut. Her lips were tingling and parted. Even when the last echo of rapture had died away, she kept her eyes closed. She had not known that she could feel like this. A savage pain clawed at her stomach. Perhaps she *was* a whore, to give herself so readily, so eagerly.

He was already lifting her from his lap and setting her on her feet. And he was—just watching her. She gathered herself up, feeling cold away from the shelter of his arms. Feeling—*terrified* at what she'd just let him do to her.

'I rather think it's yourself that you should not trust, Mrs Rowland,' he said softly at last. 'Do us both a favour by going and putting on a dress that at least covers you. Do you hear me?'

A feeling not just of anger, but of utter loss, was squeezing at her heart. 'You misunderstand and misjudge me at every turn, Captain Stewart,' she said in a low voice.

'No doubt.' He dragged his hand through his dark

hair and stood up also; he was trembling with tension, she realised, as if every muscle in his powerful body was held on the tightest of leashes. His lip curled when he saw her eyes slide, horrified, away from his skintight breeches. 'Indeed, I'm rather a handy scapegoat for all your foolhardy experiments, aren't I? You can see it's time you and I were leaving. *Now.* Go and wrap yourself in your usual drab attire, then we'll get back to the child in your care. Or had you forgotten her—again?'

That hurt. Oh, that hurt. She clenched her fists. 'It was *you* who insisted I stay here to be impressed by this place that was once your home! You who implied I ought to repay you for your dubious protection by spending two hours examining paintings, when I only wanted to get back to Katy! You are overbearing and unjust and hateful! Damn you to hell, Alec Stewart!'

He gazed down at her, his eyes bleak. 'No need. I'm already there.'

She stumbled away.

Chapter Fifteen

Alec sat there with his head in his hands. His lust for her was raging. The hardness between his thighs still throbbed.

Rosalie Rowland. Writer, courtesan and all-round troublemaker. In her way she'd been absolutely right to accuse him of trying to impress her with this magnificent place that he'd once called home. Certainly, he'd hoped to trick her into making mistakes. Yet it was *he* who had handled everything so badly.

In fact, until she'd let her damned fichu slip like that, he'd begun to feel that he'd got everything wrong about her. He clenched his jaw. Damn it, she'd had a lucky escape. One more minute of her passionate response to his foolhardy kiss and he'd have been hard-pressed to stop himself ravishing her there and then.

Alec got to his feet and paced the room like a caged animal. Why had he let things go so far?

Well, he had plenty of answers. Not least of his motivations—and certainly the worst—was his impulse to prove to himself that she was indeed any man's for the taking.

Yet once again he'd been baffled by Rosalie Rowland. Most women of experience would have realised that Alec was aroused virtually to the point of no return. Most women would have offered some sort of physical relief—but she had made no attempt whatsoever to assuage his rampant desire.

The enigmatic, tormenting Mrs Rowland. Everything about her stoked up the fire of his vital male urges—but ever since that first night at the Temple of Beauty, he'd not been able to make sense of her. He was utterly perplexed by the way she moved and spoke so gracefully, by the way she'd so solemnly examined those pictures for him and calmly delivered her judgement.

At Dr Barnard's tawdry show she'd stood out from the other jades like a pure-white wax candle burning amidst a mass of burned-down tallow ones. But how could she be unspoiled? Innocent? No. For God's sake, she'd been married, she'd been at the Temple of Beauty! She was still lying to him; he'd still be thinking Katy was hers, had it not been for Mary's suspicions— *'She doesn't even know the child's age for sure, Captain Stewart!'* And of course there was

Garrett's news that last winter Rosalie had been visiting one London theatre after another, asking for someone called Linette.

Who was Linette? Alec drove one fist against the other. Who had sent that nasty threat? Who was trying to bribe Alec's men to betray her? What the hell had he let himself in for, by offering to protect her?

Upstairs, Rosalie gazed at herself in the cheval glass. She'd swiftly got changed back into the old, drab gown, but she had yet to summon up the courage to go downstairs and face him after betraying herself yet again, this time with so much more than a kiss.

Dear God. The pleasure, the molten ecstasy summoned by his mouth, his long lean fingers...

She saw in the mirror that her lips were rosy and swollen from the harshness of his mouth. *You must tell him that Katy is your dead sister's child. You must ask him why Linette named him as she lay dying.*

Not tomorrow. Not later. But now.

She pressed her palms to her hot cheeks. One thing was certain. She could not go on much longer in this hell of uncertainty.

She went downstairs slowly, wearing her old grey mantle. Alec was at the far side of the room and he barely glanced at her. Clearly, she realised with a lurching stomach, he regretted what had just happened every bit as much as she did. He said, 'A few more minutes and we'll be ready to leave. I told Garrett to pick us up at six.'

She nodded, realising he was going round extinguishing the candles. He'd taken off his fine coat and his shirt sleeves fell back to his elbows as he reached for the higher sconces, revealing strong brown forearms that rippled with muscle and sinew.

Rosalie was about to tear her eyes away, but suddenly, in the flickering half-light, she saw an ugly, jagged scar that snaked up from his wrist. 'Oh, my goodness.' The words burst out on impulse. 'Whatever happened to your arm?'

He glanced at it almost casually. 'That? A French bayonet at Vittoria.'

Her mind reeled. 'But…'

'It was the battle that finally drove the French out of Spain,' he said tersely. 'June 1813.'

'I know.' Her lips and tongue would hardly work. 'I know… Alec, were you *there*?'

He let out a sharp laugh. 'Don't make a hero out of me. Any soldier who could hold a weapon was at Vittoria. We were outnumbered and it was a desperate struggle, full of scenes I hope you can't begin to imagine.'

'Were you with Wellington's army all that summer?'

'All that year,' he answered shortly. 'No home leave for the officers.'

The full implications of it tore through her whole being. *Dear God.* He was in Spain with the army when Linette was seduced. He could not be Katy's father...

'Alec,' she whispered. What could she say? She knew what she should say. *Alec, I have been so determined to misjudge you. I have wronged you grievously...*

He turned to her and at that very moment she saw just a man, a brave man—a hero, whatever he said, for some reason in a state of utter self-loathing. *Alec, I'm so sorry.* She went deliberately towards his tense figure and placed her hand on that ugly scar.

He caught her hand and pushed it away. He was towering over her and she felt fear scudding through her again as he said roughly, 'You have a liking for playing with fire, Mrs Rowland.'

She stood firm. He thought that her gentle caress—really an acknowledgement of her own fallibility—was just another attempt to entrap him. But now she knew. Now was the time to speak.

She lifted her head. 'Alec, you told me that Katy and I would be safe with you. And I wish, how I wish, that I'd trusted you. I—I've been foolish, I've been *wrong*... But now I want to tell you that Katy was my sister's child.'

He'd gone very still. *'Linette,'* he breathed. 'Linette was your sister.'

Her gaze flew up to meet his. 'You knew already—how?'

He was rubbing his forehead as if some tight band enclosed it. 'Damn it, I've been making my own investigations. I know you were only at the Temple for one night, but before then you'd been trailing all round London's theatres, asking questions. Asking about someone called Linette.' He pulled out a chair. *'Explain.'*

And her words began to tumble out.

'Linette was two years younger than me, Alec.' Her voice was so low, he strained to catch her words. 'She left home three years ago. She became pregnant in the summer of 1813; Katy is her daughter, Alec, and Linette, poor Linette...' her voice broke just a little '...died in abject poverty. I came to London to look for the man who did this to her.'

'You should have told me,' his voice rasped.

'I could not,' she breathed, 'I could not, because at first I thought it was *you.*'

As she uttered those fateful words, Rosalie felt as if something within her had died. Every syllable condemned her more surely in this man's eyes. Oh, how he would despise her now.

Explain, he'd said, and it all poured out: how Linette had whispered his name as she lay dying, how Linette had said he had a castle.

He had pulled a chair up for himself, and sat in the half-shadow from the dying fire, watching her. At last he said, 'She was looking for a refuge, perhaps. Sometimes we take in homeless women as well as men at Two Crows Castle. You'll have noticed them—often they help Mary with the housework, until we can find them somewhere better.'

'Yes.' She nodded, her throat still tight. 'My sister whispered, "Take me to him, please". I thought—I thought perhaps she'd loved you, but now I see that she'd not even met you, Alec. You don't turn anyone away and Linette must have heard that. I realise everything now.'

Too late.

From first seeing him, Rosalie had been drawn to his—*integrity*, that was the word. Alec had maintained Two Crows Castle because he cared about those soldiers. He had rescued her from Lord Maybury because he was concerned about her and Katy. Katy had trusted him straight away. If only she'd done the same. He would never, ever forgive her for her stupidity.

'Anyone would have told you I was in Spain with the army all through the summer of 1813,' he said, only echoing her own bitter regrets. 'And you were taking a great risk, asking your questions all around London.'

'I thought I was being careful.' She was defensive now and growing tired.

'You've managed to alarm someone—badly. Don't forget about that threat and the bribes offered to my men.'

She lifted her gaze to him. 'Is Linette's seducer behind it all?'

'I would think so indeed,' he answered quietly.

Oh, God. No word of reproach for her vile insults to him, her foolish actions, her multiple mistakes. She dragged air into her lungs. 'Alec,' she said, 'I'm sorry, to have so wrongly suspected you. I've been so stupid. Why are you being kind to me?'

He sighed, then got up and walked over to the mantelpiece to douse another flickering candle. 'Perhaps because I don't like injustice. And don't be so hard on yourself. On the contrary, I think you've been rather brave, coming to London and undertaking the search on your own.'

'Linette was my sister,' she answered simply. 'Wouldn't anyone do the same for their family?

Isn't family loyalty perhaps the most basic human instinct of all?'

He caught his breath. 'Your loyalty is indeed admirable,' was all he said. 'Do you have any more clues, apart from the fact that Linette wanted to be an actress and once worked at the Temple of Beauty?'

She told him about Marchmont's theatre, and Dr Barnard's register, hidden inside *The Myths of Apollodorus*. He listened intently.

'I'll make enquiries, as well,' he said.

She gasped. 'You *will*?'

'Put it this way—someone dangerous is after you and I'd rather like to find out who. No promises, but my men are useful at unearthing secrets.' He looked at his watch and gave her a smile that sent her spirits plummeting, because it was a sad smile, a regretful smile. 'Time to get back to Two Crows Castle, Rosalie. Though there is just one more thing. You've already understood, I think, that you must place yourself in my care, under my protection. In return, I'll make a promise to *you*. From now on, I'll ensure that you can trust me. In absolutely every way. Do I make myself clear?'

Oh, yes. She knew exactly what he meant. In other words, he wouldn't lay a finger on her again. She got to her feet slowly and an ache of sheer loss swept through her at the memory of those burning caresses to which she'd so rapturously surrendered. 'I don't think you should take any blame for what happened just now,' she whispered.

Something of her inner misery must have shown, because he touched her hand gently. 'Nor yourself, Rosalie. We'll find the man who seduced your sister, never fear—and I suspect we'll find he's the same man who is threatening you.' His hand was gone, leaving her cold. 'In the meantime,' he went on, 'my men deserve a pleasant surprise. Don't you think?' He'd carelessly pulled on his fine coat again, then picked up some empty sacks she'd not noticed before and began to load food from the table into them. Hams, pies, whole cheeses, loaves of bread—in they went, until the sacks were bulging.

She gasped. 'What are you doing?'

He grinned, white teeth flashing. 'Taking this lot back to Two Crows Castle. Jarvis brought me these sacks while you were upstairs. I rather think this food is needed there more than here, don't you?'

She thought of the hungry, ragged soldiers. 'Oh, indeed! But—won't it be missed?'

'I told you my father's gone to the country and won't be wanting any of this. So I'm helping myself. How does that rate on your journalist's scale of crimes?'

'I think it's an excellent idea! But, Alec...'

'Hmm?' He was still packing the things, but he swung round to look at her.

'Alec,' she said impulsively, 'there's always a cluster of beggars at the corner of Lothbury. We passed them on our way. There's so much food here—will you give a little of it to them, on our way back?'

'Willingly. If you'll also take a sack and put in some of those pies that are on the sideboard, I'll tell Jarvis we're leaving. And I've got something for him.' He flourished the list he'd made of the counterfeit paintings.

'The paintings! I'd almost forgotten. Oh, what are you going to do about them?'

'Make sure the originals all mysteriously find their way back here,' he assured her. 'Now, if you look outside, I think you'll find Garrett's arrived with transport.' He strode to the door. 'Jarvis!'

The elderly steward quickly appeared. 'Sir?' Alec gave him his list and had a quiet word before heading for the door. Indeed, out in the street were Garrett and big red-bearded Sergeant McGrath with a shabby old carriage.

'Some supplies, lads, for Two Crows Castle,' Alec announced cheerfully, pointing towards the sacks of food assembled in the hall.

'Yes, sir!' Eagerly the men began to load the carriage. Alec helped, too, and when they were finished he guided Rosalie out to the vehicle.

'That's about it,' Alec said to Garrett. He looked around. 'Oh, and by the way—we're going to drop a sack of food off at the corner of Lothbury.'

'Right you are, Captain.' Garrett nodded. He turned with an awkward smile to Rosalie. 'All right, ma'am? Your little 'un, she's fine, but she'll be glad to see you back!' Then he scrambled up on to the driver's box next to McGrath, who was already holding the reins.

Alec shot Rosalie a look of complete astonishment. 'My God. Garrett *smiled* at you. What magic have you worked on him?'

'I don't know really. Perhaps it's because I was kind to his dog?'

Alec lifted his eyebrows. 'You're a witch, Mrs Rowland,' he said softly, 'and in another few days you'll have us all eating out of the palm of your hand.'

Rosalie froze again. *Mrs Rowland*—oh, God. She'd told him about Linette, but she hadn't confessed to the rest of her lies—for example, her fictitious widowhood. But if she told him she was *not* married, he would perhaps start to doubt every single thing she'd ever said and might refuse to let her stay at Two Crows Castle. Might refuse flatly to help her any further.

He was watching her quizzically. 'Something wrong?'

'No!' She shook her head, forcing a smile. 'And, Alec—thank you. For offering me your help.'

'Think nothing of it.' He was about to hand her up into the carriage, but then he hesitated. 'Although one thing worries me. Even though we know—you and I—that you are quite safe with me, staying at Two Crows Castle, your reputation will be shot to pieces, to put it politely.'

She almost laughed. That was the least of her problems. 'Oh, goodness! And there was I, hoping for a top-lofty proposal or two at the start of the next Season! I'm afraid, Captain Stewart, that my hopes for a respectable future are already pretty low. And appearing at the Temple of Beauty most definitely did nothing to improve my chances!'

'You had no dreams of getting married again?' he asked quietly.

'Lord, no.'

'You feel that no one could replace your husband?'

She shrugged. 'If you wish to put it like that, yes.'

He was watching her carefully. 'Mrs Rowland—Rosalie—I hope we can at least be friends.'

She nodded mutely as he handed her in and followed behind. Out on the driver's box, Garrett and Sergeant McGrath were singing heartily as the horses pulled the laden coach briskly eastwards into darker, narrower streets. Alec joined in, his voice a melodious baritone that she instantly adored.

'Some talk of Alexander, and some of Hercules,
Of Hector and Lysander, and such great names
as these.
But of all the world's great heroes, there's none
that can compare
With a tow, row, row, row, row, row
To the British Grenadiers...'

He smiled at her. She smiled back, even joining in the chorus. But her heart was heavy. She had mistrusted him and lied to him. Yes, she now had him on her side in her struggle to find Linette's seducer. But he had also promised her that he would never touch her again and she was just realising how devastating those simple words could be.

'Horse,' said Katy, happily waving her new little wooden toy. 'Horse.'

Katy was in the parlour off the kitchen when they returned, sitting in Mary's comfortable lap. All around was evidence of a pleasant family shopping trip: gingerbread men, a penny whistle, ribbons and other toys. 'We took the children up Bishopsgate,' Mary explained. 'With some of the Captain's men, of course. I do hope you don't mind, ma'am?'

'Not at all.' Rosalie smiled down at Katy. 'Your little horse is beautiful, darling.'

'For Polly-doll.' Katy perched her little rag doll on the new horse. Alec had entered the room behind Rosalie and came over to gently ruffle the child's dark hair. When Rosalie saw the look of tenderness in his eyes for Katy, it lanced her.

'Bedtime, Katy,' she said lightly. She picked the little girl up, breathing in the sweet infant scent of her skin, and started for the stairs, but turned back. 'Thank you,' she said fervently to Mary and Garrett and all the others, 'for looking after her so well today. For looking after *both* of us so well.'

Mary beamed. 'It's a pleasure, ma'am.'

Rosalie put Katy carefully in her little bed and sang her sister's child to sleep. Alec had offered her his help and protection; therefore she had to endure living under the roof of a man who affected her as no man ever had done before. And Lord, it was going to be difficult.

Alec went to his room and cursed softly under his breath. Ever since he'd seen Rosalie Rowland at the Temple of Beauty, he couldn't get her out of his mind. And today, at his father's house, how he'd managed to control himself, he'd never know.

He could have taken her so easily. But he'd restrained himself with an iron will, because he still had not been sure of her motives. And—because, strangely, she seemed to trust him. She wouldn't if she knew *his* secrets.

He raked his hand through his hair. Earlier today, a note had been delivered for him. He'd cracked open the seal with a bitter heart, not needing to look at the signature to know who it was from, because he was already alerted by the faint scent of gardenias that imbued the expensive notepaper.

Alec. I am back in London before your father, who is following in a few days. I'm staying in Bedford Street, because the Belgrave Square house needs to be prepared. I know there are risks, my dear, but might I see you at Lord Fanton's ball? There are things I need to tell you.

It was from his stepmother. His beautiful stepmother. And Lord Fanton's ball was tomorrow night.

There was a knock and Garrett came in. 'Captain. You asked us to find out who started the fire at the place where the girl lived—and who smashed up the printing press there, too.'

'I take it you've found out?'

And Garrett told him.

After Garrett left, Alec paced the room. *Stephen's men.* In God's name, why?

He rather feared he was beginning to know the answer.

That night Stephen was at his father's house and in a raging temper. This evening's gathering was to have been a fine one for his friends: a delectable supper followed by drinking and gaming, with a few high-class whores performing their tricks at midnight.

But—there had been no food. No wine. Devil take it, Stephen's failure of a party would be sniggered over around the clubs of London for weeks to come, thanks to his damned brother!

And then Jarvis, the old fool, had directed Stephen specifically to the drawing room, where he was immediately confronted with—the paintings. The labels that had been tied to one frame after another. *Counterfeit*, those labels had screamed out in large letters. Stephen had roamed the house, his agitation increasing. *Counterfeit.* And every identification, without fail, was correct.

It must be Alec! But how had his damned brother detected it, when the whole business had been conducted with such care? Sending them for cleaning, having them copied and selling off the originals had seemed an inspiration.

Hell's teeth, would Alec tell their father?

Finally there was the fact—which he'd forced out of old Jarvis—that Alec still had the girl, Rosalie, from the Temple of Beauty, under his protection. And Stephen was beginning to guess that the child she kept with her might not be Rosalie's at all.

His threats had achieved nothing. He'd hoped to bribe some of Alec's ruffians into betraying her, but the opposite seemed to have happened. Damn it all, this could be lethal. Especially if Alec was starting to guess the truth!

Chapter Sixteen

When Rosalie came downstairs the next day, the place seemed altogether quiet. Most of the soldiers were at their various places of work and Captain Stewart was also out on business, she was told.

For a while she read stories to Katy and Mary's granddaughters, then helped with their lunch. But when it became clear that Alec would be absent all day, she grew restless.

'Please let me do something to help you,' Rosalie asked Mary, who as usual was busy in the kitchen with her baking and her laundry. 'Are there any more shirts to mend?'

'Lord bless you, I've got my two women, Janey and Bess, to help with that. But the sun's shining, it's a lovely afternoon. Why don't you take the little ones into the garden to play?'

So Rosalie did. And looking round, while the girls busied themselves setting out their toys for a tea party, she could see how beautiful this place must once have been. Ajax had joined them, sprawling hopefully in the sun while Katy and her friends feasted on milk and fresh-baked scones. Rosalie smiled at the big golden dog. 'Ajax. You are a good, good boy. Aren't you?' She slipped him a buttered scone and the dog snuggled closer to her side.

The children were absorbed in their make-believe party and the usual soldiers were around to watch them, so Rosalie, with Ajax at her heels, began to explore the overgrown thickets of shrubs that lay beyond the paved terrace. Under the ivy and sprawling wild clematis she found old stone urns, intricate paths and trellised arbours. Everywhere were vivid pockets of flowers and unpruned shrubs—blackthorns, primroses, buttercups and half-wild blue hyacinths that filled the air with their sweet scent. Flowers her mother had loved so.

As she returned to the terrace she became aware of Garrett leaning against the back door, watching her. 'I was wonderin' where that dog had got to,' he said. 'So you've been explorin' our garden, ma'am, have you?'

She seized her chance. 'Yes, and it's beautiful! I don't suppose, Mr Garrett—are there any tools I could borrow to clear it? A trowel, perhaps, and a pair of shears?'

He blinked. 'You want to clear this 'ere garden?'

'Well, yes, just a little. Nobody would mind, would they?'

Eyepatch wasn't Alec Stewart's lieutenant for nothing. Within ten minutes he'd unearthed a store of ancient gardening implements from an old outhouse and recruited four ex-soldiers who couldn't wait to take on their new role as gardeners.

Under Rosalie's supervision, her team—three of them elderly, one a young lad, Mikey—began to turn the derelict old wilderness into something rather magical. Rosalie worked as well as keeping an eye on the children, who were making daisy chains to rope round the docile Ajax's neck.

But every time she heard a man's voice in the distance, she wondered if Alec was back yet.

In the evening she bathed Katy and put her to bed as usual. And as she headed down the stairs, she saw Alec standing in the hallway talking to Garrett.

Emotion jolted her. He must have come back a while ago and changed, because he was dressed formally, in the black tailcoat and cream breeches he'd worn at his father's house yesterday. He had shaved. And brushed back his thick hair. He looked relaxed, and devastating.

Dressed for supper, at Two Crows Castle? She

thought not. 'I've got your horse ready, Captain,' Garrett was saying.

Then Alec spotted Rosalie. 'Mrs Rowland. I trust you've had a pleasant day?'

Rosalie came on down the stairs, forcing herself to sound calm. 'Very pleasant, thank you, Captain. You're going out this evening?'

'To a party,' he answered, absently fingering his starched neckcloth. 'A long-standing invitation, I'm afraid.'

A cold fist was squeezing the air from her lungs. He was going to a place that was part of his world, and of course she wasn't in it… *For heaven's sake, you little fool, once he was betrothed to the grand-daughter of a duke!*

'You sound regretful,' she said mildly. 'But I hope you enjoy yourself—and I like your Gordian Knot.'

His hand flew to his cravat. 'You're knowledge-able.'

'Oh, I once wrote an article about men's neck-wear for *The Scribbler*—' She broke off. *Idiot. He hates your writing.*

But his handsome face relaxed into a smile that made her insides turn over. 'Then I'm flattered that you approve of my choice.'

Mentally she was flaying herself. Yesterday at his father's house she'd dared to wonder if he'd put on those clothes to impress *her*. How stupid could she be?

He was smoothing his coat sleeves, glancing down to check his gleaming topboots. 'How is Katy?'

'Oh, she's sleeping now, but she was happy, very happy, with the toys you allowed Mary to buy for her yesterday, thank you. That little horse nearly went in the bath with her!'

Another flicker of a smile. 'I'm sorry I have to go out. We must find time to speak in the morning, Mrs Rowland.' He looked, for a moment, as if he was about to say something else. Then he quickly bowed his head and left.

She went to sit down in the little parlour off the hall. She'd wanted to talk to him, oh, about the garden, and about Linette, and—just *talk* to him. She felt hollow inside with his departure. She caught a sharp breath, surprised at how she could physically *hurt* so.

And then, through the open door, she heard Garrett saying in a low voice to McGrath, 'So *she's* back in town. That's why he's goin' to this fancy ball, our Captain. Dear God, she's beautiful, but she's wrecked his life, and you'd think he'd have more sense than to get within a hundred miles of her...' They wandered on towards the kitchen where the soldiers gathered in the evening.

And Rosalie had no doubt at all that they were speaking of his lost heiress. She could almost hear Alec's voice— *'She was in love with a make-believe hero and must count herself lucky to have broken it off.'* He was too proud, far too proud, to admit to anyone, let alone Rosalie, that he still had longings for what could never be.

'I hope we can at least be friends,' Alec had said to her earlier.

She felt like writing his words on her tormented heart. Friends, Mrs Rowland, you idiot. And with that, you will be content. Do you understand?

A small string orchestra played discreetly in a corner of the grand salon of Lord Fanton's house in exclusive Sackville Street and the chink of glasses punctuated the murmur of polite conversation. It had been a long time since Alec had been anywhere like this.

Lord Lucas Conistone, laconic and immaculate, was at his side—in fact, they'd arrived together— and Lucas was murmuring, 'Brace yourself, dear fellow. Can't be worse than when you and I dressed up as Spanish peasants to sneak inside French-held Badajoz!'

'How we got away with it,' breathed Alec, 'God knows. Both of us are too damned tall.'

'And your Spanish was execrable,' accused Lucas with a grin.

'At least I didn't let myself be waylaid by every Spanish señorita who gave me a pretty smile!'

'They weren't just after me!' retorted Lucas merrily. 'Good Lord, those females were baiting their traps for you, too, just as they are now!'

Indeed, people were watching them and murmuring behind raised hands. The presence of Lord Conistone was always noteworthy at any social event, and though Alec was known to be estranged for some reason from his father, society's foremost hostesses were always eager to have a handsome war hero who was also the son of an earl to adorn their gatherings.

Soon the two men were in the midst of a babble of old army colleagues, though after a while Lucas was swept away to talk politics, since some of his Whig associates were hoping to persuade him into a government post. But before he went, he was at Alec's side, saying quietly, 'All right if I move on, old friend?'

'Certainly. I'll see you later, Lucas.'

Because the conversation Alec had come here for had to be held in private.

Alec had called at his father's house on his way, to be regaled by Jarvis with the tale of Stephen's reaction last night to the missing food. 'Was my brother angry, Jarvis?'

'You could say that, sir.' Jarvis's cheeks creased in a smile. 'His guests left almost as soon as they arrived, once Lord Stephen told them there was no food or drink.'

Alec pictured the scene. 'I hope he didn't take it out on you?'

'I pointed out, Master Alec, that the tradesmen's bills were in the Earl's name and that, since the Earl was away, I'd no clear idea for whom the goods were intended. As far as I was aware, you, sir, had as much right to the food and wine as Lord Stephen!'

'You're a good man, Jarvis.' Alec looked around the big hall. 'What about the paintings?'

'Lord Stephen said nothing about them whatsoever, sir. But he noticed those labels you'd asked me to fasten on. And only an hour ago, he was back here bringing in some new ones—or should I say, the *originals*, sir—and telling me some story about mistakes having been made at the restorer's shop!'

Alec had smiled grimly at the thought of Stephen's angry confusion. And now, at Lord Fanton's, he continued to mingle with the top-lofty guests and even allowed himself to be pressed into introductions by the determined mamas of marriageable daughters. 'He's the younger son of the Earl of

Aldchester, you know,' he heard the old tabbies whispering avidly. 'There's some sort of family problem, and sweet Lady Emilia found him just a little difficult. But even so, he's a catch, my dears, a catch!'

Alec talked and smiled politely, but he never stopped watching as the guests arrived; he didn't have to wait long. He felt all his muscles tensing as she came in. She was so breathtakingly beautiful. No wonder everyone in the room turned to stare. No wonder his father had fallen in love with her so irrevocably.

Though the dancing had begun, Alec resisted suggestions that he might lead some fair maiden on to the floor. Likewise he refused invitations to a game as his friends moved through to the card room. Really he was just waiting for the moment he'd come here for.

He heard, at last, her silken voice at his shoulder. 'Alec, my dear. You got my note.'

The feline purr was all too familiar. Alec turned slowly to see Susanna, with her gleaming dark curls, her porcelain skin and sultry, dark-blue eyes.

'I got your note, yes, Susanna,' he said. 'You wanted to see me.'

She put her hand on his arm. 'And so you came. But they tell me you have not been to any affairs of the *ton* for, oh, many months! I remember you when I first set eyes on you, Alec. Dancing, laughing, surrounded by beautiful women, always—'

He drew his arm away abruptly. 'Susanna. I didn't actually come to enjoy the party.'

'Ah,' she sighed, 'the *ennui* of the times. You military men weary quickly, I think, of London's frivolities after the adventure of war.' The candlelight was glittering on her pale-pink satin gown, on the stupendous jewels—Aldchester heirlooms—that she wore to emphasise her allure. She toyed with her pearl-encrusted fan. 'Or perhaps you simply avoid society wherever you think I might be.'

His eyes grew harder. 'Perhaps I've come tonight because I heard rumours. And perhaps I wanted to know if they were true.'

She shrugged her gleaming bare shoulders. 'Ah—rumours, maybe, that you have brought my better nature to the fore, Alec! But you know, my dear, you *always* do that.'

'I wish I didn't know that was a lie,' he said quietly.

Her eyes glittered. 'If you are not careful, I vow I shall look for someone else to dally with!'

He put his hand swiftly on her arm. 'Don't, Susanna,' he said tersely. 'Don't for God's sake lower yourself with light and stupid jests, especially when you were perhaps starting to raise yourself in my estimation.'

She went still. 'So you've heard, then? That I have put an end to my—*dalliance* with your brother? It is indeed true. Alas—' she wafted her fan '—Stephen was becoming tedious. He visited us at Carrfields and I told him it was over.'

'Searching for fresh entertainment, Susanna?'

Her exotic eyes narrowed. Then she said, 'Can we move somewhere a little quieter?'

He guided her to the back of the room, away from the musicians and the dancing. And she began to tell him. 'Your brother came to us at Carrfields, for two days. But of course that man of his, Markin—' she shuddered '—was with him and my maid overheard them whispering. Something about a child, a little girl, that Stephen is desperate to get hold of.'

Alec froze.

'And do you know, Alec,' she went on, 'that changed my mind about everything.' She gazed up at him, her beautiful eyes for once clear and transparent. 'Men like you, women like me, we can look after ourselves. But I am worried about this child—I believe Stephen really intends her some harm—and I thought that you, of all people, might have the resources to do something...' She shivered suddenly. 'There. That is all. Take me into the dancing, will you? People used to say what a handsome couple we made.'

'No,' he said. 'I'm afraid I must go.'

He was already turning when she laid her gloved wrist on his arm. 'Alec. Can't you forgive me? It's how I was brought up, you know, to take what I wanted, and believe me...' she touched his cheek '...often I heartily wish it were not so! I only took up with Stephen to make *you* jealous. But I didn't succeed, did I? You are a good man, Alec, perhaps the best I've known.'

'I am a damned fool,' he broke in bitterly. He was suddenly finding the odours of perfume and pomade almost overbearing. His jaw clenched, he made his bow to Susanna and went to find Lucas in the card room. His friend was standing watching a game, but came quickly over to join him.

'News, Alec?'

'Yes, and not good. Lucas, the woman and child that I told you about, that I'm sheltering at Two Crows Castle—they could be in danger. And some day soon I may have to bring them to you and Verena. It seems the peril is greater than I thought.'

Chapter Seventeen

Alec was back at Two Crows Castle less than an hour later. Deuce take it, he thought, but he almost found the ruination of this old place a relief after the glitter of the *ton*.

Garrett came up to him as Alec heaved off his coat. 'We tracked down that oily cove Marchmont at his theatre today, Captain, like you asked us to,' Garrett announced. 'He told us—after a bit of persuasion—that he gave the girl Linette the push because she wouldn't—*oblige* him like he wanted.'

'Yet he suggested,' grated Alec, 'that she find work at the Temple of Beauty?'

'It was Mr Marchmont's *opinion*—' and Garrett's voice, too, was full of contempt '—that the experience would stand her in good stead.'

Alec ground out some words beneath his breath.

'Then we got into the Temple of Beauty, Captain—we bribed a footman who made sure the way was clear. And in the office we found that little green book what you told us about, hidden inside a heavy great thing called *The Myths of Ap— The Myths of Aplo—*'

'Apollodorus.'

'That's it, Captain. It said that your brother, Lord Stephen, had indeed been there three years ago. The summer of Vittoria. In fact, he visited several nights in a row—it was in Dr Barnard's notes. Here you are, McGrath wrote it down: *Paid particular attention to the young blonde innocent from the country. Reckon his lordship took her away for his own purposes...*'

Alec was breathing hard. That must be it. His brother, Stephen, had seduced Rosalie's sister. Was quite possibly Katy's father. That was why Stephen had been after Rosalie that night at Dr Barnard's; why he had hunted Rosalie down at the poetry reading, after setting fire to her home; why Stephen had sent that threat and offered the underworld reward for her. His damnably craven brother wanted to stop her search. Perhaps more.

How in hell was he going to tell Rosalie?

His next question—*should* he tell Rosalie?

Rosalie didn't even know that Stephen was Alec's brother. Hell's teeth, she would fly at Stephen, she would go for him hammer and tongs; she wouldn't *care* that Stephen, as well as being despicable, could also be damnably dangerous, with his money and his powerful friends.

Alec would have to deal with Stephen himself. He fisted his hands. The question was—*how*? Not, unfortunately, by telling her the truth.

Garrett was still watching him. 'She's out in the garden, Captain,' Garrett said quietly. 'And we're keeping an eye on her, never fear.'

It was a little after ten and the darkness outside was illuminated by the pale moon's glow. The lingering scents of rosemary and lavender filled the air, because Rosalie had been working earlier to uncover an old herb garden. But now she was just sitting on a bench and watching the stars come out, with Ajax lying by her feet. *Why are you waiting up for him, you fool?* He could be hours. *If* he came back tonight…

The thought stabbed her. *So she's back in town.*

Time and time again she'd told herself she was mad to allow this man whom fate had hurled in her path to hurt her so, but apparently there was no end to her stupidity. Indeed, she was just getting up to go inside when she heard the back door opening into the yard; as Ajax barked eagerly, her stomach did a painful flip-flop.

Alec came around the corner and stopped when he saw her there. The silvery moonlight outlined the stark masculinity of his features. *Be calm. Be controlled.*

He came closer. He'd taken off his coat on this warm night, so only his white shirt covered his powerful upper torso. Ajax jumped up to greet him, pawing at his tight cream kerseymere breeches and polished boots; Alec simply stroked the dog's shaggy head. 'Mrs Rowland. I thought you would be in your room by now.'

His dark, brooding gaze caused her pulse rate to race. Somehow she smiled back and gave a little shrug. 'It's such a lovely night.'

'You've been looking at the stars?'

'Looking at the stars.' She nodded.

'Tell me what you see.'

'There's Vega—the brilliant blue-white star in the constellation of the Lyre. My mother used to say it was the sign of summer returning when Vega climbed overhead—' She broke off. *Stop babbling, you fool.* 'I hope you enjoyed yourself at your party, Captain Stewart?'

He had tugged loose his cravat—the Gordian knot—and unwittingly rumpled his hair. Already, dark beard-growth was shadowing his lean jaw. He was looking like Captain Stewart of Two Crows

Castle again. And, oh, she had to resist the physical onslaught on her beleaguered senses.

He shrugged his broad shoulders. 'It was tedious. These affairs always are. So I left early.' He was looking around the garden with an air of mystification. 'You've done something to it all. It looks different.'

'To be truthful, I was glad to find something here that I *could* do,' she said quickly. 'And Garrett recruited some men to help. I hope you don't mind?'

'Twisting us all round your little finger, Mrs Rowland? No. Why should I?'

'There are so many wonderful plants out here.' She was pointing. 'My mother used to have this one—it's called *anemone pavonina*. Isn't it beautiful?'

He was looking at her, not at the scarlet flowers. She just kept on surprising him with her knowledge. With her own damned beauty. 'You told me your mother loved her garden in Oxfordshire. But surely it was only small?'

'Yes, but her home in France used to be famous for its gardens; people would travel from far and near to admire them—' She broke off, seeing his expression.

'Would travel… Where did your mother *live*?'

She had frozen. 'I thought I told you. She was born in a fine house—a château…'

'You didn't tell me *that*.' He was watching her with a slight frown. 'It strikes me you've seen even more changes of fortune than me.'

Around the lantern that hung by the back door, the moths fluttered in a distracting dance. She felt as if she were being drawn to a flame also, helpless as those poor creatures. *Alec*. She remembered his kiss. His hands caressing her. Heat flooded her at his nearness.

She eased her dry mouth and tried to smile. 'I've only really known our rather penny-pinched existence in Oxfordshire. My mother's family's fortunes vanished during the Revolution and she always told us that all her relatives fled from Paris.'

'You have lost a great deal in your life, Mrs Rowland.'

She lifted her gaze to him steadily. 'So many have lost more. You know that.'

'You're thinking about my soldiers?'

'Indeed. I know nothing about war, but I hate to hear it glorified. I know that Lord Byron visited the field of Waterloo and detested all the pointless spilling of blood. *The red rain*, he called it, that made the harvest grow, but achieved so little else…' Her voice faded away.

For one brief moment Alec recalled the horrors of the battlefield. The screams of the dying. The heaps of dead… He turned to gaze at her, unable to help himself. Such tenderness. Such—*awareness* of all the sadness in the world. So very different to those harridans who'd surrounded him at Lord Fanton's tonight, with their simpering daughters who adored a war hero in uniform, but knew nothing of the reality of war. Damn it all, he wanted to kiss her again. He wanted to take her in his arms, carry her up to his bed and soothe away the sadness in her eyes by making passionate love to her.

You fool. He clamped down hard on the arousal that was pounding through his veins. 'Rosalie. I think I might have picked up some more news about your sister tonight.'

'Oh, is that why you went out?' Immediately she could have bitten her tongue off. 'I—I'm sorry,' she stammered. 'Ridiculous of me to expect you to become as obsessive about my sister's story as me.'

'Obsessive is hardly a fair word,' he said, 'for a search after justice like yours. But will you tell me exactly what you remember about the threats that were delivered to your friend Helen?'

Her brow puckered slightly. 'When her press was wrecked? And the fire started? Let me see. The first note said, *Gossip-raking bitch.* That was all. But the second one said, *Write one more word about Lady A., and you and those close to you will be the target next, not just the house.*'

Alec was very still. 'Do you know who this Lady A. is?'

'No. But I do know that she had a maidservant whipped and dismissed for dropping a vase. Helen wrote a piece about it.' She was looking up at him anxiously. 'Does that help?'

Alec had heard that story, too. About his stepmother, Lady Aldchester. Somehow he forced a smile. 'Possibly. Look, it's getting cold, you're shivering. Don't you think it's time to go inside?'

Ajax nudged at her hand and she fondled him abstractedly. She picked up her shawl. 'Alec—'

'Hmmm?'

'Alec, I've been thinking. Up till now, my one aim has been to find this man and confront him. But now I'm starting to think that perhaps I don't *want* Katy's father to know about Katy.' She looked up at him anxiously. 'Do I sound very foolish? You see, I don't want him to have anything at all to do with her.'

His hard-boned face was grave. 'Then what do you want, Rosalie?'

'Oh, I was thinking that I'd find him and get an apology from him, perhaps. Above all I wanted to make him realise just what he'd *done* to Linette. But now?' She gave a little sigh. 'Sometimes, I wish I'd never even begun this.'

Then she realised that his hand was over hers, his strong, long-fingered hand that had wrought such wicked magic on her at his father's house. He meant it as a gesture of friendship, she knew, of reassurance, but it felt so wonderful that she hardly dared to breathe. Suddenly all she wanted was to lean into him, and lift her face to his, and perhaps he would kiss her again…

No. He is not for you. The moths were still fluttering helplessly round the lantern, scorching themselves. It was time to pull herself away from a similar fate.

Alec was saying, steadily, 'You know the story of Pandora's box, don't you, Rosalie? I'm afraid you've opened it and there's no going back. The threat is still there—my men hear the word on the streets. You still need guarding, as does Katy.'

'Yes. Yes, I'm sorry; you're more patient with me than I deserve.' She dragged herself away from him and pulled her old shawl around her with resolution. 'You're right, I really must go in now, it's getting chilly. Tomorrow, I thought perhaps we could find out if anyone remembered Linette from that place off the Ratcliffe Highway, where she died. Your men might be able to help.'

'What a good idea,' he said, heartily despising himself for his duplicity. 'I'll speak to Garrett in the morning and get him to send someone out there.'

She hesitated. 'Alec, I don't know why you're helping me like this, but I just want you to know that I'm truly grateful to you for offering us shelter here. I don't know why you became estranged from your father, but I think it is his loss, not yours!'

'Please don't make me out to be anything that I'm not.' His eyes, she saw, looked bleak. 'I must warn you again that I have nothing, I *am* nothing beyond the man you see before you. I've been living a hard life, with hard men, for years, which *alters* a person and not necessarily for the better.'

She lifted her head, her eyes bright with—what? Defiance? Obstinacy? 'I don't believe you have nothing, Alec Stewart!' she said steadily. 'I don't believe this—this façade you put up, of being of no worth to society! You have this house, for a start.'

'A wreck,' he said, shrugging bitterly as he looked around. 'A ruin.'

'No!' she persisted. 'It's of enormous value to many poor ex-soldiers! And you have your reputation as a hero of the war. Your superlative skill as a fencer. You have friends like Lord Conistone, Mary told me.'

His face softened at last. 'Lucas is one in a million.'

'And some might say that you are also,' she breathed, so quietly that she wasn't sure he heard her at all.

But unless her whole world was totally awry, Alec Stewart was good and brave and true. And she'd discovered it too late. 'Now, I really must go in,' she went on lightly. 'I've already taken too much of your time. But, Captain Stewart, I'm so *very* glad to have your help. Goodnight.' She turned to walk steadily into the house, leaving a faint trail of the scent of her skin and hair.

Alec watched her go. A flower—honeysuckle—lay close to where she'd been sitting. He picked it up, then let it drop again as the stars twinkled in the dark sky overhead. Her sweet face had brightened with such hope just now when he'd told her he might have found more news of her sister.

The dog had come to nudge sympathetically at his hand. 'Well, Ajax,' Alec said softly, 'I've landed myself in one hell of a mess, haven't I, boy?'

How was he going to tell her that the villain they were looking for was his own damned brother?

Family loyalty. Oh, God.

Chapter Eighteen

Whenever Alec came across Rosalie over the next few days, she was busy organising her small but eager band of soldiers in the garden, or helping Mary with the sewing, or playing with the children. Always she was cheerful and kind to his men, who were coming perilously close to adoring her.

Yet always now she kept her distance from him and jumped if he so much as touched her hand by accident. As well, thought Alec bleakly. He couldn't forget how she'd melted to his shockingly intimate caresses at his father's house. And he'd resolved that such a thing must never happen again.

She'd entrusted him utterly with her quest and with the safety of her tragic sister's child, and Alec was determined not to break that trust.

There were no more direct threats, though his men reported that the underworld reward was still out for her and the child. Alec didn't tell her this. He just doubled the guard on the house by night as well as day and made his men swear never to let her know that her little team of gardeners had actually been hand-chosen, by him, to protect her.

Nor did he tell her that next on his agenda was a meeting with his brother.

Stephen rose abruptly from his seat when he saw Alec entering the Pall Mall club. Though he hadn't seen his younger brother since the night of the poetry reading, he still fumed every time he remembered the way Alec had taken the girl from him. Then there was the humiliation of the party he'd planned at his father's house. And the business of the paintings.

He'd received the message this morning, to meet Alec here tonight. Alec, as he came in, looked tall. Imposing. Well dressed, for once. The doorman bowed as he let him in.

'Good day to you, Stephen,' said Alec softly. 'I thought it was time that you and I got together.'

Stephen had deliberately chosen a quiet corner; now he gestured Alec tensely to a seat. 'Indeed.' His voice was already shaky with suppressed anger. 'But first—damn you, Alec, last week I had a party arranged!'

Alec ordered brandy from a hovering waiter. 'Ah,

you're talking about my visit to our father's house. I realised that our father, being absent, must have forgotten to cancel a rather large order for party food. So I took it away.' His hard eyes fastened on Stephen. 'To a place where it wouldn't be wasted.'

Stephen's face was tense with rage. 'You interfering ruffian—'

'And as for those paintings,' continued Alec as if his brother hadn't spoken, 'it was exceedingly kind of you to arrange substitutes, while the real ones were away for cleaning. I take it you've got the originals back in time? Our father will be returning any day, I believe.'

Stephen was pale. *Yes, and it had cost him a fortune to buy back those paintings.*

'Are they all back?' repeated Alec softly.

'Yes. Damn it, yes, they are!'

'Good. Then I'll get on to my real business of the night.' Alec leaned forwards. His voice was knife-edged. 'Listen, brother mine. Those who stay at Two Crows Castle—*all* of them—are under my protection. Including the young woman you were trying to take home after the poetry reading.'

'That slut? I'd forgotten her.'

'Really? But you took an interest in that same woman a couple of weeks earlier at the Temple of Beauty, didn't you? She had a sister—is that why you were interested in her, Stephen? A sister who had a child.'

'What the hell has that to do with me?'

'I'm hoping you'll tell me. A threat has been made, on Rosalie Rowland and the child. There's even an underworld reward out for them.' Alec leaned back in his seat, but his eyes never, for one second, left Stephen's face. 'I do hope it's nothing to do with you.'

Stephen laughed shakily. 'You've got a wild imagination, brother.'

'I'm not the imaginative kind,' said Alec flatly.

'I could retaliate by asking—why is this Rosalie Rowland of such interest to *you*? Though she's a spirited jade, isn't she, if a little outspoken for a whore.'

Alec's fist stopped just short of Stephen's jaw. 'You'll never call her such names again. *Ever.*'

Stephen flinched, then began to sneer. 'Really? Why not?'

'Because,' said Alec softly, 'I'll take retaliation if she and that child are in any way harmed.'

'Is that what you've come here to tell me?'

'I think it is, yes.'

'Falling for Athena, are you?' Stephen's lip curled. 'Has she submitted to your rugged charms yet? My God, and you've still got Susanna hankering after you, too—she's had enough of me, that's for sure. Thanks to you.' His voice was bitter.

Alec caught his breath. 'Our stepmother pleases no one but herself. I don't imagine for one minute that *I* can influence her decisions.'

'But I heard you were with her at Lord Fanton's ball.' Stephen's voice was rising. 'And I know that you spoke to her when our father was taken ill, before he went with her to the country. You must have said something, to make her spurn me!'

'Perhaps it took very little. And keep your voice down, brother. You're beginning to sound hysterical.'

'Hysterical! My God!' Stephen was on his feet. People were looking. He sat heavily back in his chair. 'I think it would be suitable revenge,' he ground out, 'to tell your Rosalie *everything* about you and Susanna.'

So. The blow Alec had long expected had at last been struck. *Family loyalty.* Aloud he said nonchalantly, 'You'll not win on that one, Stephen. I don't think for one moment that Mrs Rowland would care.'

'No? Should I tell her, then?'

'By all means, if you wish,' said Alec shortly. 'It would mean exposing your own sordid secrets, remember.' He got up to leave. 'I repeat—Mrs Rowland and the child are under my protection. My warnings, as you'll know, are not to be taken lightly. You see, unlike you, Stephen, I've nothing whatsoever to lose.'

He turned to go. Stephen said, in a voice tinged with venom, 'So sure of yourself! So confident, damn you! Have you considered, Alec, what would happen if the father of this bastard child actually decided, quite legally, to claim his brat?'

Alec swung round to face him, jaw clenched. 'Let him just try it, brother mine,' he breathed. 'Let him try it.'

After Alec had gone, Stephen ordered another brandy and sat alone. He most definitely could not afford to have any more dirt raked up over his past; he'd been flying too close to the wind anyway because of Susanna and he'd always half-suspected that she only used him to get closer again to damned Alec!

But now this widow, Mrs Rowland, had emerged and things were looking more dangerous by the minute.

Most of the gentry paid for their pleasure from time to time, or kept discreet mistresses. But Linette had been a mighty big mistake, because she had been gently born and a virgin.

The stupid girl had thought Stephen would marry her. Kept pestering him, until he'd paid her off—generously, he'd thought—and by God, he'd taught her a few skills she'd find useful in earning her living keeping other men happy! But he'd not known she'd been pregnant and had gone to her grave lamenting him. If word got around that he'd abandoned her, that she'd died in deep poverty...

He could deny it! But hell's teeth, there was a child. Damned Alec had clearly worked it all out. And now, Alec had taken both the child and Rosalie Rowland under his wing.

Alec was, unfortunately, pretty unassailable in his fortress-like house that was, not without reason, called a castle. Alec was considered a hero amongst his band of ex-soldier ruffians and didn't give a damn what society thought of him. But if the child really was Stephen's, which seemed all too likely—what should he, Stephen, do?

What would a true gentleman do?

Stephen's lip curled in an unpleasant smile. He would do just what he'd hinted at to his brother. He'd admit, sorrowfully, that he'd sadly lost contact with the mother whom he'd adored, but announce that he was willing to provide for the child. To claim her as his own, in fact.

Oh, how Alec and his pretty little widow from the Temple of Beauty would hate that.

Francis has news, my dear, such surprising news, of your family...

That night while Alec was out, Rosalie received a letter. It had been delivered earlier to Two Crows Castle—Sergeant McGrath had taken it from the post boy, grumbling at the charge—but then Mc-Grath had been called out and forgotten it; it was past nine in the evening when Mary spotted it lying on the kitchen table amongst a heap of bills and brought it to Rosalie.

The letter was from Helen. As Rosalie opened it, another folded-up missive slipped out; she put it aside and started on the first one.

Helen's letter began with the usual expressions of concern for herself and Katy *in that place*. Rosalie could almost hear Helen's disdain. There was news of Toby, who was well, and good news, too, of the church school that Francis had been asked to set up. There were also fervent wishes that Rosalie and Katy would join them in Oxfordshire—in time for Helen and Francis's marriage!

Rosalie was glad because she felt that Francis was ideal for her old friend. Helen went on to tell her that the first banns had already been read.

But then came the real bombshell.

You know, of course, Rosalie, that Francis has contacts in Paris and lately he received interesting news about the Lavalle family.

Rosalie's hand tightened on the letter as she remembered how her sister, alone in London, had called herself Linette Lavalle—their mother's name, before she married.

Francis asked me to enclose another letter for you, Rosalie, from an attorney in Paris... Swiftly Rosalie unfolded the second missive. And felt her world changing, for ever, around her.

When Alec got back to Two Crows Castle half an hour later his men melted away rather hastily at the sight of his brooding expression. Only Ajax came up to nudge sympathetically at his hand.

Garrett pulled the dog away quickly. 'Think I've found 'im a new home, Captain!'

'What?' Alec was looking abstracted.

'A new home. For Ajax.'

'You're getting *rid* of him?'

'Thought that was what you wanted, sir.'

Alec shook his head. 'Oh, no. He might as well stay. After all, he's doing no harm.'

He didn't see Garrett's secret smile of satisfaction, but went straight up to his own room and tugged off his coat. Running his hand through his hair, he went back down the stairs to the kitchen, where Mary was tidying up for the night.

'Where is Rosalie?'

'She's just in the parlour, Captain.'

He went through. Somehow she'd made this little parlour into a different place, tidying it in the indefinable way that women had. Evidence of her quiet feminine touch was everywhere.

But there was also danger everywhere.

She was arranging a bowl of flowers on the window sill, and at first she didn't see him. He thought that she looked—*different* somehow. As if she was hiding something, and whether it was good or bad, he could not tell. She was so self-contained, so strikingly lovely, even though she refused to believe it...

And you are no damned good to her, Alec Stewart.

Faint colour tinted her cheeks as she spun round. 'Captain Stewart...'

'Mrs Rowland. Have you had a quiet day?' he enquired.

She nodded. 'Indeed, but I've had a letter, from Helen and Francis. Such good news—they are going to be married, Alec, and the school Francis has set up is going well...' She hesitated.

'And they want you to go and join them, I imagine. Is it close to where you used to live?'

'A few miles or so. I would like to see it all again. My mother is buried there.'

'Of course.' His voice was calm. 'So what will your answer be?'

She met his eyes directly. 'Some day it would make sense for us to go there, I feel. But—' she looked up at him '—you warned me, Alec, that the person who threatened me might trace us there. Might trace us *anywhere*.'

He looked around. 'Do you mind if I sit down? Were you in a hurry to retire?'

She put the flowers aside and sat down herself. 'No. Not at all.'

He sat opposite her, on the sofa. 'Rosalie,' he said, his face shadowed in the candlelight, 'have you ever considered that the man who seduced your sister might have a legal claim on Katy, as her father?'

She looked absolutely stunned. 'Oh, no. But— why would he *want* to make such a claim, when he abandoned both mother and child so cruelly?'

'He could say that the mother left him of her own will and he didn't know the child existed.'

'Yes. Yes, I see...'

Pity for her twisted rawly in Alec's gut. She took a moment to calm herself before going on, 'Alec, could this man—would he be allowed to take Katy away from me?'

'If he's her father, it's possible, yes.'

Her hands were clasped tightly in her lap. 'Would money help?'

'What money?' he answered grimly. 'That's one commodity neither of us has and for once I'm sorry.' *Stephen, damn him, has enough money to buy up lawyers by the score.*

Rosalie nodded, biting her lip. 'What do you think I should do?'

Alec regarded her steadily. 'I know you will hate this. But there is one solution. Agree to a betrothal.'

'A—' She looked even more stunned.

'A betrothal. With me.'

Dear God. She looked—horrified. He raked his hand through his hair and tried again. 'Look. It need only be a temporary arrangement. You and I would always be aware of that. But if this man should try to claim Katy, you do need to assume respectability. I may not be rich, but I am an Earl's son—and a betrothal to me would strengthen your reputation, Mrs Rowland, in the eyes of the world.'

Rosalie sat very still. *Do you really think that you—a courtesan who writes for a gossip rag—would be taken seriously at the magistrates' court?* Those caustic words of Alec's still seared her. 'So— you would pretend that you'd asked me to marry you…'

'Exactly. It's not going to be so very surprising to anyone, is it? You have, after all, been married before. And people already know that you're living here.'

Rosalie lifted her head at last. The scent of the flowers on the window sill seemed almost overpowering now. 'They already assume I'm your mistress?'

'I'm afraid it's inevitable.' He saw the tinge of colour under her fine skin.

'Is there nothing else I can do?' she asked quietly. 'No alternative?'

How she hated the idea. 'It's the best way, I fear. We would need to make a formal announcement, of course, in the papers and so on, but I'll give you the night to think about my proposition. I can see you hate it, so let me remind you that once the danger is over, you can break it off any time you want.'

And he went, not even glancing at her as he left the room. Dimly she heard him in the hallway talking to Garrett, his mind already on other things, no doubt.

She gathered up those letters from Helen that she'd thought of showing him and clutched them to her, feeling quite sick.

She remembered overhearing Garrett saying

sourly, *'So she's back in town. Dear God, she's beautiful, but she's wrecked his life...'*

Alec had offered her this betrothal even though clearly he detested the notion. And she *must* agree to it, for Katy's sake. But, oh, it was going to be difficult.

She looked again at the letter from France.

It reminded her that her mother was part of the Lavalle family, who'd owned land, châteaux and great vineyards in the Loire region of France, but lost them in the tumult of the Revolution so long ago. Rosalie had always assumed that the wealth of the Lavalles had gone for ever.

But six years ago, this letter told her, her family's fortune had been restored by the Emperor Napoleon in a deliberate ploy to gain the political backing of France's foremost aristocratic families. And the letter told her that a portion of that fortune—not vast, but large enough to make a difference to her life—might be hers.

She folded the letter in her fingers and gazed into the dying embers of the fire.

Even if this was true—how could it help her, now? For she had lost her heart to a man who was scarred for ever by a past commitment and who felt nothing but pity for her.

And if he knew all her lies—he wouldn't be able to bear to have her near him.

Chapter Nineteen

That night Katy lost her much-loved rag doll. Rosalie had realised Polly was missing at Katy's bed time and was apprehensive, because she clutched the battered toy in her sleep every night. But Katy had fallen asleep so very quickly that it had slipped from Rosalie's mind.

Until, a little after midnight, Rosalie was woken by Katy's woeful cry. 'Polly-doll. Gone.'

Rosalie scrambled out of bed in her nightgown and hurried to comfort the little girl. 'I'll look for her, darling. Don't fret—I'll be back very soon.'

Her fault for not doing it earlier, she reproached herself. Quickly pulling a shawl over her nightdress, she took a candlestick and tiptoed barefoot downstairs. She was aware that a rota of Alec's men kept watch both inside and out, night and day—a relic of their old army routine, she assumed. But the sleeping house was quiet as she hurried down the staircase and along the unlit passageway to the parlour off the kitchen where she guessed the doll was most likely to be.

Indeed, the rag doll was lying half under a chair. Retrieving it with a sigh of relief, she set off back up to Katy, and a watery smile was her reward.

'There, darling.' Rosalie stroked Katy's cheek. 'Everything's all right now. Sweet dreams, my love.'

As soon as Katy was asleep again Rosalie tiptoed back to her own room. So stupid of her to go without shoes, for she'd somehow caught her left foot on a splinter of wood—on the rough staircase, perhaps—and now it was bleeding slightly. She wrung out a cotton handkerchief in cold water and knotted it tightly around her foot to cover the small wound. Then she remembered she'd left the candlestick burning on the landing and limped out to fetch it.

And nearly collided with a tall male figure. Alec.

Shock quivered through her veins at the raw masculinity of his body, so close to hers.

'I thought I heard someone,' he was saying. 'Is anything wrong?' He was assessing her sharply, taking in her shawl flung over her nightgown, her pale face, her loose hair.

'Katy woke up just now and realised she hadn't got her rag doll.' Somehow she kept her voice calm. 'Major crisis, of course. So I've just been down to find the doll, then I remembered I left this candle out here...'

Her voice trailed away. She hadn't realised, and she should have done, that he wasn't all that fully dressed himself. His lean, hard-boned face was shadowed with beard growth. His white shirt had been hastily thrust into his tight buckskin breeches, but was unfastened almost all the way down his chest, and... Oh, Lord, she could see, as his shirt gaped, that astounding musculature. His sculpted shoulders and chest, the bronzed gleam of smooth male torso, that line of silky dark hair that ran down towards his abdomen and...

Don't look as though you're about to faint at the sight of a half-naked male body, you silly fool. He thinks you a widow and a whore.

'So Katy's all right?' he asked.

'Oh, yes, indeed—she's fast asleep, now, and quite happy, thank you!' She gave a brief nod and turned to go.

His hand was on her shoulder. 'And what about you, Mrs Rowland? Perhaps you'd like to tell me why your nightgown is spattered with water and there's a handkerchief tied around your foot?'

'I caught it on the stairs just now. So stupid of me. It's only a scratch. I'm sorry I've disturbed you—'

His voice was softer. 'You must stop blaming yourself, you know, for everything.'

Something tight caught in her throat. 'Who else *should* I blame?' she whispered.

His hands were warm and strong on her shoulders. 'Listen to me. *No one* could have done more than you for your sister. You've searched high and low for her, you've taken extraordinary care of her child…'

'But I had to. *I had to.*' She gazed up at him in despair. 'Because it was my fault, Alec!'

'For God's sake! What was?'

'It was my fault that my little sister ran away from home!'

His gaze was steady. 'I really find that very difficult to believe,' he said.

'Then you must,' she told him bleakly. She dragged herself away from him. 'Why do you think I care so desperately for poor Katy? Because it's the only way I can make amends!' She was trembling. 'You've been so kind to me, you and your men, but I've drawn you into all this on a lie, because I should have told you everything from the very beginning, I've *deceived* you… Excuse me, I've disturbed your sleep. I'll go back to my room now.'

But she couldn't go anywhere, because he'd caught her again by her arm.

'Rosalie. This is an order. You're not going any-where until I've looked at your foot.'

She stared down at it blindly. 'No, really, it's just a splinter…'

'Then it needs removing. You'd better come to my room. And at the same time you're going to tell me—*everything*.'

After it happened, Alec reviled himself bitterly. But what else could he have done? He couldn't leave her so obviously in pain, though she tried so hard to hide it. Couldn't leave her so full of *contempt* for herself.

And he couldn't take her downstairs, where any of his men, as they made their nightly rounds, might see them. But he was playing with fire. And he damned well knew it.

She followed him to his room. He could tell by her uneven tread that she couldn't put her weight prop-erly on her left foot. He saw her glance at his bed and catch her breath before perching on the edge of a chair with her nightgown buttoned up to her throat. But her lovely pale hair was loose, as it never was by day, and—*damn*, he thought. Damn, didn't she realise, with that lamp glowing away behind her, that despite that garment being long and all-enveloping, he could see almost *everything* through that sheer material? She looked exquisite, with her slender legs outlined beneath the filmy fabric, her pert breasts jutting...

Dear God, you're no good for her. Remember it, you fool.

He fetched a low stool on which she could rest her foot and bent to swiftly examine the damage. Yes, there was a splinter—tiny, but if it wasn't removed it could turn nasty. Her foot was small and soft. Clenching his teeth, he fetched water. Then, bringing a lamp very close, he said, 'This will hurt, just a little.'

Rosalie nodded, biting her lip. His strong, warm hand cupping her foot was such sweet torment that it sent a surge of longing through her veins. With swift skill he eased out the splinter and she suppressed the low cry that forced its way to her lips.

He glanced up at her, concern and reassurance in his dark eyes. 'That's it,' he said. He bathed away the slight trickle of blood, knowing it would cleanse the wound, then tied one of his laundered neckcloths around her foot and stood up. 'Better?'

She lifted her chin staunchly. 'Thank you. Much, much better. I'll go back to my room—'

'Not just yet,' he said quietly. 'You were going to tell me—remember?—about your sister.'

And so she began. He reminded himself, as he

watched her, how young she was, how vulnerable still. Twenty-one and a widow, with her life in tatters around her. He stood with his back to the window, hoping that the distance across the room might help to quell the physical arousal of which he was all too aware.

She clasped her hands together. She raised her face to him and said quietly, 'Alec, I loved Linette, so very much. But I've already told you that everyone was unkind to my mother for being foreign—even for being *pretty*. And Linette was just like our mother—so sweet and lovely, wanting everyone to adore her, and not understanding why they didn't.'

'And so you took it upon yourself to defend your little family?'

'My father asked me to.'

'Your father? But—how old were you when he died? Seven, I thought you said?'

'My age did not matter—I'd promised!' She gazed at him almost defiantly, her blue eyes dark with emotion. 'And as I grew older I did what I could to protect my poor mother from those who—wished to hurt her. Helen was my one good friend; she was the village schoolteacher. I loved my lessons, I loved learning about—oh, about *everything*. And I used to write stories. They were my way of escaping a rather cruel world, I suppose—Linette used to love hearing them.'

She took a deep breath. 'But Linette didn't enjoy school at all. And as she grew older, she grew very pretty, not like me.'

Alec found himself about to say something, but stopped.

'Then Linette realised that a lot of the local boys and men were starting to notice her,' she went on. 'I couldn't blame her for enjoying their flattery, but I just asked her to be careful...' Rosalie shook her head and blew her nose with the big, clean handkerchief Alec had silently offered her. 'I'm sorry, Alec, you must find this tedious!'

'No,' he said. 'What happened? To make her run away?'

He saw the pulse fluttering in her throat, the faint colour that tinged her exquisite cheekbones. She moistened her lips. 'There was someone in the village...'

'Go on.'

'And he used to lend me his books. His name was Thomas—he was the local squire's son. He often came riding past our cottage, and when he saw me, he would stop and talk. I thought he was—a friend. I was eighteen, nearly nineteen—he told me he would protect us, against the troublemakers.'

Alec listened. 'And he didn't?'

She shook her head quickly. 'I was a fool. I'd gone to tell him that some men were persecuting my mother again—oh, in little ways, harassing her for being a foreigner as she walked to the village shop and so on. He told me to meet him that evening, in the churchyard, and he…he tried to seduce me.'

Alec had gone very still.

'I *told* him that I'd only agreed to meet him because he'd promised to help us. But he said—' she clenched her hands '—he said I was deluding myself if I thought that anyone would trouble to defend a French trollop and her brats without—some sort of reward.' She shuddered. 'And he told me I was too thin for him anyway.'

Too scrawny to give a man a comfortable ride had been his exact words. She could still remember the horrible wet thickness of his lips as he'd tried to thrust his tongue into her mouth, the hateful grabbing at her breasts. She'd kicked him away, panting with nausea. 'And then,' she went on rather desperately, 'he said I had been deliberately leading him on. Which I hadn't! I'd no *intention*—'

Alec had hardly moved. 'He sounds a pleasant specimen. Was that the last you saw of him?'

She was struggling to be calm, but he saw her chest rising and falling rapidly beneath her nightgown. 'Unfortunately, no. A few months later, I discovered that he had been meeting my sister and giving her gifts.' She lifted her blue eyes to Alec's; he saw how they burned with distress. 'I don't know what, if anything, occurred. But we argued, terribly. She told me I was jealous and had wanted Thomas myself; I told Linette she was being very foolish.'

'Couldn't your mother have said anything to your sister?'

She shook her head. 'Our mother was by then not at all well. When I warned Linette that his intentions could *not* be honourable, she said I was making life unbearable for her. And a few days later she'd gone. Packed some things and taken the carrier's cart to Oxford.' She caught her breath. Despair etched her features. 'I knew that she wanted to be an actress, so I guessed she'd gone to London, and I went there again and again to look for her, but it seemed hopeless. And then I had to go back to my mother, for she was very ill, and bed-bound; she passed away last summer. But last October, I got a note from Linette to say that she was in trouble. I found my sister, with Katy, just before she died. And it was *my fault...*'

Rosalie was standing up, running her hands through her long hair. 'So now you see why I'm not worthy of your kindness, Alec—you who are so generous to waifs and strays. I drove my sister away. I'll understand completely if you no longer wish to help me.'

She was already limping towards the door, her head held high.

Something in him—some iron band of self-control—snapped in that instant. Something was wrong. Something was *very* wrong in the story she'd just told him. Yet all that mattered now was that she was in distress. In utter despair.

He blocked her way. He put his hands on her shoulders. Feeling her start to tremble, he tilted up her small chin with one warm finger. 'Rosalie. Listen to me. You were just trying to guide her in the right direction, as a caring parent does with a wayward child. And—forgive me—your sister left home without a word, which must have caused untold distress to your unwell mother. Not an act of consideration on her part, surely? You did everything that you could. Do you hear me?'

'You are being kind.' She shivered. 'But you must still hate me, for failing my sister. Perhaps Thomas was right—I *was* jealous of Linette, because she was so pretty, and I am not.'

'Not pretty?' Alec stared at her. Her low opinion of herself was beyond belief. 'Why in God's name do you *persist* in believing that?'

She shrugged, meeting his gaze defiantly. 'I'm too thin. My face is all bony. My nose doesn't turn up prettily like Linette's did, my eyes are too big, my hair is too straight.'

'You list those things as if they're *faults*,' breathed Alec. 'Listen to me. Your bone structure is exquisite. Your high cheekbones, your perfect nose, your figure...'

Alec was stunned to find himself having to say all this. If there was one thing the females who had been his mistresses in the past were aware of, it was their own allure. They were always fishing for compliments and Alec would oblige—or not. But this time—this time he found, to his astonishment, that he really *meant* it.

'Rosalie,' he said. 'Many women are pretty—but you are beautiful.'

His hands were still on her shoulders—*dangerous*. The tightness pulling at his loins was a heavy, throbbing ache.

'You must despise me, then,' she said almost defiantly.

It was no good. Her lips, tremulous, were barely inches from his own. Her lovely, turquoise-blue eyes that were so wide with despair melted all his carefully built defences.

He bent down to kiss her. It was meant to be a gesture of reassurance. Of tenderness.

Damn. It was anything but.

Something else that was entirely wrong. She was supposed to be a *widow.* All that had been just slightly askew, slightly off kilter about her accounts of her past, now fell into place.

Never once had she told him about…her husband!

Too late. Too damned late. She was opening to Alec's kisses like a tender flower yearning for the sun.

There was no way in the whole of this world that he could pull back from the inevitable now.

Rosalie felt the caress of his warm lips through every fibre of her sensitised being. Every nerve she possessed was sparked by that one instant. Licking flames of desire surged through her veins, burning her up. Alec's hands pulled her closer, sliding down her back to span her tiny waist, hauling her against him. Then he reclaimed her mouth with a low growl of male hunger and Rosalie found herself responding, parting her lips to accept the thrust of his tongue.

The warm male scent of him all but overwhelmed her. The hard ridge of arousal pressing at her abdomen tormented her with sweet desires. His tongue was plundering her mouth strongly, sweetly. She wanted to nestle into his big, muscled arms and melt into him, to be one with him…

At one point she realised that Alec was, with a great effort, pushing her away. Was trying to say, through clenched teeth, 'This should not be happening.'

Her cheeks were burning hot, but inside she felt so cold. *French whore's daughter.* Perhaps what she'd told him about Thomas repelled him. Her eyes were wide and haunted as she stared up at him. 'Of course. I'm so sorry. You were only being kind to me and I'm behaving like a fool—'

'*Kind* to you!' grated Alec thickly. He cupped her sweet face and tilted it up so his eyes blazed forcefully down into hers. 'You think this is kindness?'

Her heart fractured. 'Just—don't send me away,' she whispered. 'Not now.'

'Rosalie, I'm trying to *warn* you.'

'Alec, I feel safe with you. As safe as I've ever felt in my life.'

Her hands had stretched up round the nape of his neck, daring to feel the dark hair that grew so closely there, sliding down a little to caress his strong muscled shoulders beneath his shirt. With a low groan he'd pulled her to him again to hold her close against his aroused body, while his other hand unfastened the buttons of her nightgown until he could push the cool linen aside and cup the aching fullness of each rounded breast.

Rosalie clung to his shoulders as her nipples peaked and her whole body sang with longing. Alec swept her up in his arms and carried her tenderly to his bed, where he laid her down as if she was something precious. Then he lowered himself to her side, still kissing her. Instinctively she arched her whole body towards him, her head falling back in rapture as she pressed her own flat palms against his strong, naked chest, feeling the smooth skin stretched over swelling muscles, feeling his heartbeat.

This was like coming home. Like something she'd dreamed of, all her life. This might be all she could have of this incredible man. But she would remember it, for ever.

She shivered with exquisite sensation as he tenderly eased her nightgown away; gasped with delight as she felt her breasts pressed against the hard wall of his chest. And all the while she was aware of his lips on her hair, her forehead, her cheeks…

Quickly he pulled down his breeches, then drew her now-naked body close again. His strong, hair-roughened thighs were against hers, while he kissed her throat and murmured her name. She felt his aroused manhood and shock thudded through her.

But with an achingly tender touch, he caught her gasp with his kiss and continued to caress her breasts with his hands, sending wave after wave of pleasure through her. Then he dipped his dark head to catch one stiffening bud in his mouth and drew it in, laving it with his tongue.

She cried out as sensation pulsed through her. She raked her fingers across his wide shoulders and, as his tongue worked at her nipple, she wanted more, *needed* more. The hunger spiralled from deep within her, surging through her blood like a fever. *'Alec...'* Then her breath stopped in her throat as he trailed his hand beguilingly down her abdomen and began, using gentle fingertips, to explore the very heart of her femininity.

Dear God. She arched against him, eyes squeezed shut, her legs opening instinctively to his hard lithe body as he shifted to take his own weight on his arms and eased himself between her slender thighs.

She glimpsed it, in the candlelight, the proud essence of his masculinity, the dark, lengthy shaft, its silken head positioned just at the secret heart of her. Then he was lowering his head to kiss her again, his lips and tongue taking hot, needy possession of her mouth. At the same time he was gliding into her, inch by powerful inch. At first she was afraid, but then she was awash with pure sensation, pure need, as he gentled her, stroking her hair, her breasts, kissing her face and eyelids, murmuring, *'Rosalie. Sweetheart...'*

For just that one moment in time, it was almost possible for Rosalie to pretend that he loved her.

Then something happened. Then Alec encountered—resistance. He froze. His suspicions clenched at his insides. 'Rosalie. What—?'

'Don't stop,' she pleaded, pulling him to her, arching herself to meet him in raw hunger, revelling in the sensation of his hard length at her core. 'Alec, please don't stop now!'

And indeed, how could he? He surged in deep. She uttered one sharp cry, which he cherished with his kiss, then he pulled her to him, coaxing her into his rhythm. And Alec made love to her, being as gentle as a man of such power could be, caressing her, soothing her with his mouth on her lips and breasts, his fingers working skilfully at the core of her being as she was caught up in a surge of incredible pleasure she thought could rise no higher, until there began a soaring, glorious, impossible ecstasy as he took her over the edge.

Alec reached his own powerful release moments later. Hard reality began to creep in. He pulled himself up, breathing thickly. He'd been right. *She had not known any other lover.*

Hell. How could he have made such a blunder?

Easy. Because he had believed her when she'd told him she was a widow. The alarm bells had only begun to sound tonight, with her anguished tale of the young brute who'd tried to seduce her.

Which he himself had now done, most effectively.

He got up and started heaving on his clothes. 'Oh, Rosalie.' His voice was harsher than he'd meant it to be, because this was his fault, his stupid mistake with which to lash himself mentally. 'Rosalie, why, in God's name, didn't you *tell* me? How was I to perform some miracle of mind-reading and to know that you were, in spite of your much-vaunted widowhood, in spite of everything—a *virgin*?'

Her face was so white that it was as if he'd taken to her with a whip. She sat up on the edge of his bed, pulling on her crumpled nightgown, fastening it with frantic fingers. She tossed her head in that defiant way of hers that smote him utterly. 'I—I pretended to be a widow for Katy's sake. For her safety, Alec, and for mine! And somehow the time never seemed quite right to tell you...'

'Not even in my damned bed?'

'I'm sorry,' she said quietly.

He dragged his hand through his hair. Deceit all round, then. For wasn't he deceiving *her*, by keeping the truth from her about his despicable brother?

'What about practicalities?' he said tiredly. 'When was your last monthly flow?'

The blush of utter mortification flooded her cheeks. 'It ended three days ago,' she whispered.

'Little chance of pregnancy, then,' he said. 'That's something.' He sighed and drew her near. 'We will talk properly tomorrow. Shall we? Hmmm?' Gently he tilted her face towards his and saw there were shadows of sheer exhaustion under her lovely eyes.

'Tomorrow,' she echoed. She looked—frozen.

Something twisted in Alec's gut. He kept his arms around her. 'This isn't the end of the world,' he said. His eyes were grave, but his voice was gentle. 'We'll find some way forwards, trust me. But in the meantime—we'll speak of this to absolutely no one, do you understand? Now, I'll just check that the way is clear before I see you back to your room.'

He left her there, while he went to look out on the corridor.

Oh, God, thought Rosalie, sinking to the edge of his disarrayed bed. What had she done *now*? He'd offered to stop, after that first kiss. But she'd lied to him. She'd encouraged him. She'd longed for him, even though she *knew* he could never love her.

And she had dared to criticise Linette for her behaviour all that time ago! Alec had been so kind.

But he would be thinking now, *She is a slut, like her sister.* She drew in a deep, shuddering breath.

Then she saw the letter, lying open on his desk. It was written on fine paper, in a beautiful script, and from it drifted the faint scent of gardenias. Something fateful dragged her towards it. *I know there are risks, my dear,* she read, *but might I see you at Lord Fanton's ball? There are things I need to tell you...*

She tore her eyes away. Remembered Garrett muttering, when she wasn't supposed to hear, *'So she's back in town. Dear God, she's beautiful, but she's wrecked his life...'*

The letter must be from the woman he was once going to marry. The woman he'd loved and lost—only, perhaps he *hadn't* lost her.

Alec was coming back into the room. 'All's clear,' he said. 'And I've been thinking. I'm going to send you and Katy to some friends of mine in Mayfair, where you will be safer.'

'Safer...'

'Yes.' He gazed at her steadily. 'In all possible ways. I've been considering it for a few days.'

She could hardly speak. 'I see. Do I take it you also wish to end the pretence of our betrothal?'

'No!' he answered sharply. 'More than ever I'm afraid we must make our betrothal public, to safeguard your reputation, and in case it comes to a legal action for custody of the child. I'll send you to my friend Lucas's house tomorrow.'

Oh, God, she thought. He hated all this. She met his gaze steadily. 'You are high-handed, Captain Stewart.' Her voice broke, just a little. 'I take it your friend Lucas has been consulted?'

'I have spoken to Lord Conistone about it, yes.'

'Lord Conistone…' Mary had told her he was one of Alec's friends. He was also head of one of the most prestigious families in England and a member of the Prince Regent's set.

'Indeed,' went on Alec, 'Lucas understands the situation, though I've not burdened him with all the details. His wife, Verena, is extremely kind and discreet; they have two children, a boy and a girl, who are just a little older than Katy, so she will fit easily into the nursery there.'

'Lord Conistone is generous.'

'He is my friend.' Alec escorted her back to her room then, his face set. Just as she was turning to go in, he said, 'Rosalie. I can see that you are flaying yourself over the secrets you've kept from me. I should even the score by telling you that I've lied to you also.'

Her eyes flew up to his. *He was going to tell her about that letter.*

But it wasn't what she thought. 'I have a brother,' he went on. 'An older brother. I've told you that. What I *haven't* told you is that he is—Lord Stephen Maybury.'

She just stood there, frozen. At last her lips moved. 'Why didn't you—?'

'Tell you before?' His voice was heavy. 'There were reasons. But what you need to know, *now*, is that my brother is not to be trusted in any way at all.'

She said quietly, 'So you hate him and he hates you. Am I—was *tonight*—part of your campaign against your brother?'

He ground out some words under his breath. 'For God's sake, Rosalie! You must not believe that, ever!'

'Then what am I to believe?'

He said, between clenched teeth, 'That I count the welfare of you and the child as one of my chief responsibilities!'

Rosalie dragged in a deep breath. 'And if I could relieve you of that responsibility, I would. Oh, believe me, I would.'

What could he say? He ushered her to her room. Then he went back to his own chamber, feeling sick with himself. Haunted, by her words.

If I could relieve you of that responsibility, I would.

So there it was. She had deceived him and he had deceived her. A recipe for utter disaster.

But he would never forget how she had given herself to him. The way that her whole being splintered into rapture at the crisis of her pleasure…

Never again. *That* was why he was sending her to Lucas's. Because it must never happen again.

For Rosalie, sleep would not come.

It seemed she wasn't the only one to keep secrets. Alec, and Stephen Maybury—brothers! Yet it all made sickening sense. Their bitter familiarity. Their deep-rooted enmity. Alec's warning: *Promise me you won't throw yourself away on a brute like Maybury.*

She suddenly remembered how she'd even thought they'd resembled one another, ever so slightly, when she first saw Lord Maybury at the Temple of Beauty… Oh, why hadn't Alec *told* her? Then again, why should he tell her, when she'd clothed herself in such lies?

Tonight, just for a fleeting and magical hour, her dreams had seemed within her reach. *Never again.* The clock struck down in the hall. His words tolled in her ears. He'd blamed himself—but she was the one truly to blame, for so stupidly giving away her heart to a man who could never return her love.

Never again. The bleakness of utter despair tore at every fibre of Rosalie's being.

Chapter Twenty

If Rosalie had thought that she would never see again the kind of love that existed between her mother and father, she was proved wrong at Lucas and Verena's house. For their utter devotion to one another was evident in every word, every gesture.

It made her sad, for what her parents had lost. It made her happy, that such love could indeed be found. Perhaps, if she and Alec had met in another place, another time…

No. Best not to think of that.

But it was cruel indeed that everyone thought she was betrothed to him.

Rosalie had been terrified on arriving at this palatial place in Mayfair. Lucas had at first looked so haughty, so aristocratic, and Verena, too, seemed dauntingly refined. But they had welcomed her so very warmly. Katy was fussed over by Verena and the servants and had quickly grown used to sharing the nursery with Verena's little girl, Isobel. If her hosts knew that Rosalie was not a widow, they were far too polite to mention it.

The notice of betrothal between Captain Alec Stewart and Mrs Rosalie Rowland had appeared now in the papers and Alec visited every day. He was unfailingly kind to her, but was careful never to be alone with her for long. She burned to ask how his men were progressing in their hunt for Linette's seducer, but she sensed that the quest was a heavy burden to him now.

Watching him in Lord Conistone's company made her realise just how highly Alec was regarded in society. Sometimes she would catch snatches of conversation between Alec and Lucas's top-lofty visitors, often government ministers and senior army officers. She heard them talking politics, discussing the new European boundaries that had been drawn up at the ending of the war. Though more often, during those bright spring afternoons, she found herself in the garden of Lord Conistone's lovely house, with Verena and her children, Isobel, who was three, and four-year-old Adam. Adam looked after Katy with the kind of tender gravity that reminded Rosalie of her father. The garden here was an exquisite place, its shrubberies and flower-beds kept pristine by a team of skilled staff. But she would rather be in the overgrown, scented garden of Two Crows Castle any time.

'We'll take care of all your plants, don't you worry, miss,' the soldiers had assured her when she bade them goodbye. 'You'll come back and see us, now, won't you?'

'I'll certainly do my best.' She smiled. The youngest of them, Mikey, shyly gave her a posy of flowers that sat, fading, in her bedroom here.

She doubted that she would ever set foot in that garden again.

So many mistakes. Too many mistakes.

One evening Alec had stayed on for dinner, because Lord Conistone had some important guests who were interested in Alec's opinions about the unjust fate of the many unemployed soldiers. Alec was sitting some way down the vast table, so she had no chance to talk to him, but she could see him. He looked so darkly handsome, so charismatic as he talked to Lucas and his guests. Once he glanced her way and caught her looking at him; he smiled and her heart was wrenched.

He would not even touch her hand now. There was a look of strain in his dark eyes when they spoke, and lines of tension bracketed his mouth. To be so near to him still, to have to present herself as his betrothed and know that he could never love her, was apt punishment indeed for her mistakes.

After dinner, she and Verena left the men to their port. 'They are sure to join us later,' Verena said, misunderstanding Rosalie's low spirits. 'Perhaps then you will get a chance to speak to Alec alone, my dear.'

'Perhaps, but I'm afraid I feel rather tired tonight. I think I have a headache coming on. Will you tell Alec so, please, if he should ask?'

'A headache? Would some powders help? Our housekeeper has various tisanes, or sometimes a lavender cologne can be soothing!'

'Really, no, thank you. But you've been so very kind.'

'Any friend of Alec's is a friend of ours,' said Verena earnestly. 'You must be very happy, to be marrying him.'

'Indeed.' Rosalie managed to smile.

She had almost reached the broad landing that led to her bedroom when Alec caught up with her. 'Rosalie?'

Why was it that just the sound of his husky voice so weakened her usual stubborn resolve? She turned to face him, her heart pounding as his dark eyes scoured her. 'Rosalie,' he went on, 'Verena told me just now that you were not well.'

She shook her head slightly. 'It's a headache, that is all.'

'I hope you're not worrying too much. You know that Katy and you are perfectly safe here. I'm sorry that we've had so little opportunity to talk.'

She lifted her head so her eyes locked with his. 'Then here's our chance. I told you before,' she went on, her voice ragged because of the pain that gripped her, 'I don't think I should continue this search. I don't *want* to know who Katy's father is!'

He broke in then, his voice harsh. 'And I've told *you*, it's not a matter now of mere curiosity. This man could claim Katy as his child. That's why it's so important that our betrothal stands, that we appear in public together, that you have the public approval of figures in society like Lord Conistone and his wife. I thought you understood all this!'

She put her hand to her forehead. 'For how long must this pretence go on?' *This torment?* she added silently to herself.

'The end might just come sooner than we think.' His voice was abrupt. 'In the meantime, we must keep up appearances. That's what I've come to tell you. We have been invited to a ball at Lord Stoke-say's in three days' time, along with Lucas and Verena.'

'Do I have to endure it?'

His jaw clenched. 'We must make this betrothal convincing. We must proclaim to the world that you are under my protection. For I have sworn to keep you and Katy safe, and I've no intention of break-ing my word.'

Hateful though it was to him, thought Rosalie in despair. He might as well have said that. His eyes said it, his curt nod. His back as he turned to leave her. And after he'd gone Rosalie felt as alone, as full of despair as she'd ever been in her life.

Alec rode back to Two Crows Castle that night, the blood thundering in his ears. *You fool. You co-lossal fool.* Wouldn't it be better to tell her *every-thing*?

No. Because then Alec would have to tell her about—Susanna. And the crisis was at hand, any-way, for Alec had learned today, from his loyal men of Two Crows Castle, that Stephen was preparing his own desperate attempt to get his revenge on Alec. An attempt in which the child would be the innocent pawn.

* * *

'Try on this one, dear Rosalie! Yes, the lilac silk. Oh, you look adorable in that colour!'

'Do you really think so?' Rosalie touched the exquisite gown with trepidation. Verena's dressmaker had arrived earlier at the Mayfair mansion with a range of gowns for her to choose from and Rosalie was overwhelmed. She had never worn anything as fine as this, ever.

'It looks *wonderful* on you!' declared Verena, laughing. 'I grew up with three sisters and a vain mama forever fretting about fashion, so believe me, I know what I'm talking about!'

It was four in the afternoon, on the day of Lord Stokesay's ball. The children had gone on an excursion to St James's Park to feed the ducks; Rosalie had demurred a little, hating to let Katy outside the safe haven of Lord Conistone's house.

But Lucas Conistone had strolled in then and said, in his elegant drawl, 'You don't think I'd be lax about the safety of my own children, do you, Mrs Rowland?'

'No. Of course not, my lord.' Rosalie hung her head.

'Your anxiety is understandable, my dear,' Lucas said more gently. 'But Alec has everything in hand, believe me. You must trust him.' Then he added, quietly, 'I always have.'

Perhaps *she* was the one who was untrustworthy, because earlier that morning she'd lied again, or at least omitted a rather crucial truth, by asking Verena if she could borrow one of the footmen to accompany her into the city. 'I have a small business affair to attend to,' she'd explained.

A letter had arrived for her while she was breakfasting with Verena. It was from Hathersleighs' bank in Seething Lane, requesting that she visit them at her earliest convenience. Verena had insisted that she make her journey in Lord Conistone's coach, with three of his men in attendance.

When Rosalie had returned, she'd found Verena arranging flowers in the drawing room. 'Is everything all right, my dear?'

'Indeed.' Rosalie had forced a smile. 'Thank you.'

But everything had changed. At the bank they'd told her the exact size of her inheritance. Once all the details were settled, and suitable investments made, she would be able to lead an independent life, with Katy. Without Alec.

But an iron fist squeezed at the core of her being at the thought of never seeing him again.

Meanwhile, Lord Stokesay's ball loomed large. 'You can borrow my cream pelisse to wear over that gown tonight, my dear Rosalie,' Verena was chattering on happily. 'The lilac suits your colouring so well, I declare you will set a new fashion!'

'No one will notice me, surely!'

'You underestimate yourself,' said Verena softly. 'You look beautiful. Do you know, you're about the same size and height as my youngest sister, Izzy,' she went on, smoothing down the ruffles on Rosalie's dress, 'who drove all her suitors mad during her first Season, since she fell in love with someone new once a week at least!'

Rosalie tried to pull herself together and return Verena's warmth. 'Did you meet Lucas during your first Season?' she asked shyly.

'Oh, Lucas's estate bordered ours, in Hampshire.' Verena's eyes softened with what was almost adoration. 'I never needed a Season. I think I always knew he was the one for me.'

Rosalie felt her heart constrict. *It had been the same with Alec.* The minute she saw him, standing at the back of the hall in Dr Barnard's stupid show, she'd known.

But since then everything had gone so terribly wrong.

'Of course,' Verena went on, putting the muslin pelisse aside and adjusting a trailing cream ribbon on Rosalie's sleeve, 'my sisters and I knew Alec, as well, because he was Lucas's best friend. We all adored him; in fact, my youngest sister, Izzy, suffered several months of being utterly in love with him, until he kindly made it plain she was not the one for him. Dear Alec! You know, he could have made a good career for himself in the War Office, but instead he chooses to champion the cause of the poor soldiers.'

Verena continued to sing Alec's praises, talking about his heroism in battle and how respected he was by officers and men alike. She meant well. The lilac gown, Verena enthused, was the one and Rosalie agreed just to please her kind hostess, for her heart had gone out of the topic of ballgowns altogether. The dressmaker was called upstairs to take in the waistline. 'Madame has such an exquisite figure!' she exclaimed over Rosalie as she got out her tape measure.

There was then much fussing over the gauze overgown and the elbow-length kid gloves. Rosalie was glad when it was all over. She wanted to go back to her room, to gather up her courage to appear in public as Alec's betrothed, when she knew he was doing this out of a sense of duty. When she knew that he would never love her.

And then she heard the noise out in the cobbled courtyard that adjoined Lucas's stables.

Horsemen must be riding up, a dozen of them at

least; as she ran to the window she saw they surrounded the open barouche just drawing in from the roadway, in which sat Katy and Verena's children, with their nursemaids. She saw that Alec was amongst the riders and was already dismounting from his horse, while talking rapidly to Garrett. Alec held a cloth to his right temple, from which a scarlet stain was spreading.

Something had happened. Her heart stopped. What had Alec said to her? *'The end might just come sooner than we think...'*

Rosalie had already gathered up her lilac-silk skirts and was running, running downstairs, with Verena hurrying after her.

Katy.

Chapter Twenty-One

Alec had lifted Katy from the carriage and was holding her tight in his arms. Garrett and the rest of the men—some of them Alec's, some Lucas's—were talking in muttered voices as they saw to the horses.

A quiet trip to the Park?

She didn't think so.

Rosalie hurried across to Alec. 'What has happened?' she breathed.

She reached for Katy, but Alec shook his head. 'Let Katy go with Verena and the children,' he mouthed to Rosalie over Katy's head. 'You're frightening her. She doesn't even realise anything's wrong.'

By now Rosalie was terrified. Verena had come up and reluctantly Rosalie saw Alec pass Katy to her. Rosalie turned back to Alec, her heart thudding. He'd put his handkerchief to his temple again;

it was still bleeding. 'Are you going to explain, Captain Stewart?'

'An attempt was made to kidnap Katy.'

A sharp pain clamped her ribs. 'You promised me she would be safe!'

'And so she was.' His tone was curt. 'We were expecting the attempt, you see. We let it be known that the children were going to the Park, with just two nursemaids.'

'You—*encouraged* this?'

He looked around. By now the courtyard was empty except for them. 'We set up a trap,' he said. 'It's not as crude as it sounds. As well as myself and Lucas, at least a dozen of Lucas's and my men were within fifty yards of the children all the time in the Park—posing as passers-by, horsemen, whatever was necessary. The minute that Katy's would-be kidnappers started moving towards her, our men were on to them. The children were not even aware of it.'

'Who were they?'

'There were four of them and they're being questioned at the Queen Street police office right now. But I already know whose pay they were in.' He tensed his muscles. Looked at her steadily. 'It was news I was prepared for, I'm afraid. The would-be kidnapper was my brother, Lord Stephen Maybury.'

Her first emotion was incredulity. For a moment the world seemed to stop. But already she was starting to realise what she should have realised a long time ago. And now the truth of it all—the terrible truth—punched the air from her lungs like an iron fist. 'Oh, *no*,' she breathed. 'You mean—Lord Maybury and—*Linette...*'

He'd clenched his hands. 'I know what you're going to say—I should have told you. But if I had, you'd have tackled him head on, wouldn't you? And he's dangerous, believe me.' Already he was helping her towards a bench, where she sat down, her brain reeling. Yet it was all becoming dreadfully clear.

'So Stephen found me deliberately at the Temple of Beauty, and at the poetry reading.' She looked up at Alec. 'Oh, I walked straight into his *hands*.'

'Yes. And once he knew that *I* knew, Stephen became extremely frightened that I would expose his brutality to your sister. But I just wanted Katy—and you—to be safe. When Stephen heard that you and I were betrothed, I think he resolved—in sheer desperation—to try to kidnap Katy. As a hostage? For revenge on me?' His face was grim. 'Fortunately, someone...' he hesitated a fraction '...let me know that he intended to use Katy in his plans. So I decided there was only one way to put an end to his dangerous mischief. To lay a trap.'

Sickness pooled coldly in her stomach. 'The poetry recital—I was so *stupid*. I should have guessed...'

'How could you? My brother's good at deception—thanks to years of practice,' said Alec curtly. 'So far he's got away with his iniquities. But not for much longer. Rosalie, if you can bear it, I think it best if we continue as though nothing has happened, because I want to know how Stephen will react to the arrest of his men.'

'Will he be charged?'

'I imagine he'll have done everything through a third party, just as he did with the threats, and the reward for you. But he'll know that I know.' He turned to her. 'If you're sure you can face it, we'll still go together to Lord Stokesay's tonight as planned. Being with me is your best defence, much as you may hate it.'

She heaved in a tight breath. Alec had done all this, regardless of the gulf it would doubtless widen between him and his already estranged family. For Katy. For *her*. Why? Simply because of his overpowering sense of justice. His integrity. How she'd misjudged him. A leaden weight seemed to be crushing her shoulders.

Be sensible. Be practical. 'Alec,' she asked calmly,

'how, when the time comes, will we break off this—betrothal?'

Some impenetrable emotion flickered across Alec's face. 'It will be up to you, of course. You can think of what's appropriate—for example, that we've decided we're ill suited. I believe that's a common enough reason.'

Ill suited. Dear God, she hadn't thought so when she was in his arms. When he was making passionate love to her. But that had been a wild stupid dream.

Somehow Rosalie swallowed down the ache that squeezed her throat. 'Of course. Oh, Alec, that cut to your forehead, it's still bleeding, here, have my clean handkerchief...' She pushed it towards him, hoping he wouldn't notice how her hand shook. 'Your poor face, what happened?'

'That?' He dabbed with the handkerchief. 'I had one of Stephen's brutes cornered. He managed a punch before I felled him.'

She tried to joke. 'Clearly you needed me there. I came to your aid at the Temple of Beauty, didn't I?'

'Swinging that little table at them.' He smiled back and her heart shook. She hurried to rinse her handkerchief at the nearby pump and came back to bathe the cut, fussing over him. *This was probably the closest she would ever get to him again.* Tenderly she pushed back his dark hair from his forehead, aware of the warmth of his skin beneath her fingers, the strength of him, so close to her, yet so impossibly distant.

'You must keep my handkerchief until you can get a proper bandage on it.' She was blinking the stupid tears back from her eyes even as she placed it tenderly across his temple. 'There!' she said brightly. 'You look fit for anything now, even a ball, Captain Stewart!'

He stood up and gazed down at her. 'Is that the gown you'll be wearing tonight?'

'I—yes, it is.' She faltered. 'Is it all right, Alec?'

'More than that,' he said. His face was suddenly grave. 'You look exquisite.'

She stared at him, her heart pounding as she searched for words that wouldn't come. 'Ridiculous man,' she uttered lightly. But inside something was breaking.

'I must go and change my clothes,' Alec said, then hesitated. Touched her cheek, with fingers that lingered. 'Rosalie. Oh, Rosalie. I don't think you'll ever know how much I wish that things could have been different.'

Then he was gone.

It took her a little while to realise that Verena had come to lead her back into the house.

'I don't think I've ruined the gown,' Rosalie said somehow. 'But it was a close thing…' She fought the sudden sting of tears.

Verena took her hand. 'I told you that you should trust Alec,' she said, squeezing it warmly. 'Lucas and I do.'

Rosalie nodded blindly. But she hadn't. She hadn't, and that had been her utter downfall.

It was early evening and Rosalie was alone in her room. She'd had her bath and the servants had gone. She was wearing a cream silk wrap Verena had lent her; the lilac gown lay ready for her on the bed.

She hated it now. It seemed a symbol of all she had lost.

At seven Verena knocked and came in, her bright smile somehow making Rosalie's world even darker. 'The children will be going to bed soon,' Verena announced, 'then it will be time to set off.' She hesitated. 'You'll still be upset, I know, by what happened this afternoon. But Katy and you couldn't be in safer hands than Alec's—I've heard Lucas saying it often!'

His hands. Oh, God. Rosalie remembered his exquisitely tender lovemaking and fresh pain surged through her. She tried her hardest to smile. 'To be honest, I'm slightly daunted by the thought of to-night's ball. Though you've been so very kind.'

'No kindness is too much for a friend of Alec's!' declared Verena, sitting cosily on the bed beside her. 'Once Alec actually saved Lucas's life, did he tell you? In the Pyrenees. Lucas had injured his leg and was likely to freeze to death in the snow, so Alec got his men to build a rough stretcher and between them they carried him miles across the mountains in winter, to safety! I somehow *knew* Lucas was in trouble. But I also knew that with friends like Alec, Lucas would come home to me.' Verena patted Rosalie's hand. 'Now, I'm going to send my maid to you again, to help you to put on your gown. And I have an amethyst necklace and ear-drops you may like to borrow. They will match the lilac of your gown quite beautifully—I'm sure Alec will think so...' She hesitated again, then went on, 'Alec might sometimes seem a little distant, a little cold. But life has treated him harshly, you know. His family— well, his family quite frankly do not deserve him. What are your plans, my dear?'

Rosalie tensed. 'Plans?'

'I mean—when will the two of you be married?'

Rosalie forced out each word as if it drew the life-blood from her. 'I am not sure now that the marriage will take place.'

Verena's face said it all. 'But we thought—Lucas and I thought you were made for one another! Oh, I know Alec seems distracted often. He worries about the funding of his soldiers' hostel—the hostel was his father's idea, you know, but his father abandoned it, so Alec had to take it all on. And unfortunately he refuses all offers of help from friends like Lucas. He is too proud!' She shook her head. 'Now, I know it's really none of my business, but Alec thinks the world of you. Didn't you *see* the look in his eyes, when he saw you in that gown?'

'He was betrothed once before, I know. I think he is so wary of another commitment…'

Verena's brow creased in perplexity. Then—'You aren't thinking of Lady Emilia?' Verena raised her hands in amusement. 'She was a silly little thing; he never had a shred of anything except *pity* for her. You didn't really imagine… Oh, my goodness, I can tell by your face that I've said quite enough. I'll go and fetch that jewellery.'

When she'd gone, Verena's maid came to help Rosalie put on her lilac ballgown, then dressed her hair. '*Madame* looks beautiful!' she enthused. 'I will just pin up your hair—*so*—and leave a little of it trailing down your neck, like this—*madame*? Are you listening, *madame*?'

Rosalie was miles away, gazing at herself in the

mirror. 'You look exquisite,' he had told her just now. And Verena: *Didn't you see the look in his eyes, when he saw you in that gown?*

Rosalie sat very still. The beginning of an unfamiliar emotion—hope—was just beginning to tingle through her veins.

For months afterwards, Lord Stokesay's ball was talked about as one of the most splendid events of the Season. 'The food! The guests! The gowns!' everyone was fond of exclaiming as they reminisced over it. 'Do you remember how the garden was lit up like a Venetian carnival? And there must have been over five hundred people in the ballroom! Of course, the Prince Regent was there, with the elegant Lord Conistone and all the other members of the royal set. And even Prinny looked dazzled by it all!'

Rosalie, sitting inside the Oxford mail coach the next day with Katy in her arms, gazed unseeing out of the window as London's western suburbs turned into rolling green countryside. Katy, who'd been sleeping, was looking around at the other passengers with a frown. 'Tick-tock man?' she asked Rosalie.

'We won't see tick-tock man for a little while, darling,' she said with an ache in her throat. *For ever* would be more like it.

She had so much to thank him for. It wasn't his fault that Rosalie's heart had been broken into little pieces. That her whole being *hurt* so, every time she remembered his smile, the touch of his fingers, his kiss…

All over, now. She blew her nose hard on a handkerchief—it was Alec's, she'd laundered it and kept it from that night when… Oh, Lord, those stupid tears were coming again. People were looking at her.

She sat up straight and pointed out of the window. 'Look, Katy. There are some sheep. And some calves, do you see them?' *What a fool she'd been.*

Last night Rosalie, Verena, Alec and Lucas had travelled to Lord Stokesay's ball together. Lucas was as charming as ever, paying compliments to Rosalie on her gown, though his eyes burned with passion when he turned back to his much-loved Verena. Alec was courteous, but distant. Their only chance to speak privately came as they lined up to be presented to Lord and Lady Stokesay, when Alec said quietly, 'I'm so sorry you had to find out, in such an abrupt and unpleasant way, about my brother's wickedness to your sister.'

Her hand was on his arm—so warm, so strong— and the painful thudding of her heart made her realise just how much she was starting to *hope*. 'I understand,' she said quickly. 'And Alec, I understand how hateful all this has been for you, as well as dangerous. Oh, your poor face!'

Her eyes had flown up to the bandage almost, but not entirely, hidden by his wavy dark hair. 'You patched me up beautifully,' he said. He reached to touch a stray curl that brushed her cheek and the intimacy of his touch jolted through her. 'The main thing is,' he went on steadily, 'that you can now be quite sure Stephen will never dare to threaten you again. He knows that I hold all the cards now.'

'Because you could expose his attempt to seize Katy?'

'Indeed. The kidnapping of a young child—whatever the motive, whatever the relationship—is unforgivable, whatever one's rank.'

Vividly across Rosalie's mind flashed the imaginary scene of a terrified Katy, delivered to a man—Stephen—who told her he was her father. Unforgivable. *Unbearable.* Her hand tightened just a little on Alec's arm; he looked down at her with concern etched across his features. 'Are you all right?'

'Thank you, yes. I'm fine.'

'One thing,' went on Alec in a level voice as the queue moved slowly forwards. 'I've just heard that my father and his wife might be here. Had I realised it, I would have declined the invitation. I hope you are not embarrassed by it.'

All she knew about Alec's father was that he had withdrawn his support for Two Crows Castle and cut Alec off, both financially and socially. An older version of Stephen, she'd assumed with scorn. She lifted her chin stubbornly. 'Your friends are not embarrassed to be with you. Far from it. So why should I be? It's your father's loss.'

'Thank you,' he said quietly.

At first Rosalie was terrified of being introduced to all these grand people, but she curtsied and spoke clearly, aware always of Alec's firm hand on her arm. And to her surprise, she found she was beginning to attract admiring glances.

She'd always considered herself too thin. Straight fair hair like hers was not fashionable, she'd thought. Men preferred lively, curvaceous women with curling locks and flirtatious conversation—didn't they? People came up to speak to Alec, of course, not her. But his friends' eyes would slide to her and widen. 'Congratulations, Captain Stewart!' she heard one of them say. 'You're a sly dog—glad you've brought your intended out in public at last!'

Verena spoke to Rosalie as she passed by on her

way to the dancing. 'I told you that you looked beautiful!' she beamed.

'Ah—flattery.' Rosalie smiled back, waving her hand lightly in self-deprecation.

But Alec's eyes were warm whenever he looked at her and he seemed relaxed, almost happy. Until his father and stepmother arrived.

Alec and Rosalie were sitting down to supper with Lucas and Verena and all their friends when the late arrivals were announced. 'The Earl and Countess of Aldchester.'

Rosalie saw that Alec went very still. Verena said worriedly, 'I had not thought they would be here tonight...' The conversation was restarted by Lucas talking lightly to Alec across the table. But Rosalie watched as Alec's father and his wife came in.

He was a distinguished figure, in height and profile more like Alec than the hateful Lord Maybury. Yet he and Alec were estranged. Why?

Then she saw the beautiful woman at the Earl's side. Could she *really* be the Earl's wife, Lady Aldchester? But she was so young, only a little older, surely, than Rosalie! She had curling dark hair and a pale, exquisite face. Her gown, a precious thing of pink silk covered with layers of gauze and embroidered with pearls, revealed satiny bare shoulders and the curve of a perfect bosom.

An inexplicable cold warning tingled down Rosalie's spine.

But it appeared that father and son were happy to avoid one another's company; after supper Alec took her into the room where the dancing was, to lead her into a cotillion. There was just a moment, with his hand holding hers as he smiled gravely down at her, that she felt like confiding in him about her plan. But then he'd said, as the music stopped, 'Will you be all right with Verena and her friends for a short while? There are some people I need to speak to, you see.'

He led her to the edge of the dance floor, where Verena's friends crowded round Rosalie as she watched Alec's tall figure disappear. 'You are fortunate,' some of them sighed. 'We've all of us had our eye on Captain Stewart, at one time or another.' They chattered on and she tried to concentrate on what they said. But it was very warm in here, too warm; she didn't like the noise and the heat, and she missed Alec. She moved nearer to an open doorway, fanning herself.

Out there was a veranda and the night air suddenly tempted her. She walked slowly along it, gazing at the lit-up garden, the sparkling fountains. *Linette would have loved all this.* She would have loved the dancing, the beautiful house, the people strolling along the paths just below her...

And she saw them there. Alec and—his stepmother.

They were talking in low voices, intent only on each other. Rosalie was frozen to the spot. His stepmother—*so beautiful*—had her palms pressed to Alec's chest and looked as though she was pleading with him; while Alec, his expression grave, was shaking his head. His stepmother spoke a little more, then reached up on tiptoe to kiss him lingeringly on the lips. After that she turned and walked swiftly along a path that led back into the house— and Alec stood very still, as though he might never move again.

Half-remembered words were tumbling in chaotic confusion through Rosalie's brain. *'So she's back in town! Dear God, she's beautiful, but she's wrecked his life.'*

And that letter. *I know there are risks, my dear, but might I see you?*

Desperately she tried to make sense of it all. Perhaps Alec had loved this woman years ago, before she was married. And then she chose his father, for his title and money, thus embittering Alec for good. Yet still she toyed with him, summoning him with a scented note, a silken look...

Lady Aldchester was so very lovely. Rosalie felt

her stomach pitching with nausea as she somehow got back into the house to find Verena. Her lips seemed to be refusing to form the right words as she said, 'I'm not feeling very well. I'm really sorry to be such a nuisance, but I wonder, would your carriage take me back now?'

After that, it was easy. The next morning she got her things together, then found Verena and told her, 'I received an invitation a few days ago, from an old friend who's moved to the country. I've decided to go and stay with her for a while.'

Verena was bewildered. 'But Alec… Is your betrothal at an end? Aren't you going to speak to him before you go?'

Rosalie couldn't bear to. Her heart would surely break. 'I think he will understand.'

Verena looked grave. Disappointed in her. 'I hope you'll leave a note to tell Alec where you will be?'

Rosalie hesitated 'Of course.' Not that he would need it. He would realise, surely, that she knew his secret at last. *I don't think you'll ever know how much I wish that things could have been different…*

Quickly she wrote down Helen's address; Verena took it, tight-lipped.

So here she was, on the mail coach to Oxford, with a new life ahead of her. And she knew she would never stop missing Alec Stewart for as long as she lived, but now she understood. Why his betrothal to Lady Emilia had been so brief. How he'd tried to stay away from his lovely stepmother. Why he'd deliberately excluded himself from polite society, to live an austere life with his soldiers.

But that woman clearly still held his heart in her smooth white hands.

Katy was sleeping again as the coach rocked on its way and Rosalie held her close. With her portion of the Lavalle fortune, she was free to do as she wanted. To live where she wanted.

And she wished, she wished she was back at shabby old Two Crows Castle, with Alec. In Alec's arms. In Alec's bed.

Chapter Twenty-Two

Two days later Alec was striding up the front steps of the house in Belgrave Square. A footman opened the big door, then Jarvis was hurrying towards him. 'So *very* glad you could come, Master Alec! Such news, such dreadful news...'

'My father said very little in his message. What's wrong, Jarvis?'

'I think your father would prefer to tell you himself, sir. Would you mind waiting a little, until I can inform him you're here? His man of business arrived a while ago and they are still closeted in the library.'

'Shall I wait in the parlour?'

'Very good, sir. I'll let you know the moment his lordship is free.'

And so Alec had time to remember the conversation between himself and Susanna at Lord Stokesay's the other night.

She had looked so self-conscious, so artificial in that over-elaborate gown of pink silk and gauze. She'd also looked tense. She'd begged him to come with her into the garden, for privacy, and once there she'd murmured, 'I realise you find it difficult to trust me. But I helped you last time, did I not, with my news about Stephen's intentions towards the child?'

'You did,' he answered curtly, trying to keep his senses clear of that over-strong scent she used.

'That little girl. Is she safe, Alec?'

'Most certainly.'

She let out a breath of relief. 'At least, then, I can feel I've done something of use, before I leave.' She sighed.

'You're leaving the ball already?' Alec asked sharply.

'Not here—London, I mean! Oh, Alec, I have decided that your father does not deserve my wickedness. You are the one honest member of this family and I want to tell you that I am leaving England for good. I'm going back to Italy. Please tell your father I am sorry. And I know, my dear, that I do not deserve your good wishes, but I hope you believe me when I say that I truly wish you well.'

One lingering touch of her silken mouth upon his lips that left him cold and she was gone, leaving behind only her scent and the rekindled memories of the night he'd so bitterly regretted ever since.

In the winter of 1814, Napoleon was a prisoner on Elba, and London had become a city of parties and frivolity. By then Alec's father was besotted with Susanna, the Contessa di Ascoli. Alec had been forced to acknowledge she was enticing indeed, with her soft raven curls, her ripe mouth and her sultry, dark-blue eyes. But he was wary, too, because he read lechery in the sidelong glances she cast his way.

That Christmas his father was at Carrfields, holding a house party that was to continue into the New Year. Alec, whose engagement to Lady Emilia was already faltering, had promised to come from London, but would stay for just two nights. He was due back with his regiment in early January, because Lord Wellington did not expect the peace to last.

By the time he arrived at Carrfields he was dogtired, and dismayed by his father's news that he and the Contessa—who was there as a guest—were engaged to be married. Last time Alec had met her he'd heard her saying that she would die if she had to stay in the country. But here she was at Carrfields, his father's betrothed.

Alec had forced himself into his usual lightheartedness, drinking toasts in champagne to the happy couple with the rest. But thanks to his fatigue the drink had gone to his head and he was glad to make his excuses at midnight and retire to his room, where he'd fallen asleep the moment his head hit the pillow.

He thought he heard his door open two hours later, but imagined it, in his alcohol-induced languor, to be a dream. He stirred and muttered something, but the dream persisted; he imagined that someone was there in his room, a sinuous creature with long dark hair, who was starting to ease off her satin nightgown, then lowered herself to bed beside him, her silken hands stroking his powerful naked shoulders, her scent enveloping him.

'Alec. Oh, Alec. How I desire you,' she breathed.

Alec was aware of trying to fight his way through the confusion of heavy sleep, his mind still hazed by champagne and exhaustion; but in his dream the dark-haired nymph was pushing back the sheets to reach for his thickening member and twisting her lithe body to slip astride him. Uttering little cries of delight, she coaxed him and passionately caressed him into the act of love, then lay curled in his arms.

He'd woken before dawn to memories of that shadowy, erotic dream. His manhood was pulsing again, troubling him…

Then he realised. Someone was pressing herself against him, fondling him with languorous fingers, her tongue sliding between her lips and her dark-lashed blue eyes hot with invitation—

His soon-to-be stepmother. His naked, soon-to-be stepmother. He'd jumped from the bed. Hell. This nightmare had been only too real.

She watched his naked body as he started reaching for his clothes, her eyes lingering on his erection. 'It's early. Come back to bed,' she'd murmured.

He was already struggling to pull on his breeches. Self-disgust fractured his being. 'My God,' he'd said through gritted teeth, 'I hope you're not still seriously considering getting married to my father.'

'Why not?' she'd queried softly. 'Surely you are not going to tell him about this?' She'd slid out of the bed and swayed towards him; he continued pulling on his clothes. She put her hands up to his chest, toying with the buttons of his coat. 'We can do this again, whenever it's convenient, can't we? Your father need never know.'

'You're joking.' Alec had pushed her away.

He'd set off back to London before the rest of the house was astir, filled with self-disgust. Surely his father could not marry this woman?

He'd tried to warn his father, before he was sent abroad again on his last spell of active service. The result was total estrangement between father and son. And the young Lady Emilia, already peevish at Alec's devotion to his army duties, and bewildered by his increasingly sombre moods, hastily broke off their betrothal.

The Earl and Susanna had married in the summer of 1815, the summer of Waterloo. When Alec returned from the war he went to live at Two Crows Castle, effectively cutting himself off from his family.

That autumn he'd gone to a house party in a grand Kensington mansion, hosted by an officer of his regiment—Grenville—whom Alec hadn't seen for some time. Alec had been under the impression it was to be a kind of army reunion, but clearly the event had grown in size. And Grenville hadn't told Alec until he arrived that night that he'd also invited Alec's father and his wife.

As it turned out, the Earl, unwell, had been unable to attend.

'A shame about your father,' Grenville had said to Alec. He was either unaware of father and son's estrangement, or was bent on causing mischief. 'But your stepmother's turned up. Your brother offered to bring her, you see.'

Alec was deciding he liked Grenville less and less. And—Stephen, with Susanna? It wasn't unknown, of course, for a male relative to escort a married woman to a social event. So Alec, trapped in a situation he had not foreseen, was curt to Stephen and coldly civil to Susanna. He stayed for barely two hours, then made his excuses to leave.

Like the other guests, the intention had been that he stayed overnight, so he first had to go upstairs and get his things from the chamber he'd been allotted on arrival. It was a little past eleven; his mind was already on his journey home.

But he'd pulled up with a jolt of utter disbelief when he came upon Stephen and Susanna, stealing out of a nearby bedroom.

To Alec it couldn't have been plainer that they were fresh from intimacy. 'My God,' he'd breathed.

Stephen, straightening his neckcloth, had drawled, 'Say one word about this, little brother, and you're finished. I know from Susanna that you have no reason whatever to preach virtue at me.'

'At least she wasn't my stepmother at the time!'

Stephen said, 'Do you think that would matter if our father were to find out?'

So Stephen had been able to hold that knife to Alec's throat ever since.

Jarvis came into the parlour where Alec waited. 'His lordship is ready to see you, Captain Stewart.'

'My thanks, Jarvis.'

The Earl was still in his library, pacing the floor. When Alec entered, his father came almost hesitantly towards him.

'Alec,' he said. 'You were so right, my son, to warn me about—about...' He suddenly gripped Alec's hand. 'God help me,' he whispered, 'I've been such a fool.'

'No, sir,' said Alec quickly. 'Never that. Please. Sit down.'

'A fool is what I am,' repeated the Earl bitterly. He sank into the chair to which Alec guided him and ran his fingers through his greying hair. 'She's gone back to Italy. She as good as told me it was tedious, living with an old man like me. And she's taken all the family jewels!' He began to laugh, a hollow sound. 'Well, there's no fool like an old fool, they say. And do you know? Stephen has set off after her. He says it's to get the jewellery back. Says he feels huge concern for me and all the rest of it...'

Alec had gone very still. *Stephen*, gone after her. To get the jewels? To get Susanna? Or was it because he realised that, thanks to his attempt to kidnap Katy, Alec could now expose Stephen for the blackguard he was?

Alec said, 'It's good of Stephen to try to get the jewels back for you, sir.'

His father looked up at him in utter despair. 'There's no need to gammon me any longer, Alec. Stephen and she were rutting together whenever my back was turned. Weren't they? Weren't they, damn it?'

Alec braced himself. 'For how long have you known this?' he asked quietly.

'There were signs I'd ignored, for months.' His father clenched his hands. 'But I knew for certain when Stephen came to visit me in the country. They thought I was in my bedchamber. I came downstairs and saw the two of them whispering together. *Touching* each other. God damn it, I tried to pretend I didn't realise what it meant...' The Earl shook his head. 'Of course she probably cares for him even less than she did for me—he'll just be an idle diversion for her. You, Alec, realised what she was from the start—that was why you tried to warn me off her, before our wedding—' He broke off, coughing.

Now. Now was the time. 'Sir, there is something I must tell you.'

And Alec told him the story of that one despicable night. He made no excuses for his own behaviour. 'It was unforgivable of me,' he said quietly.

After a long silence his father turned to Alec and said, 'You did try to tell me, didn't you?'

'I did, sir, but not strongly enough.'

His father waved his hand dismissively. 'Ah, I was an old besotted fool, I wouldn't have listened to a word anyway.' He got up and went to the window, his shoulders rigid. Then at last he turned round and said, 'Did you take all your war diaries away, my son?'

'Almost all, sir. But there were just a few left, which of course I intend to remove as soon as possible.'

'You know, Alec…' his father's voice was hesitant '…you never did tell me about Waterloo. I wonder, are you free for an hour or so?'

'For as long as you wish, sir,' said Alec quietly.

'Perhaps,' his father said, 'you would spare a little time to go through the battle with me? I find myself rather in need of company. And, you know, I never did understand why Wellington said that the whole outcome of Waterloo turned on the Coldstream Guards holding some damned gate at a place called Hougoumont…'

Alec went over to the bookcase for his father's maps, spread them out on a nearby table, then pulled up chairs for himself and his father and started pointing out the battle lines. 'Here's Hougoumont, below the escarpment. It was a farm with gated grounds that Wellington had fortified, a crucial position—the French attacked it all day.'

'And is that the north gate?'

'Yes. There the enemy might have broken through were it not for Macdonnell and his Coldstream Guards defending it hand to hand. Then Halkett's Hanoverian Brigade reinforced Macdonnell's men and they somehow held on, despite heavy losses.'

'Ah, Halkett's men.' The Earl nodded.

'Indeed, sir. Lord Wellington always said that between them they won the battle for him there...'

Alec was in no hurry. He had all the time in the world spreading out empty before him, now that Rosalie had gone. For he had realised what he should have acknowledged weeks ago: that he simply could not bear to live his life without her.

Yet clearly—she couldn't have made it plainer—she wanted nothing at all to do with him. Had removed herself entirely from his life. *Why had she left so suddenly?*

Alec knew that the attempt to kidnap Katy, and the news that Alec's brother was the villain, had shaken her badly. Perhaps she'd been right and he should have told her earlier about Stephen. But surely she'd forgiven him, when she realised how thorough had been Alec's preparations to safeguard the little girl? Hadn't Rosalie tended Alec's slight injury herself, her eyes full of something like tenderness?

But she'd gone, and there was no message for him, only an address—Helen's address—that he gathered she'd been reluctant to give. Perhaps Rosalie had decided she could no longer bear to be in the company of someone who would always remind her of Linette's evil seducer. Remind her of Katy's father, God damn it.

It was as well she'd never know how he'd betrayed his father with Susanna. Or—perhaps she did. His stomach pitched as he realised—*that could be it.* At Lord Stokesay's ball—somehow she'd realised. She'd somehow found out—and that was why she'd left.

Oh, God. Who could blame her?

Meanwhile, he'd neglected his fencing lessons lately for the other matters, and day after day more soldiers came to Two Crows Castle begging for shelter. Alec knew it was possible now that his father might offer to restore his aid. But in the meantime drastic action was called for, if they were not to close down within weeks.

After leaving his father, Alec rode to his bank in the Temple, to ask for more time to pay his bills. As he was ushered into a private office, he braced himself.

Then a senior clerk hurried in, smiling. 'Captain

Stewart. This is indeed a lucky chance! I was about to contact you…'

And Alec listened, almost in disbelief, as the clerk told him that a large sum of money had been given into the bank's care—for the benefit of the soldiers at Two Crows Castle. And the donor wished to remain completely anonymous.

His father? His father would have told him, surely! The clerk refused to say any more. But Alec, on his way out past the rows of junior clerks at their desks, was stopped by a scrawny lad in black, sweeping the floor.

'Captain Stewart?' the boy whispered eagerly. 'You remember me, don't you, Captain Stewart? I got a job here now, Captain, running errands and the like!'

'Mikey! You stayed at Two Crows Castle for a couple of weeks, didn't you?'

'I did, and it was thanks to that place I got this job. And funnily enough, I saw someone else here from Two Crows Castle only the other day, Captain!'

'You did? Who was he?'

'Not a he, Captain,' said Mikey importantly. 'But a *she*.'

As Mikey explained who, Alec began to understand. And—to hope.

Chapter Twenty-Three

It was a warm May afternoon and Rosalie was in the orchard at the back of Helen and Francis's pretty house, sitting on a rug in the shade of a blossom-laden apple tree while she read stories to Katy and Toby.

She had been here for a few weeks now, renting a cottage close to the village of Heythrop. The banns had been read three times in Heythrop's pretty church; Helen and Francis were married now and Helen had welcomed Rosalie like a lamb returned to the fold.

'Oh, my dear Rosalie, I knew you'd see sense in the end!' she had cried.

'Captain Stewart proved to be a true and honourable friend,' Rosalie had replied quietly. 'And he helped me to find Katy's father.'

'So—is the villain going to be made to pay for his wickedness to poor Linette?'

'I think he *has* paid, Helen.' Rosalie could still hardly bear to think of the kidnap attempt on Katy. 'Though the fewer people who know of it, the better. And Katy and I are quite safe from him, thanks to Captain Stewart.'

Helen had kept hugging them both, and laughing and crying, and trying to ask more. But sensible Francis had drawn his wife aside gently. 'Give Miss Rowland time to get her breath, Helen! You'll be tired, my dear,' he added to Rosalie, 'after your journey.'

'I'm fine.' But Rosalie had smiled at him, in gratitude. 'Mr Wheeldon, I cannot thank you enough, for putting me in touch with my mother's family. And I want to tell you and Helen that I would like to give some money towards your school—no, I will not allow any arguments! There will still be more than enough for me and Katy, I assure you!'

And for Two Crows Castle. She hugged that thought to herself over the next few days, remembering her visit to the bank. It was so strange that she'd bumped into Mikey there, who told her how much he'd enjoyed working in the garden. She'd had to hurry away, because of the stupid tears brimming in her eyes.

She and Katy had settled quickly into their little cottage. The fact that it was less than ten miles from the place where she grew up gave her a sense of peace, of redemption even, to be here again with Katy. To visit her mother's grave, and their old home, which was inhabited now by a pleasant young family. To watch Katy, so happy in the places like the riverside where she and Linette had played.

Helen had offered to send over their daily maid-servant to help her in her new abode, but Rosalie preferred to do everything herself, brushing and sweeping from dawn till dusk. Action was a neces-sity, for a great ache of loneliness—of sheer *loss*—filled her almost unbearably whenever she thought of Alec Stewart.

Once the cottage was neat as a new pin, she helped Helen in the school, teaching the small ones to read. But now school had finished for the day, which was why she was in the orchard with Katy and Toby, equipped with buttered scones and a pitcher of lem-onade for when the storytelling was over. Helen and Francis had taken a trip into Chipping Norton in their dog cart to visit the shops there, so she was surprised to hear the sound of steady hoofbeats ap-proaching.

Katy heard it, too, and wandered off towards the low hedge that separated the orchard from the lane. She turned back to Rosalie, her little face alight.

'Tick-tock man!' she cried in joy.

Rosalie felt her heart do a topsy-turvy somersault. *No. It could not be...* She got slowly to her feet.

But it was. It was Alec. Lithely dismounting, he looped his horse's reins over the gatepost and was striding towards her, his hair rumpled, his boots dusty from the road, but still so handsome that her breath caught thickly in her throat.

Katy was the first to reach him; he swung her up in his arms and kissed her cheek. 'How's my girl?' He smiled.

But his eyes—his dark, burning eyes—were on Rosalie. 'I've come to thank you,' he said to her. 'For what you did for Two Crows Castle.'

She'd scrambled to her feet, knowing her straw hat was askew. 'But you weren't supposed to *know*...'

'And no one deliberately betrayed your trust,' he assured her. 'But...' And he explained about Mikey.

'Of course,' she said wonderingly. 'I saw him there.'

'He misses the garden. And you,' he told her. There was something in his eyes, in his voice, that made her dizzy with an emotion she didn't dare to name.

Then Katy was tugging at his hand, and Alec sat with them all in the orchard, sharing their lemonade and scones. Afterwards he showed the children how to roll pennies along the smoothed-out rug, making Toby laugh with delight at his success and guiding little Katy.

Rosalie watched his long, lithe figure as he sprawled in the grass in his shirt sleeves, the sun hot on his brown forearms, one of them marked by the jagged scar she remembered so well. Though a tight ache of longing squeezed at her chest, she tried her hardest just to be content that he was here, that he turned to her every so often with a look of such warmth in his dark eyes that her foolish heart leapt.

He has only come to thank me for the money, she warned herself. *Nothing else has changed. His heart is not free. Soon he will be leaving again.*

When Helen and Francis got back they were surprised to see him here. But Francis warmly invited Alec to eat with them and Katy was put to bed in the room next to Toby's so the adults could dine together that evening. Francis was aware of Alec Stewart's work with homeless soldiers; now he openly showed his interest. As for Helen—well, Helen was melting, slowly but surely.

'He is rather charming,' she confided reluctantly when she and Rosalie were alone together in the parlour after the meal, while the men took a glass of port. 'And so *very* handsome… Obviously I'd got hold of the wrong end of the stick about him. An earl's son, you say? And he dealt with the villain who wronged poor Linette. Hmmm.'

Rosalie didn't even want to think about Stephen now. All that filled her mind was Alec. Alec was here. *It means nothing. You know it means nothing...*

The men joined them very soon afterwards, and Helen began to say, 'You may stay here, of course, Captain Stewart, we have a bed made up!'

Alec looked at his watch. 'I actually planned on staying at the Heythrop Inn tonight. But on my way back, perhaps I could escort Miss Rowland home.'

'Oh, Francis will do that, won't you, Fra—?'

But Rosalie would swear that Francis had, most definitely, given his wife's arm a warning pinch.

Tomorrow, Alec would be leaving her life again. He'd only come to thank her for the money, hadn't he?

It was less than a quarter of a mile back to her cottage, and a beautiful, moonlit evening. He led his horse, and as they walked she told him lightly about the school and how well Katy had settled in here. He waited while she unlocked the door, then she turned to him.

He was going to leave her again now. She gazed up one last time at that proud, handsome profile that had stunned her at the Temple of Beauty. 'Thank you for seeing me home,' she began. 'Now you will want to ride on to the inn.'

Something blazed in his dark eyes. Some emotion that caught at her quivering heart, pounded through her veins, melting her very bones.

'Rosalie,' he said, 'why did you leave London so suddenly?'

Her throat seemed to have closed up. 'I really think you must guess why…'

'No,' he said. 'I can't. May I come in? Just for a brief while? We really must talk.'

She couldn't answer.

'Go inside,' he urged gently. 'I'll see to my horse. Is there a stable?'

'Round the back. A neighbour uses it sometimes, everything's there.'

She went inside. Her throat felt as though it could hardly drag air into her lungs. Tension made her sick. She'd just lit the fire that was ready laid in the grate when he came back in, bowing his dark head a fraction to enter the low-beamed door.

'Please tell me everything,' he said simply.

What had she to lose?

He joined her on the sofa, not too near, not too far. He was very quiet as she told him how she'd seen him with his stepmother at Lord Stokesay's ball. She began to shiver again. 'I saw how beautiful she was, Alec,' she said. 'And I'd heard your men talk about someone who had hurt you badly in the past. I'd assumed it was your fiancée…' Her clear voice, so steady till now, faltered at last. 'But that night I realised that you must have loved *her* and were devastated when she married your father…'

He said, 'That is not true. You must believe me. I never loved my stepmother, ever.'

And she began, at last, to hope.

A slow tide of exhilaration was surging through Alec's veins. He remembered Mikey's words. *'She went dashing out, Captain Stewart, with tears in her eyes when I talked about you and Two Crows Castle!'*

Those tears were precious. The money—her gift—had given him the excuse to make this journey. Rosalie's tears had given him hope.

He must not press her. He mustn't overwhelm her. Hadn't she endured enough, in her usual calm, courageous way? But she did, at the very least, deserve the truth.

Steadily Alec told her the whole sorry tale. How Susanna had come to him that one wretched night, when she was already promised to his father, and seduced him when he was befuddled with drink and fatigue. How he had tried to warn his father away from her, but had only alienated the Earl, badly. How he'd discovered that Stephen, too—Rosalie let out a low cry at this—had shared that woman's bed, often.

She listened to him intently and he saw the colour tinting her cheeks as his story unfolded. She clasped her hands in her lap throughout; only at the end did she say, 'But when I saw her with you at Lord Stokesay's, she—she looked as though she still *loved* you…'

His face became hard briefly. 'Perhaps she does care for me in her own way. But she was saying goodbye to me, Rosalie.'

'Goodbye?'

Again he saw the emotions fluttering across her delicate face like shadows. The anguish in her eyes as she absorbed all this. *Gently*, he told himself. Gently. She is not sure she can trust you, for God's sake.

Alec wanted to enfold her in his arms and soothe away her suffering, and tell her she was safe. But this wasn't over yet. Instead he took her hand in his and said, 'She left my father the day afterwards to return to Italy, taking the family's jewels with her. Stephen went after her.'

'To get them back? To get *her* back?' she whispered.

He held her hand fast and said, 'Ostensibly to get the jewels back. But who knows—perhaps Stephen felt some kind of affection for her? However, I think he probably seized on it all as a convenient reason to leave London for a while. He would have been afraid, you see, that I would spread the news about his attempt to kidnap Katy. That I might make known the whole, shameful business of his seduction of Linette and his efforts to silence *you*, Rosalie.'

'But if you'd told Linette's story, your family's reputation might have suffered. You would have sacrificed that?'

'Without hesitation,' he said steadily.

A jolt shook her heart. Was it possible that she meant so much to him? Or was it his sense of honour, of justice, that prevailed? Her hand still lay in his and the warmth, the strength of his grip, tingled through her veins, setting off that familiar, so-painful longing that tugged at every fibre of her being. Fighting it with all her strength she lifted her face to his to ask calmly, 'What will happen, Alec, when Stephen comes back?'

His hard-boned face was grim now. His voice devoid of emotion. 'He won't come back. He drowned when the ship on which he was sailing foundered in a storm off Brest. I'd have come so much sooner, but you'll understand my father needed me.'

'*Oh...*' The shock of it travelled through her. 'Oh, Alec. Stephen was Katy's father and your brother...' She was silent, wondering. 'Yet—yet everything about him was the very *opposite* of what you stand for.'

He'd gone very still. 'What do you think I stand for, Rosalie?'

'You stand for courage,' she said steadily. 'Honesty. Duty.'

Her words resonated through his body, bringing light somehow to the darkest recesses of his soul. He heaved a deep breath. 'Stephen's story is sad indeed,' he acknowledged quietly. 'He could have been so much more.'

'Your poor father—he will be grief-stricken!' Her blue eyes lifted suddenly to his face. 'Unless—he *knows*?'

'He's gone to his country home at Carrfields in Hampshire for a period of mourning. But, yes, he knows. I didn't have to tell him about Stephen and Susanna, for which I thank God. My father knows also about me and that one hateful night with her.' He shook his head, as though banishing dark dreams. 'We are reconciled again, my father and I. And he wants me to bring *you* to Carrfields, Rosalie.'

'Me?' A pulse was beating very faintly in her throat.

'Indeed. You,' he said softly. 'And Katy, too, of course. We are betrothed, remember?'

Again Rosalie felt an agonising surge of hope. Hope that she'd crushed remorselessly, again and again, until her body felt battered with emotion.

She tried to smile dismissively. 'Alec, I know you only made your offer of betrothal out of duty! It was to keep Katy and me safe from your brother—but there is no longer any need. Besides, now that Stephen is dead, you are the heir to an earldom and marriage to someone like me is out of the question!'

That decided him. If he'd had any doubts at all about the complete *rightness* of this, they were gone. Vanished. Yes—his brother's death made him one of the most eligible matches in England. And only Rosalie—his enchanting, courageous Rosalie— would turn him down for that very reason.

He drew her into his arms, as he'd been longing to do since seeing her in the sunshine of the orchard that afternoon. 'Rosalie. Listen to me. I want you. I need you. I would have told you long ago, but I knew that you believed so very much in loyalty to one's family and I thought that my past—my shameful past—would repel you for ever!'

She'd lifted her hands to his cheeks now, outlining his dear, familiar features with her fingertips, feeling ripples of desire surging through her every nerve end as she traced his hard cheekbones, the stubble-roughened skin of his jaw, the soft sensuality of his lips. 'Alec, I did a dreadful thing in driving Linette away from home, remember?'

'You were trying to *save* her. You searched all of London for her. You risked so much for her daughter's sake. No one could be as loyal or as brave as you.' He drew a deep breath. 'When I realised that you'd left Lucas's house, I was terrified that you'd found out about my stepmother and hated me. And I couldn't endure it. I want to know—I *need* to know—if you feel that you could, some day, come to love me, Rosalie.'

Her heart was almost too full to speak. '*Love* you! Alec, I think I've loved you since that night that I saw you at Dr Barnard's!'

'Really?' He was speaking huskily now, his desire for her pounding through his veins, heating his loins. 'You're telling me that Ro Rowland, fellow about town, writer of scathing pieces about London's gentry, lost her heart to a patron of the Temple of Beauty?'

'Ro Rowland, fellow about town, was—quite frankly—captivated by a handsome soldier simply known as the Captain,' she breathed, running her hands across his shoulders.

'And I by you. Oh, God, *Rosalie...*'

In that same instant he gathered her in his arms. His big hands spanned her ribs, encompassing the slenderness of her waist beneath that old gown, feeling her tremble at his touch; then her arms were round his neck and she was breathing his name. He let one palm cup her breast, his thumb stroking the right nipple until it tensed and hardened beneath his touch.

She was lifting her face to him like a flower, her lips already opening for his kiss. Their mouths brushed once, twice, then were joined in a gliding of lips and tongues that had his body burning for more. Her kiss was delectable—shy, yet passionate. He roved deeply within the silk of her inner lips while he pulled her harder against his own body, until her breasts were crushed against the wall of his chest. The old sofa groaned and creaked. Alec broke off the kiss, swearing under his breath. 'This is *not* a good idea.'

He saw the desperate disappointment in her wide, desire-hazed eyes. Saw the way she drew herself back, her arms clasped across her bosom. 'Of course. I'm sorry. What you must think of me...'

'I meant,' he said softly, his dark eyes burning with need for her, 'that I think a bed would be far more comfortable.'

'You were going to the inn...'

'They're not going to lose sleep over my absence.'

Her sweet face lit up again. Her eyes danced with laughter. 'Oh, Alec. Let me just lock the door and put up the fire guard...'

'We'll do that together,' he said, his thumb still deliciously circling the sensitive skin of her palm. 'When you've explained one more mystery to me, Rosalie Rowland.'

'A mystery?'

'I've already thanked you for your donation to Two Crows Castle. But—forgive me—I thought you were penniless.'

And so she told him all about Francis Wheeldon's enquiries and her Lavalle legacy.

'Oh, Rosalie Rowland,' he breathed, 'fellow about town, I am fascinated. I can't wait to begin finding out the rest of your secrets... Oh, hell and damnation!'

'What?'

'I don't suppose I should touch you, let alone kiss you. Devil take it, now I've learnt you're a French aristocrat, I suppose I should ask permission from *someone* to court you!' His eyes danced with laughter and something darker that thrilled her soul—burning, all-male desire.

'My dearest Alec,' she whispered, pulling his head down to hers, 'you'd have to travel a long way to find anyone who'd trouble himself to fight for my honour. And I've told you—you are an earl's son and should be looking amongst England's aristocracy for a suitable wife!'

'God damn it all—' he frowned '—I will *not* face the Marriage Mart at Almack's! Please, Miss Rowland, don't put me through that!'

She put her head on one side. 'On second thoughts,' she murmured, her eyes dancing, 'I *might* take pity on you. And if you do not kiss me this very minute, I swear I will most definitely have to seduce you!'

'Are you sure?' He was still holding back. 'This isn't all too—sudden for you?'

She ran, light-footed, to lock the door, then came back to wrap her arms around his neck. 'I'm fine,' she murmured, 'apart from the fact that I have missed you, my darling Captain Stewart, so very, very badly.'

He swung her up in his arms and carried her up the twisting stairs to her bedroom. 'Mind the beams.' She was laughing. 'Alec, I don't think anyone of your height was ever meant to live in a cottage like this—be careful of the doorway, and that old cupboard there—oh!'

'I was *made* to be in a cottage like this. With you,' he said. He deposited her on her bed and began to kiss her.

Rosalie had told herself all evening that all she wanted now was his touch and one kiss, no more, but it felt so wonderful to be held by him again. Inevitably her hunger deepened, burned like a flame as she pressed her lips to his warm skin and ran the flat of her palm over his dear, familiar face, his muscled shoulders.

He pulled off his shirt, then his breeches; already his desire was evident. He helped her to unbutton her gown, because sudden shyness made her fingers clumsy, but he reassured her with the kisses he traced from her throat up to her earlobes and lips.

She breathed, 'I want you, Alec. Come to me, now. *Please.*'

His dark eyes intent, he joined her, seeking her mouth with his in gentle cajoling, giving her pleasure and reassurance with every touch of his hand, every caress of his lips. Sweetly he suckled at the tightened crest of her breast, while letting his fingers trail downwards to the heated core of her. Letting out a low moan of need, she wrapped her slender legs round his muscular, hair-roughened ones, urgently seeking him.

Whispering her name, he drove himself into her, sheathing himself in her warmness; she clutched him and moved with passion and love, until her whole being was shattered by a delirious extremity of pleasure in which he exulted even as his own climax convulsed him.

For a long time afterwards they lay breathing as one, hearts beating as one.

And still Alec's blood pounded with the urge to kiss her, caress her. By God, he'd fought his love for her. He'd been so reluctant to lay himself open, make himself vulnerable. But Ro Rowland had stolen her way into his heart and he had no intention of losing her, ever again.

She was stirring dreamily in his arms, her lissom body curled half-naked against his own hard-muscled form.

'Tired?' He kissed her throat tenderly.

'I shall not sleep all night,' she whispered. 'I shall always remember lying here like this, with you, Alec.'

He raised himself on one elbow, gazing down at her as the moonlight filtered into the low- ceilinged cottage bedroom. 'I've told you,' he said steadily,

'I love you, Rosalie. I want to spend the rest of my life with you.' He cupped her face with his hand and gazed into her eyes with a kind of raw and aching tenderness that set all her nerve ends tingling again with the need for his possession. 'Are you, or are you not, going to marry me?'

So much. He meant so very much to her. 'I really need to remind you,' she said huskily, 'that I've appeared on stage, at the Temple of Beauty, which is truly outrageous!'

He gave a shout of laughter and gathered her close. 'So you did,' he breathed, 'and that's when I realised what was missing from my life. The goddess Athena, in the form of the adorable Miss Rosalie Rowland!'

She was beginning to laugh, too, tenderly. She was shifting beneath him, eager for his embrace again. Eager to feel the delicious weight of him, feel his virility pleasuring her, joining with her in a completeness she'd scarcely dreamed of.

'Try getting me to leave your life, Captain Stewart,' she whispered, pulling his face to hers to kiss him sweetly.

And Alec felt, after years of travelling through an uncharted wilderness, as if he'd come home at last.

Epilogue

Their wedding was in November and the reception was held at the Earl's Mayfair home. The six-month delay was inevitable, for the Earl and Alec were in mourning for Stephen, and an unspoken grief was felt by both, for the man he might have been. No one ever spoke Susanna's name again.

Prior to the wedding Alec moved back into the Bedford Street house that was originally his home, for Susanna's mother had followed her daughter to Italy. Alec left Garrett to manage Two Crows Castle for him, which he did most efficiently. The Earl had offered to fund the hostel fully and Alec had wanted to return Rosalie's money, but she refused.

'I'll think of it as my memorial to Linette,' she told him and he understood.

At the party after the wedding all the guests agreed that Rosalie looked radiant in her gown of white tulle, while Alec was splendidly, darkly handsome in his black tailcoat. But it was also agreed that little Katy stole the show, for she refused to be parted from Alec's side, and had to be cajoled away from the party and to her bed with the promise that she would see him again the next morning.

After an idyllic week spent in the countryside at Carrfields, Rosalie, Katy and Alec returned to Bedford Street. Katy had been invited to Lucas and Verena's house for the afternoon to play with their children, so Alec showed Rosalie around. On the first floor she espied a sun-filled room with a bay window that was furnished with some as-yet-empty mahogany bookcases and a beautiful old writing desk. Rosalie turned to Alec with questioning eyes.

'For you,' he smiled. 'A study, for Ro Rowland. I know you'll never want to give up your writing.'

'Alec, it's a beautiful room. But you know I'll stop writing if you want me to!'

'Perhaps you could try something safer, like poetry?' he teased. 'My love, I don't want you to ever stop writing. You'll have some spare moments to fill, after all. We won't be at parties and balls *every* night, and when we are old and grey we'll have perhaps got over spending most of our days in bed together.'

She nestled against him. 'Mmm. Most of our days.

Oh, good. And I'll be careful,' she promised, 'with my writing. I'll be *especially* careful not to tackle down-at-heel soldiers about rackrenting!'

'Wise of you,' he murmured. His strong hands, which had been caressing her breasts, were already starting to deftly unbutton the bodice of her pretty sprig-muslin day gown. 'Because one of these days, Ro Rowland, intrepid adventurer, exposer of wrongs, you might find that you've taken on more than you bargained for.'

She touched his wide, sensually curving lips. 'And so, indeed, might you—Alec! The servants!'

'Are well trained,' he grinned, undoing another button.

She sighed with happiness and ran her fingers over his shoulders, deliciously conscious of that powerfully masculine body beneath the formal shirt, of the way his breeches moulded his lean hips and powerfully muscled thighs. She could see that he wanted her. Was aroused for her, as she was for him.

She said softly, 'Here's an order, Captain Stewart.' She moistened her own full lips. 'I want those clothes off.'

'Wanton,' he said, shaking his head a little, 'utterly wanton…'

'Do I detect insubordination?' she retorted, a wicked gleam in her eye.

The look of mischief in her sparkling turquoise eyes made his throat go dry, his skin tingle. For answer he swung her up in his powerful arms and carried her to the bedroom, while she clasped her hands tightly around his neck and pressed her cheek to his chest, where she could hear his heart beating.

For her.

Tenderly, powerfully, he made love to her. And she indeed matched him in his ardour as he took her to the pinnacle of pleasure and beyond, until she felt herself shattering into a million shards of starlight.

Wrapped in his strong arms, she recalled the perilous, often sad journey that had brought her here. Alec was watching her, stroking her cheek with one finger.

'Not tears, sweetheart?' he whispered.

'No. Oh, no! At least—not tears of *sadness*. I love you, Alec, so very much. I just hope I will be worthy of you.'

'You've proved that and more, a thousand times,' he told her gravely, stroking a curl away from her temple. 'When I realised you'd left me, after that ball, I faced an abyss. And I knew then that I could face anything—anything at all, Rosalie—except the loss of your love.'

She nestled tighter into his arms. 'You have that for ever,' she breathed.

He kissed her tenderly, his lips warm on her cheek. 'For ever and always,' he echoed.

Rosalie twined her arms around his neck with a little sigh and her heart overflowed with pure happiness. For ever, with her darling Captain Stewart, was all that she could want, or need.

* * * * *

Discover Pure Reading Pleasure with

Visit the Mills & Boon website for all the latest in romance

Buy all the latest releases, backlist and eBooks

Find out more about our authors and their books

Join our community and chat to authors and other readers

Free online reads from your favourite authors

Win with our fantastic online competitions

Sign up for our free monthly eNewsletter

Tell us what you think by signing up to our reader panel

Rate and review books with our star system

www.millsandboon.co.uk

 Follow us at twitter.com/millsandboonuk

 Become a fan at facebook.com/romancehq